'WARE THE
DARK-HAIRED MAN

Borgo Press Books by ROBERT REGINALD

THE NOVA EUROPA FANTASY SAGA

THE HIEROMONK'S TALE
1. *Melanthrix the Mage*
2. *Killingford*
3. *'Ware the Dark-Haired Man*

THE ARCHQUISITOR'S TALE
4. *The Righteous Regicide*
5. *The Virgin Queens*
6. *The Prince of Exiles*

THE PROTOPRESBYTER'S TALE
7. *Brother Theo's God*
8. *Questions and Questings*
9. *"Whither Goest Thou?"*

THE HYPATOMANCER'S TALE
10. *The Cracks in the Æther*
11. *The Pachyderms' Lament*
12. *The Fourth Elephant's Egg*

Plus: *Academentia: A Future Dystopia* * *The Attempted Assassination of John F. Kennedy* * *Dead Librarians and Other Shades of Academe* * *The Elder of Days: Tales of the Elders* * *If J.F.K. Had Lived* * *Invasion!* (War of Two Worlds #1) * *The Judgment of the Gods and Other Verdicts of History* * *Knack' Attack* (Human-Knacker War #2) * *The Martians Strike Back!* (War of Two Worlds #3) * *The Nasty Gnomes* (Phantom Detective #2) * *Operation Crimson Storm* (War of Two Worlds #2) * *The Paperback Show Murders* * *The Phantom's Phantom* (Phantom Detective #1)

'WARE THE DARK-HAIRED MAN

THE HIEROMONK'S TALE, BOOK THREE

BEING THE THIRD ROMANCE OF NOVA EUROPA

ROBERT REGINALD

THE BORGO PRESS
MMXIII

'WARE THE DARK-HAIRED MAN

FIRST EDITION

Published by Wildside Press LLC

www.wildsidebooks.com

DEDICATION

In memory of my grandfather, Roy P. Burgess.
I saw him just a week before he died, when
he took me down to the main railroad tracks,
so we could watch the trains go by. I'm still
watching them sixty years later, Grandpa!

and

For Mary,

who has given
so very much
of herself—

to my life,
to this book,
to everything.

CONTENTS

L'ENVOI

The Evil Gods are raging storms,
Ruthless spirits created in the vault of Heaven;
Workers of woe are they,
That each day raise their evil heads for evil,
To wreak destruction.
> —*Utukki Limnuti* (Old Babylonian poem)

The chess board is the world, the pieces are
the phenomena of the universe, the rules of the
game are what we call the laws of Nature. The
player on the other side is hidden from us.
> —Thomas H. Huxley

AUTHOR'S NOTE

For those of you who care about such things, this novel is an alternate history set in a Europe whose geographic features are similar or even identical to our own, with the major (but not sole) divergence from our timeline having occurred in the year 363 AD, when Roman Emperor Julian the Apostate, Constantine I's cousin, was *not* killed in battle against the Persians (as he was in our world), but lived on for another forty years.

For the geographic and personal names herein, I used mostly Slavic, Hungarian, German, and Greek models; there are no silent letters in such constructs. Forward accents are intended to provide guides to stress in Slavic words, such emphasis often appearing in locations unfamiliar to westerners; in Hungarian names, however, the accents merely indicate differences in vowel sounds. I've employed circumflexes in Greek words to distinguish between the letters epsilon and êta, and omicron and ômega. Umlauts can denote gutteral vowel sounds—or dress up otherwise pedestrian names. The letter "ß" stands for "ss."

In the end, of course, I have my own ideas about pronunciation, and each reader will undoubtedly have hers or his. Mangle them as ye will, folks, and no one will be the wiser, unless you actually hear me read a passage someday, and then you can tell me, with as haughty an air as possible, that I've got it all wrong! I do try to have fun when creating these things; some of the names here have been invented from the flimsiest of constructs, bearing no discernible relationship to anything that anyone but I will ever be able to determine. Oh, well!

PROLOGUE ONE
"NOW WE COME TO IT AT LAST"

Anno Domini 1242
Anno Juliani 882

"And now," Queen Grigorÿna said out loud, "now we come to it at last."

She looked at the pile of parchment sheets scattered on the tables before her, some of them bound together into heavy, authoritative volumes of brown leather, while others were arranged in stacks of loose pages, roughly corresponding to the latter stages of the Great War of A.J. 845—those sections of her manuscript that had yet to be completed.

It had taken her the better part of three years to reach this point. When her aunt Arrhiána had passed to her reward some five years earlier, she'd left her incomplete history of Kórynthia to her niece, with the hope that Grigorÿna could complete the narrative of the last hundred years.

But the Queen was only really interested in what had happened when she was a little girl at court, during the time when Pommerelia had warred with Kórynthia, to the great detriment of both countries.

King Kipriyán III had seemingly been driven by the events of the winter and spring of that year—a series of murders at court, crimes that had never been solved, but which he'd ascribed to a mythical creature he'd called "The Dark-Haired Man"—into promulgating a *jihad* against their ancient enemy: the Papist-loving pederasts of the West.

He'd proceeded with the enthusiastic support of the population and nobility of the kingdom, mobilizing the levies of the counts and barons, and gathering them first at his capital city of Paltyrrha, and thence moving to a temporary base on the eastern flank of the Carpates Spinæ Mountains, the formal dividing line between the two states.

In June the King had finally invaded Pommerelia with a force comprising tens of thousands of soldiers and support brigades, with his Pretender to the throne of Pommerelia slipping over a pass far to the north.

Initially, both incursions had met with little resistance.

And then—and then—came Killingford, the great battle in central Pommerelia that had devastated each side of the conflict almost equally—and ultimately forced the surviving Kórynthi forces to withdraw back to their own border.

The kingdom was still paying the lingering price for its foolishness, even decades later.

But what actually had happened during the late summer and fall of the year 845, after the king and his surviving noblemen had returned to Paltyrrha? Something strange, she knew very well—because she'd been a small part of it herself. She needed to know—she *had* to know—all of the events that had been hidden from the world, in order to settle the raging waves of anger and bitterness that ever threatened to consume her, in order to silence the whispering voices that she could never make go away.

"Why, why, why?" was all she wanted to know. Was that overmuch?

But finally, she'd found someone who'd been present there at that time, who'd been a young baron at court during those crucial days and months when everything had changed. His name was Hastur Lord Baniszow, and he'd been waiting to see the Queen for at least five hours now.

It was good to let the men wait: they became more eager to please as a result. Particularly old men, whose bowels became tied in knots after just a few hours of perching their scrawny butts on those hard, hard wooden benches.

"Master Svyet!" she shouted, knowing that the old major-domo was going a bit deaf. "Call for Lord Baniszow!"

"Yes, Majesty," came the response from his alcove near the entranceway—and she could hear his sandals scuffing the tiled floors as he slowly made his way down the long corridor leading from the Yellow Room.

"'Yes, Majesty'," she repeated to herself, smiling a bit at the thought. Svyet knew what she wanted, all right. She never had to worry about *him*!

PROLOGUE TWO
"THE 115TH INDIVIDUAL TO MAKE SUCH AN APPLICATION"

Hastur Lord Baniszow slowly made his way into the reception room. He used a cane to help balance his seventy-year-old body, and from the grimace etched on the lines of his face, even that effort kept him in constant pain.

Still, he displayed remnants of the man he'd once been: he yet sported a full head of gray hair, sprinkled with spots and streaks of ochre, neatly gathered together behind his neck by a silver ring fastened with an azure pin of lapis lazuli from the East. He kept his beard trimmed down to the rim of his jaw; its sole purpose appeared to be to cover his old-man jowl.

The baron quietly bowed his respect, and at a gesture from the Queen, settled himself carefully on a be-cushioned chair to the right of the monarch.

"You are well, I trust," Grigorÿna said.

"I am ever Your Majesty's true and devoted servant," he replied softly.

"So I am told," she said, "although I rarely see you at court these days."

"My, uh, ailments prevent me from traveling overmuch, I am very sorry to say, my Lady. My son and heir, Noble Krikor, acts in my stead most of the time."

"And yet, I was very interested to note"—she nodded to a slightly curled parchment on the small table to her left—"that you have joined the chorus of nobility petitioning for my hand in marriage."

"That is so, Your Grace."

"In fact, you are the 115th individual to make such an application in the last year, since my Council approved the solicitation of possible suitors for my hand. They evidently feel that I should be wed as soon as possible, while I can still bear children. Why should I consider your petition any differently than the others?"

She smiled slightly as she said the words, but noticed that he paid no attention to her facial expression. Instead, he quite suddenly coughed, long and loud, a hacking, chest-wracking paroxysm that sounded halfway fatal.

"Do you require a physician?" the queen asked. She was suddenly concerned that he might not be able to leave the Yellow Room without assistance—or a stretcher.

He held up his hand as he cleared his throat over and over again, trying to regain some small control over his breath.

"Your Majesty will excuse me," he managed to say. "An old ailment."

He coughed again, more feebly this time, cleared his chest once again, and then sat up straight.

"Uh, if...if I may ask...," he almost whispered. "Your other suitors—what kind of men are they?"

"What do you mean?" Grigorÿna asked.

"They are young...or no more than, say, middle-aged." It was a statement, not a query.

"Yes."

"They are rich...or powerful...or foreign...or, well, to put it more bluntly, ambitious," he said.

"Yes."

"They would attempt to subdue your authority, with the assistance of all or some of your Councilmen."

"Yes."

"They would question your decisions and interfere with your rule."

"Yes."

"They would, in short, be a continuing problem to you until you were forced to take quick, brutal action against them—or they against you."

"Yes."

"I would do none of these things."

"Why?" she said, leaning slightly towards him. Clearly, she was intrigued by this novel approach.

"Because I do not want them," he said. "Look at me, Majesty. Look...at...me! I am old, I am worn out, I am ill, I am destined to die in two or five or ten years, after much sickness and debility. I have no ambition at this point in my life. I have no need to prove anything to anyone.

"My small fief is insufficient to engender greed in others: and yet I have enough of all that I need to enjoy whatever life yet remains to me. I have a loving family, with four living children from my two deceased wives, and numerous grandchildren on which to dote. I have enough to eat, a pleasant place to live, and the respect of my peers. I ask you, what more does any man require? I am grateful every day to Almighty God for having been so generous with his gifts to me, a man who deserves nothing.

"And yet I bring you the experience of my years surviving political intrigues at court and in my region, *if* you choose to seek my advice—I certainly will not try to force it upon you. I am incapable of generating additional offspring, however much I might desire them, and so your marriage to me carries with it no danger of 'accidents.' By the time I die, you'll be past child-bearing age."

"And just what do you require in return?" the queen asked. She was amused by this preening relict of the past.

"My son and heir to be advanced to the rank of Count, such title to be passed in due course to his heirs male or female, with myself to receive the title of Duke Consort *ad personam*; a stipend of 1,000 gold angels to be paid to me annually, so long as I shall live; a seat on your Council of State; and the wine concession for the southern half of New Pommerelia."

She chuckled out loud at the latter request; this very bold, bald display of out-and-out greed provided a greater window into the old Baron's soul than anything else he had said.

"You seem to have thought this through very carefully, Lord Baniszow, but you're no saint."

"I have never claimed to be, My Lady. I may be unwell physically, but...."—he tapped the right side of his head with the index finger of his right hand—"...I still have something left up here. As I say, I could be a hidden asset to you...but I promise you that at least I will never be a liability."

"So you aver," she said. "Indeed, so say them all. I will consider your request, sir, and give you a response in due course.

"In the meantime, if you have such concern for my well-being, you could start by helping me *now*."

He cleared his throat once again. "Anything, Majesty."

"You were present at Court, I understand, in the latter half of the Julian Year 845."

Hastur raised one bushy gray eyebrow; clearly, he wasn't expecting her question. "I, uh...yes, that is correct, Your Highness. The small contingent of troops from Baniszow, left to my command by my late father, Lord Pastor, had only reached a few leagues beyond Paltyrrha when we received word of the great Battle of Killingford. The Old King returned to Court with the surviving members of the High Council not long thereafter. Our advance was subsequently halted, and I returned to the capital."

"I know that," the queen said. "What I don't know is exactly what happened subsequently. And I need to understand these things better in order to complete my history of this era. Can you help?"

The old nobleman briefly dropped his head down on his chest, and for the first time looked every bit his three score years and ten. Finally he said: "I was present, to be sure, during all of those proceedings, but My Lady, I was not privy, being of lower rank, to much of what happened."

"But you *are* Psairothi," she said.

"I am, but you understand, Majesty, that I was the heir to a minor fiefdom of the Crown. I never...."

"But you have had, my ambitious little lord, damn near forty years to reminisce and consider what occurred in those days, and to discuss these matters *ad nauseam* with your friends and colleagues; and I have no doubt, none whatsoever, that you did so, at length, because you were *not*, as you have so frequently observed to me already this day, a dunce.

"So, if you wish your petition to succeed with *me*, Hastur son of Pastor, you will pay this price: you will tell me all you know over the next few days, until you can talk no longer about these events; and then you will allow me to probe your mind, your emotions, every thought, as thoroughly as one of my scullery maids might clean the royal privy, or you will gain no privilege from this discussion. Do you understand?"

He sat back a moment, a flare of despite passing over his wrinkled face like a cloud obscuring a bright summer's day; and then coughed again, as he was wont to do to gain a moment's respite to regain his sensiblility, a trait she had already noticed in him.

She smiled to herself once more. She had purchased him— land, life, and all. She looked into his eyes, and knew suddenly that *he* knew—and that he accepted the deal.

"Very well," he finally intoned, "I will make my bargain with the devil, Majesty, and God forgive us both our sins overt and covert."

"So mote it be," she said, sealing the arrangement.

He requested a flagon of wine, and when it was put before him by Master Svyet, cleared his throat for the thousandth time, sipped his drink, and stated:

"In the days following the Old King's return to Court...."

CHAPTER ONE
"I SEND YOU GRAVE TIDINGS"

Anno Domini 1205
Anno Juliani 845

Prince Zakháry and Father Athanasios rode hard throughout the rest of the day, camping overnight near the Spargö River. They started again at daybreak. Although they spotted several unidentified riders from a distance, they encountered no one except official Kórynthi patrols and organized supply trains heading north.

Late on the afternoon of that same day, the Feast of Saint John the Baptist, they finally reached the city of Borgösha. Zakháry immediately produced his credentials and took command.

Everything was filled with chaos and confusion, with men constantly coming and going; the Skopélosz Pass was clogged with troops, war materiel, and supplies. The contingent of soldiers from Arrhénë had just arrived in Borgösha on the previous day. Prince Zakháry ordered Count Sándor to deploy his brigade south and west to block any possible advance of Pommerelian soldiers from Körvö or Dharmagrigg. More supplies were sent north to aid the returning Kórynthi army, flanked by larger-than-normal patrols to safeguard their transit.

* * * * * * *

The Archpriest Athanasios spent the night in Borgösha

sleeping the sleep of the righteous. In the morning, he was given a new mount, and sent on his way to Myláßgorod. Before leaving, he met privately with Prince Zakháry.

"Father," the prince said, coming forward to grasp his hand, "I've certainly enjoyed traveling with you, despite the circumstances. *Bonne chance* for the rest of your trip."

"Thank you, highness," the priest replied. "May God bless all your endeavors, now and in the future."

The next day was the Feast of Saint Maximos. Although Athanasios started through the Skopélosz Pass shortly after sunrise, the way was so crowded that it took him all day to make the journey. The side of the road was littered with broken-down wagons, discarded baggage, and garbage left by the many travelers. The blueberry bushes and ferns that had flourished in the highland meadows when they had climbed through the pass a month earlier had now been trampled into a tangled ruin. It would take many seasons for nature to restore the beauty that had been lost here.

Not long after the dinner hour, he finally reached open country, and rode the last few miles in relative peace, at times cutting through undisturbed fields to avoid the traffic. He reached Myláßgorod at sundown.

At once he sought out Count Zygmunt and presented his credentials, plus a personal message from the hereditary prince, which he handed over immediately.

"My master orders you to stop the flow of men and supplies through the pass at once," he added, "and to keep secret the reasons why you're doing so until he reaches home, about a week from now. Is this understood?"

"Yes, father," the little man replied. "I will do exactly as he says."

"For myself, I request some water for cleansing, a new robe, and something to eat," Athanasios added. "I'll also require the use of your *viridaurum* later this evening."

"Anything, father," Zygmunt indicated, and clapped his hands to bring his servants nigh.

Two hours later the priest transited to Tighrishály Palace in Paltyrrha, and requested a private meeting with Princess-Regent Arrhiána. He was conducted immediately to the council chambers, where the princess was waiting.

"You look very tired, father," she commiserated.

"I've been traveling for days, highness," he acknowledged, "but I do appreciate your concern. I was sent on ahead by Prince Arkády to bring you news of the war. First, I must give you this private message from your brother."

He handed her the missive he had drafted for his master at Saint Paulinos's Abbey.

The princess opened the paper carefully, without breaking the wax seal, which she realized immediately had a special psychic message embedded in it. First she read the written letter:

"Dearest Sister:

"I send you grave tidings. We have met the enemy at Killingford. Both sides have suffered terrible, irreparable losses. Since we cannot continue to prosecute the war in our present state, we have decided to withdraw, carrying our wounded with us. Of the thirty thousand soldiers who started on the trek to Pommerelia, barely five thousand survive. Patriarch Avraäm, King Humfried, Prince Pankratz, Prince Ezzö, and our brother, Prince Nikolaí, are dead, and Prince Norbert is captured by the enemy. Father lives, but his mind is uneasy. We move with all possible speed towards home. I send this letter to you via my trusted servant, the Archpriest Athanasios.

"Your Brother,

"Arkadios Prinképs"

"Oh, Nicky!" was all Arrhiána was able to utter, crossing herself. "God have mercy on all of us."

The cleric murmured a short prayer of remembrance, to which they both said "Amen."

Then Arrhiána pressed her *psai*-ring into the seal. The message buried in the wax further directed the princess to keep the details of the message secret, and to assist the archpriest in locating and retrieving Princess Arizélla.

"I am also ordered, highness," Athanasios continued, "to inform the *Locum Tenens* of the Holy Church of the patriarch's passing, and to secure the Forellëan heir. Do you know where I can find the princess?"

It took Arrhiána a moment to reply. The dimensions of the Kórynthi losses were still swirling around in her head: *Twenty-five thousand men! The cream of the nobility gone! Half the Holy Synod dead!*

"F-father, I think she's, uh, somewhere in Dnéprov," the princess replied, abruptly sitting down with a thud. "I'm sorry, I just don't know where. You'll have to transit down there and find out."

"I'm terribly sorry for your loss, princess-regent," the monk ventured. "I'm particularly saddened about the death of your brother. He was a fine man and a good soldier. I admired his spirit and bravery. It's said that he saved the hereditary prince's life by sacrificing his own."

"That sounds just like Nicky," Arrhiána responded, "always venturing out before anyone else. I just...."

"I understand," the priest said. "I'll take my leave, now, if you please, highness. I must report forthwith to Metropolitan Timotheos."

Arrhiána offered Athanasios her hand, which he kissed, and then he departed. She sat there for half an hour, looking out the window and crying to herself. She would never see her dear brother Nikolaí again on this fair earth.

CHAPTER TWO
"SO MANY, SO VERY MANY"

An hour later, the Archpriest Athanasios walked to the Abbey of Saint Theophanês in Paltyrrha, next to the Cathedral, where he asked to see the Metropolitan Timotheos. He was ushered into a small antechamber a few moments later, and was joined by his old friend not long thereafter.

"Arik!" he exclaimed, dropping to his knees and kissing his mentor's ring.

"How good to see you again, friend Afanásy," the older man replied, lifting the priest to his feet. "You look a bit worse for wear."

"I've seen better days," the archpriest agreed. "I have sad news, holiness. The Thrice Holy Patriarch Avraäm IV has gone to his heavenly reward. He bade me give you this, and commended you as his successor to the Holy Synod."

He pulled the signet ring from his finger, and handed it to the metropolitan. Timotheos turned it over and over in his hand before pocketing it.

"I am the Alpha and the Omega," he said with reverence, bowing his head in respect. "He was a kind and good and gracious man, one of our greatest leaders, I think, although little appreciated by his contemporaries. He knew he was dying, and he undertook this onerous journey anyway."

The archbishop sat down on his stool and shook his head in disbelief. Then he turned back again to Athanasios.

"What of those members of the synod who accompanied the

expedition?" he asked.

"All have perished, metropolitan."

"Then only six remain, including myself," the prelate stated. "I presume this information is to be kept secret until the king returns."

"That is what I was told," the priest confirmed.

"Who else?" the metropolitan inquired.

"Prince Nikolaí, King Humfried, Prince Pankratz, Prince Ezzö, and twenty-five thousand others died. Prince Norbert was taken, and is not expected to survive."

"So many!" Timotheos exclaimed, exhaling with a loud huff, "so very many. When do you expect the king to return?"

"A week, maybe less, depending on the roads," the younger man noted. "They also carry with them a great many injured men."

"I will pray for the recently departed and those recovering," the metropolitan said, "and quietly make arrangements for their return. Will you stay with us for a while?"

"Alas, that I could," the priest said, "but another mission awaits me. I do need a place for the night, though, if you don't mind."

"It will be our pleasure," Timotheos responded, rising and embracing his old comrade. "It's good to have you back, Afanásy, even for a short time."

The metropolitan went to the door, opened it, and stuck his head into the corridor.

"Brother Bogdán," he ordered, "please prepare quarters for Father Athanasios."

Then, turning back to Afanásy: "Now, my friend, if you'll join me in the dining room, we can probably scavenge a cup of herb tea and a slab of old Dürny cheese."

"But that stuff really stinks," the priest responded, making a face. "Yech."

"Not the old kind," Timotheos said. "It still has some vigor left in it. It's just the newer variety that has a certain *odeur* about it. Come along, now, you'll see."

And they spent the rest of the evening together, talking about that other war that Arik had experienced so many eons earlier, until Athanasios suddenly found himself unable to speak further, as the events of recent weeks finally overcame his emotions.

When the metropolitan urged him to unburden himself, the younger man just shook all over and said, "I cannot," taking himself off to his bed. There he found himself reliving the horrors of the battlefield all over again, waking screaming in the heart of the night as the great green globe consumed thousands of lives in just an instant.

For he understood quite suddenly that this had been no accident of fate, that the deaths of his comrades had been an intentional act on the part of another, and that the terror was not yet ended.

CHAPTER THREE
"I AM *NOT* THE HEIR!"

The next morning, Father Athanasios celebrated the Feast of Saints Salvios and Souperios with his mentor and the monks of the abbey. Despite the half-forgotten agonies of the previous night, it filled his soul with joy to be able once again to lift his voice in song to the Lord, harmonizing with his brothers' polyphony. He hadn't realized until then how much he had missed the all-enfolding sanctuary of the church. Perhaps seeing the death and destruction at Killingford had been an epiphany of sorts after all. He had suffered a crisis of faith there, but his faith had survived intact or had even been strengthened.

He embraced Metropolitan and *Locum Tenens* Timotheos, he who had once been Arik Rufímovich, again before departing. His friend was growing old, Athanasios thought, but he still had something further to contribute to the growth of the Holy Church.

"I too believe that you are the man to lead us through reconstruction," Athanasios stated, looking his mentor in the eye, "and I will pray that the Holy Synod has sufficient wisdom to realize this."

Arik laughed. "And *I* will pray they don't, Afanásy. Take care on your journey. Come see me again soon."

Athanasios used the *viridaurum* mirror just off the vestibule of the Chapel of Saint Kasdôê to transit himself to the Cathedral of Saint Phaustos in Dnepróvgorod, the capital of the County of Dnéprov. The Metropolitan having been one of those who had been summoned to the capital, Athanasios sought out the Archbishop Aphrikanos, the *Locum Tenens* of the metropolitanate, and an old acquaintance from Saint Svyatosláv's Abbey.

"Afanásy Ivánovich," welcomed the prelate, "how pleasant to see you."

"Nazáry Kriskéntovich," the archpriest responded, "you look the same as you did thirty years ago."

"I should hope not!" Aphrikanos chuckled, rubbing his big belly and watching it bounce. "So what brings you out to our deserted city?"

"Running errands for our king, as usual," the priest noted. "Now he wants me to make certain that King Humfried's sister is safe. I don't know how she could be any safer than in Dnéprov, but you know how it goes. We do what we're ordered to do."

"Isn't *that* the truth!" the archbishop agreed. "So what do you need to know?"

"Specifically, where the Princess Arizélla is located," Athanasios said. "And, of course, I have to verify that she's all right."

"Well, I know she has a *dacha* somewhere down the coast, and she may still be living there," Aphrikanos indicated. "She's a bit of a hermit, you know, and I haven't heard anything specific about her for quite some time, oh, maybe six months or a year, at least. Father Pompeios, one of my aides, can give you specific directions to her place. He's been down there on a couple of occasions to say mass.

"Oh yes, and you'll need some transportation: I don't think she has a *viridaurum*. I'm afraid that all we can provide is an old donkey, if that's all right. It's about a twelve-mile trip into the country.

"Can you stay for lunch?" he added.

"I'd be honored," Athanasios agreed, not knowing how to get out of the invitation without appearing too obvious.

As they ate, the priest avoided questions about the war, just saying that the king was still in the west on campaign.

After the meal, the priest bade his farewells to his old

comrade, and rode out into Dnéprov Town. It was a clear, clean day, with the cool wind blowing in off the bay, and gulls as large as chickens screeching insults overhead. Laundry was hung from some of the windows of the two-storey houses that lined the cobblestoned streets of the city. He followed the main road down towards the waterfront, and as he descended the long hill, he could see the tiny ships coming and going from the piers.

A few blocks before the road dead-ended at the quay, it intersected with a major cross-street, and he turned to the left there, following the new street out of town. As he neared the eastern edge of the port, he noticed the beautifully-kept manor houses of the wealthy merchants and shippers, stacked up the hillside one on top of another. He followed the road into the country as it became a well-traveled, dusty wagon path, filled with farmers bringing their vegetables into town.

Gradually, the shoreline began to lift, and the road with it, until the drop from the cliff was several hundred feet down to the crashing waves below. He could smell the myriad flowers blossoming around him. Everything was green and lush.

Outside of town were a series of large estates set far back from the road, but further on he encountered mostly the small freeholdings of local farmers, interspersed with the occasional summer *dachas* of the wealthy.

After traveling most of the afternoon, with the sun still shining but low in the sky, Athanasios finally espied the landmark he had been given by Father Pompeios: a large formation of twin rock pillars poking out of the sea just a few hundred yards off the coast, the so-called Breasts of Loryù, named for one of the pagan gods of the Elders, who had supposedly once visited or resided at this place. Their rounded tops made a spectacular sight as they were rouged by the rays of the declining sun.

Around the next bend, he finally saw Princess Arizélla's *dacha*, and turned in at the path that led to her door. He was exhausted, and sincerely hoped that he hadn't come all of this way for nothing.

No one seemed to notice his arrival. He tied up his donkey, and pounded on the door. Still no answer. Then he walked around the small place, and onto the back terrace, which over-looked the wine-kissed sea. A middle-aged woman was seated there, her back to him, her gray-streaked hair braided down her back to her waist. She was drawing the vista with a piece of charcoal on a thin section of wood or paper.

He started to speak, but she cut him off with a harsh, "Sssh!"

So he waited patiently, and when the sun had finally set, she finished what she was doing, and said: "What do you want?"

"Are you Princess Arizélla?" he asked.

"Who wants to know?" she demanded.

"I am the Archpriest Athanasios Hokhanêmsos...," he began, before being cut off again.

"Well, Archpriest Athanasios Hokhanêmsos," she repeated, "you've found her. So I'll ask you again: what do you want?"

Father Athanasios didn't know what to make of this prin-cess. Women were a mystery to him anyway, and this one was unlike anyone he'd ever known. She seemed to have none of the sophistication of the women he had met at court.

"Highness," he finally iterated, "I bring you sad tidings. Last week there was a battle in Pommerelia at a place called Killingford. We suffered terrible losses. Your brother, your nephew, and your great-nephew Pankratz were all killed. Prince Norbert was captured by the enemy, and was certainly executed, or will be shortly. *You* are the next heir to the throne of Pommerelia, and I have been asked by the king to bring you back to court."

"I am *not* the heir," she growled. "Little man, you don't even know your royal genealogy." She slapped her wrist. "Damn bugs come out when the sun goes down. We'd better get inside. Follow me," she added, and he had no choice but to obey.

Her *dacha* consisted of three small rooms and a kitchen. There were no servants. She lit an oil lamp and set it on the mantel. Then she motioned to the one good chair in the place.

He hesitated to take it, this not being the kind of manners one offered to a lady, until she barked, "Would you *please* sit down." So he did.

"Well, I can't say that I'm going to miss my pipsqueak of a nephew or his two brawny babes," she admitted, "but I'm sorry to hear about Ezzösh. I tried to talk him out of going, but his mind was too far gone to listen to a mere woman. Didn't used to be like that, you know. He was a good man once, until his brains turned to mush.

"You want something to drink?" she asked.

When he shook his head "no," she added: "Well, I'm going to have one anyway."

She put some clear liquid from a jug into a pewter cup.

"Sure you won't try some of this stuff?" she inquired. "It'll take some of the dust off your hide, that's for sure," she added, quaffing it down in one swallow.

"All right," he allowed.

She poured him a cup, and handed it to him. He sipped it and choked, spitting it out. When he had recovered, he could hear a gurgling sound, and realized that she was laughing so hard, she couldn't speak.

She pulled up a stool, and poured herself another.

"Look, priest," she said, "even if they're all dead and buried, there's still silly Salentína, Humfried's little girl. She comes before me, and she's welcome to it, by God."

"Well, they say that she's the offspring of a morganatic marriage," he noted.

"Bullcocky!" the princess spat. "Hogwash and hokum. She's got no royal blood in her on her mother's side, to be sure, not that any of that ever seemed to matter much to our family if their hips were wide enough, but Lady Pulkhériya *af* Jutta comes from a noble family with a pedigree as long as your leg. It may be a foreign title, but it's as ancient and honorable as anything we have here. So, where *is* Princess Salentína?"

"They say she was captured with *Junior*," Athanasios stated.

"Well, no wonder, then," she snorted. "If they haven't got one, they'll substitute another. Sorry. I have better things to do with my life, little priest. Go away and leave me with some of that proverbial peace of yours.

"Would you like some sun tea?" she added, suddenly changing her mood. "You look a little green around the gills."

"Please, highness," he said. He was still trying to get the taste of whatever it was out of his mouth.

"Just a moment," she replied. Humming a ditty under her breath, she went into the kitchen, and began fumbling around amongst the jumble of things out there, with a clang and a bang and a rattle of pots and pans.

His eyes had finally adjusted to the dim light, and wandered around the room while he was waiting for her. He noticed many sculptures and busts and paintings attached to the shelves and walls of her cottage, and took the opportunity to examine them more closely. He assumed that she had fashioned most of them, and although he was no connoisseur, some of them seemed to him quite evocative.

"Like my stuff?"

He jumped from the sound of her voice, seemingly right behind him, and twirled around, but no one was there.

Again he heard her laughing, like a tinkling of silver bells. She was certainly unlike anyone else in her family. Arizélla came out of the kitchen, holding a container of warm herb tea.

"Neat trick, huh?" she quipped. "My father taught it to me when I was a little girl. Don't have a chance to use it much anymore. Here's your tea," she added, pouring him a cup. "I think you'll find it a wee smoother going down than the old rotgut. I also brought you some fresh cakes and honey. I keep the hives right across the road."

"Hmmm," he murmured, "now *that's* good."

"'Course it is," she agreed, her eyes twinkling. "It's all natural, see, fresh from the sun and the rain. That's all I've got around here. Don't eat any meat."

She went to light another, much larger lamp.

"Sorry about the smell," she added. "All we have is fish oil, lots and lots of fish oil. You could take a bath in the stuff, if you wanted to, not that anyone ever would."

Then she showed him all of her things, clearly delighted that someone, *anyone* was interested in her creations.

"Well, there's not a lot to do around here," she continued, "other than contemplate your navel, and you can only do that for so long before you get an *ouroboros* from it. Still, I like the peacefulness of the place. Nobody tells you what to do.

"See, priest, if I go back, then everybody's going to want something out of me all of the time, just nit nit nit, if you know what I mean. I really got tired of the 'life,' as we royals call it, after my pretty girl Tamára died. And when my hubby passed on too, well, I got me this place, and gradually started spending more time here than anywhere else. I really like it. Now you're going to try to ruin me, aren't you?"

Athanasios didn't answer her directly, but instead pointed to a small ring of bronze attached to one wall.

"Did you make that?" he inquired.

"Nah," she scoffed. "Give me more credit than that, little man! I only kept it because of Papá."

"How do you mean?" the archpriest asked.

"That old nag Zubayda had a thing about memorial rings," Arizélla responded. "I guess they're common back in Tôrtous, where she came from. Anyway, when Papá and King Makáry and his two sons were killed at Dürkheim, she immediately had a set made for the royals, and everybody in the family got one. The inscription's supposedly written in one of the ancient languages of the east, although I've never met anyone who could read it. Each of the rings was personalized. I was told that mine said, 'Arizélla, daughter of Kazimir.' Here, take a closer look."

She pulled it off the peg on which it was hung, and handed it to him. He examined it carefully, memorizing the inscription. Except for the lettering, it was *absolutely identical* to the torc he still kept in his trunk as a remembrance from his earliest days.

"In fact, you can have the piece if you really want it," she added, stirred by his interest. "Zölla's got one of her own hidden away somewhere, and no one else in my family would be the least bit interested. That's true of all this junk."

She waved her hand around in a wide semicircle.

"You see, everyone was rather embarrassed by them. They reminded people of a very bad time, and as soon as Zubayda was dead, away they all went into storage closets and such. I only kept mine out because I have so little left of Papá to remember him by, and he was such a good father to us three. I cried and cried when he died."

She abruptly sat down, suddenly downcast.

"So tell me, priest, how bad was it this time? Tell me of the awful things my family has done to the good people of Pommerelia so we can make life perfect for them again."

He sat down heavily in the hand-stuffed chair, the only one in the *dacha*, and sipped the sun tea this lovely lady had prepared for him, and ate her bread and honey. He suddenly felt very sad, as if all the cares of the world were piling up on him. Then he began talking to her, unraveling his soul, and he continued until the whole story was told, what he knew of it, which was not everything; and for no reason that he could ever identify, he started to cry, very silently, for all the dead soldiers and all the dead civilians he had met on his journeys this past year, and all the dead souls he would visit in the future.

Will it never end? he thought to himself. *Will it never pass?*

He felt the slight whisper of a handkerchief brushing away his tears, and the press of her soft lips on his brow.

"I do not think so, father," she replied from the safety of her stool.

She sighed very heavily, and looked poignantly and lingeringly around her cottage.

"I will return with you to Paltyrrha," the Princess Arizélla spake. "There are things to be done and words to be said, and they *do* matter, little priest. They do. You'll understand that someday, when you begin making choices that affect people's lives. But I will miss my pretty *dacha*, that I will."

Then she became *la belle dame sans merci* again, her eyes flashing, her mouth laughing.

Had I met this woman when she was young, Athanasios thought, *I would never have become a priest.*

"Time for bed, Father 'A,'" she merrily chirped. "We retire early out in the sticks."

"I, uh, I'll use the s-stables," the priest stammered out.

"You'll do no such thing!" she snorted. "We don't even have a stable, but I do have a spare cot in my cot, or were you thinking I meant something else, eh?"

The princess giggled.

Athanasios blushed beet red.

She grabbed his hand, and pulled him up.

"Come along now, I'll show you where everything is," Arizélla chuckled, leading the way.

My God, he thought to himself, *if she kisses me now, I'll gladly spend the next twenty years here.*

But of course she didn't, much to his silent regret, because although she liked him, she didn't play those kinds of games with people.

Although he didn't expect to, he slept quite soundly, being awakened in the morning by the sound of mockingbirds singing and the smell of eggs cooking.

It was the Feast of Saint Zôïlos, and he said his prayers with joy in his heart for the first time in a month.

"Sleep well, did you? The country'll do that for you," Arizélla observed. "Come now, I've got some good eats to put some pounds on those skinny limbs of yours."

She put down on the table a huge platter of fresh food—eggs, bread, cheese, and milk—the likes of which he had not seen in a very long time.

"This is...ambrosia," he managed to choke out between bites.

"Why, thank you, dear priest," she returned, smiling. "Tell me, what do your friends call you?"

"My original name is Afanásy, but I also go by Athy."

"Athy, eh?" She turned it over on her tongue like a bit of dough. "Pithy enough, even for a priest. Some folks 'round these parts call me Élla. You may do so also, as long as we're by ourselves."

"Princess, uh, Élla, I only have one donkey, which of course you're welcome to use," he fumbled, "but how do you propose that we get back to town quickly."

"Well, if it's Dnepróvgorod you're heading for, there's no quick way about it, Athy," Arizélla noted. "We're about a dozen miles away, and I don't have anything here but a couple of milkers. When I really need something, I just use the transit mirror."

"The mirror?"

He felt like a schoolboy again. It had never occurred to him that she might have a private *viridaurum* in her *dacha*, but of course, she had to have one.

"Yes!" she emphasized. "We can go anytime you want, *after* I've cleaned up a bit and let the neighbors know I'm going to be gone for a while."

A coal black cat came wandering through the open back door.

"Sybélla," she murmured, "there you are, my pretty kitty!"

She picked up the feline, and began stroking her. Athanasios could hear the purr clear across the room.

"She always shows up when she wants something," Arizélla said.

She put some milk into a small tray, and set it out. The cat immediately started slurping.

"You see what I mean? We're not so different," the princess noted. "Very well, priest, I can see you're impatient to go, now that one of your hungers has been satisfied. Pah, men are all alike. Sit down over there"—she imperiously pointed to the one good chair—"out of the way, please, while I do what must be done."

For the first time in his life, Father Athanasios understood, in a small way, what he had missed and what he could have had, if his choices had been different.

But then, he thought, *he wouldn't have been the same person. No regrets*, he added, *none.*

CHAPTER FOUR
"YOU'D BETTER OBEY ME"

Back in Paltyrrha, the Princess Royal, Her Serene Highness the Lady Grigorÿna Arkádiyevna von Tighrisha, was entertaining the Doll Family to luncheon. She had managed to find twenty-two of them stashed in different places around the palace, and had set them all before a long, low table which she thought perfectly appropriate for the high lords and ladies at court.

Of course, her own family had the primacy of honor at the head of the table: herself, Lady Louisa, Lady Sylyána, Lord Bánya, and Lord Philogón. These she had dressed out in all their best finery. For herself, she had put on her prettiest court dress. On one dainty white arm she wore a gold band with a snake design engraved 'round it, a bracelet that she had found in a distant, unused room of the palace; and on the other a small bronze ring etched with funny characters on the inside. This one had come from the dregs of an old trunk. Hung about her neck was a chain of white metal, from which dangled the silver bell of calling.

"I say, Lord Phil," Bánya intoned, "would you be so good as to pass the *borscht* and the *shchi*?"

"Quite pleased, old chap," Philogón replied. "What news of the war?"

"It's going well, I hear," Lord Silyán noted. "We smash the bloody fiends wherever we can find them, which is often. Hear, hear! Waiter, more *kvass*!"

Lady Ouisa was already bored with all the men talk.

"Sylyána," she interjected, "I hear Lady Aventína has been seen with Prince Parsival."

"No!" Sylyána replied. "And I thought he was seeing Lady Denÿsya! The wicked wretch!"

"Would you like more wine, Lady Ouisa?" Princess Grigorÿna inquired, ever most politely, as befitted her exalted status as the sponsor of this party.

"Why, thank you, no," Louisa said. "But I was wondering how you and that curious Doctor Melanthrix are getting along."

"Well," the princess replied, "he's not back from the war yet. I do expect him quite soon!"

"It wasn't very nice of him to go away when your brother was ill," Ouisa noted.

"He had to!" Grigorÿna exclaimed. "Grandpapá needed him."

"A likely story!" Lord Bánya stated. "Why, he's not even a military man. No credentials, what?"

"Too true, old thing," Philogón agreed. "He would only have been in the way. He would have served the glorious cause much better by tending the Hereditary-Prince-To-Be."

"But Ari's all right now," the princess emphasized.

"No thanks to Melanthrix," Lady Konstántsiya chirped.

"No thanks to Melanthrix!" they all agreed.

Princess Grigorÿna looked around the table in consternation.

"This is no fun," she said. "We're supposed to be having a party."

"How can we have a party when Melanthrix is absent?" Ouisa inquired. "Why don't you call him?"

"Mamá says I'm not supposed to use the bell 'cept in 'mergencies," Grigorÿna noted.

"Well, this looks like an emergency to me!" Lord Rádost stated.

"This looks like an emergency to me!" they all chimed in.

"*Stop it!*" Rÿna ordered. "*Just stop it!* This is *my* party, and I can invite whomever I please. And you'd better obey me, too, or

I'll send all of you home. *All of you!*" she shouted.

After that they were all as silent as death.

The Princess Royal, Her Serene Highness the Lady Grigorÿna Arkádiyevna von Tighrisha, smiled. Sometimes you just had to show them who was in charge.

CHAPTER FIVE
"TOO DAMNED QUIET"

At mid-morning on the following day, the Feast of Saint Eirénaios, the retreating Kórynthi army finally reached Karkára. They had actually been in contact with Prince Kiríll's patrols and supply wagons for several days now, and the prince himself was waiting for them at Lüstern Field.

Several hundred men had perished from their injuries during the five-day trek, but another thirty or so missing soldiers had drifted into camp along the way back, happily telling their stories of escape and adventure around the evening campfires.

"Hail, King Kipriyán!" saluted Kiríll, as the lead elements of the army finally came to a halt.

But the king just stared dully off into space, making no response.

Prince Arkády reached over and grabbed his younger brother's elbow in the ancient manner of two warriors greeting each other.

They talked privately for a moment.

"Any change?" quietly asked Kiríll, nodding at the king.

"None," Arkády whispered. "He's been like that, off and on, since Killingford. It's when he starts shouting orders for us to charge the enemy that I have to have Melanthrix sedate him again. It makes the men nervous. What news here?"

"Quiet. Too damned quiet, to my way of thinking." Kiríll shook his head. "We've got the supply spigot shut off up north, and managed to save most of the wagons that were on their way down to Saint Paulinos's. I've ordered General Khydión to withdraw his forces back to Lockenlöd Castle and environs. He really doesn't have enough soldiers to do anything else.

"Down here," he continued, "we've set up a series of temporary forts along the Spargö, which have virtually stopped the attacks by the irregulars. Zack and I have also established a series of patrols between Karkára and Borgösha."

"Well done, brother," Arkády noted. "We need to get the king back to Paltyrrha as quickly as possible. News about the battle will start circulating soon in Kórynthia, and the royals have to be seen again by the *hoi polloi* there before that happens. The king and I will stay overnight in Karkára. Tomorrow you'll join us in riding down to Podébrad. We can use one of the mirrors there to transit to Paltyrrha. I'll leave General Rónai in charge here; he's now recovered well enough to resume command. We'll send the remnants of the army south to Borgösha; the Skopélosz Pass is much easier on the vehicles, and many of our wounded are still wagon-bound. Those who haven't perished yet will probably survive."

He turned in his saddle.

"Lord Rónai!" the prince shouted.

When that officer had reported, Arkády said: "Have the men camp here overnight. Tomorrow, we'll march them south to Borgösha under the command of General Zinón Karélovich. The King, Doctor Melanthrix, Lord Gorázd, the servant Siméon, and I will return to Paltyrrha via Podébrad, together with Prince Kiríll. *You* will take command of our forces around Karkára. My orders are to continue our patrols for a week, and then withdraw to Lüstern, establishing a perimeter here at the base of the canyon.

"By the way," he added, "how's your leg?"

"Much better, highness," the officer responded, "and thank you for inquiring. Now I'd best get to my men. May I be excused?"

Arkády waved his hand, then turned back to Kiríll.

"Let's ride out," he said. "Rónai's quite capable, and doesn't need my supervision. I'm very concerned about father, Kir. He needs all the rest he can get."

Then they headed up the pass with the king and Melanthrix and several aides in tow.

CHAPTER SIX
"I TOLD OUISA"

In Paltyrrha, meanwhile, Princess-Regent Arrhiána and Dowager Queen Brisquayne were privately and carefully questioning Princess Grigorÿna.

"Do you remember, Rÿna," Arrhiána was asking, "when we visited Granny's house in Kórynthály, and we were talking about Great-Aunt Mösza?"

"Oh, yes, Auntie Rhie," the girl replied. "I had lots of fun there."

"Did you mention her name to anyone?" her aunt continued.

"I told Ouisa," Rÿna ventured. "I tell her *everything*."

"Who's Ouisa?" the queen inquired.

"Would you like to meet her?" the little girl chirped. "I'll go get her."

Grigorÿna rushed off and came back a few moments later, dragging the rag doll in one hand.

"This is Lady Louisa Doroféa," Rÿna exclaimed, forcing the doll to bow. "She's the Vasílyissa of Pargamón."

"Where's that, Rÿna?" asked Brisquayne.

"Oh, somewhere far away to the east, I think," the girl stated. "I'm not too sure."

"May I see her?" the queen insisted.

When the princess handed the doll over, Brisquayne centered herself on her *psai*-ring, and suddenly dived into the eyes of the image. The rags twisted in her closed hands, trying to escape the probe, but the queen held on tightly. She was relentless in her pursuit, chasing the thing 'round and 'round the interior of the doll's head, until there was an audible "squawk" and rip, and out popped a small, coal black toad.

It jumped before anyone could react, then leapt again, heading right under a low table. Arrhiána tried to move the furniture away, but Brisquayne stopped her.

"You'll never catch it," the queen sighed. "It's gone already. Once you lose sight of the bloody things, they're impossible to find again. It's already gone back to its master."

"What was it?" Rhie asked.

"A little bit of nastiness from the east," Brisquayne noted, smiling slightly. "They call them *ifrits*. Think of them as minor dæmons, and you'd be close enough. Sometimes, if you know just how, you can catch one and bind it to yourself and make it your slave. That's what this was: someone else's pet. I think we can all guess whose. And there was something further, Rhie."

She picked up Louisa, who had fallen to the floor during their minor drama. The queen held the doll face-up on her palm, so they could see the two shining, emerald crystals sewn as eyes onto its forehead. She ignited a flame on the rings of her left hand, breathed the word "*árnyék*," and then reached with her five fingers into the space between the two "eyes," pulling out of the doll's head a larger third one. It was dark green and pulsing, like the heart of a chameleon, and it looked alive.

Brisquayne threw it to the floor, uttered the word "*halál*," and crushed it beneath her foot. Arrhiána thought she heard a thin scream fading into the distance.

"Something different?" Arrhiána inquired.

"'Different' is the right word to use," the queen agreed. "They call them *xixiegui yanjing*, and they come from the land of the yellow men, a long, long ways to the east. There are two different agencies at work here, Rhie."

"Spies spying on the spies, eh?" Arrhiána commented.

"It rather looks that way," Brisquayne said.

"But what about Ouisa?" Rÿna cried.

"She's just fine," her aunt stated, handing the doll back to her. "She was just a little sick, that's all, and now she's all better again."

"Can I go play now?" the little girl asked.

"Of course you can," Arrhiána allowed.

When Rȳna had left, the princess posed another question.

"Is there any way of tracing these 'things' back to their starting points?"

"There probably is," the queen indicated, "but it's way beyond my knowledge or abilities."

"Could there be more around?" her granddaughter asked.

"Possibly," Brisquayne nodded. "I'll check her other toys over the next few days. But this kind of thing is insidious. Whoever put these little trinkets here could easily withdraw them, leaving no trace, and then reinsert them somewhere else when our guard is down again. There are supposed to be stringent rules that forbid the cross-use of magical elements from other traditions, but enforcement is often lax. These things are surprisingly easy to come by if you know where to ask for them. There's a marketplace in Kharrákh...."

The door suddenly popped open, and the steward appeared.

"Very sorry, highness," he intoned, "a visitor to see you."

"Who is it, Mögh?" Arrhiána asked.

"Some personage named Élla. *That* is all she would say, highness," he stated, clearly displeased, "together with some minor cleric called Athanasios."

"Show them in, Mögh," the princess ordered, trying to keep from laughing.

"Very good, mistress," he responded. "The Lady Élla, the Archpriest Athanasios," he announced, then withdrew.

"Arizélla!" Arrhiána exclaimed, rising from her chair and embracing her cousin.

"Dearest Rhie, you haven't changed a bit," Élla replied. "Too damn many Ari's in this family to keep them all straight. Arizélla, Arrhiána, Arión, even my cousin, Ariélle. And *she* had a daughter named Arilándra, now gone, alas."

She glanced into the corner.

"My God, is that *you*, Quayne? Haven't seen you in *years*. Put on a few pounds, huh? Well, haven't we all?"

"Élla, thank the Lord some folks never change," the old woman replied. "You're always a breath of fresh air in this dusty old palace of ours. Now just come over here and give me a kiss."

They hugged each other like the old friends they were, and then drew back a little.

"What brings you to these parts?" the queen inquired. "I'd heard you'd become a kind of hermit somewhere."

"Well, I *was!*, too," Élla said, "until that blasted priest rousted me out. Said I had to come back."

"Who?" Brisquayne asked.

"Him!" Arizélla pointed to the doorway, where Athanasios was standing.

"Good morrow, ladies," he stated, bowing low. "I'm sorry to intrude."

"Oh, come on in, little priest," Élla blurted out. "He's just the most delightful humbug you ever did see, ladies. We had a *great* time in Dnéprov."

She raised her eyes suggestively.

Father Athanasios blushed bright red. "I, uh...," he mumbled.

For the first time in a great many years, he had absolutely no idea of what to say.

"Why, *father*," the Princess Arrhiána said, totally amused at his discomfiture, "am I to understand that *you*...."

"No, *of course not!*" he exclaimed, more hurriedly than he needed to. "There was *never* any...."

"Any *what?*" asked Brisquayne, chuckling to herself, keeping the game going.

"I, uh," he mumbled, looking miserably back and forth at all three women. "I really don't know," he finally admitted.

"That's pretty obvious," the queen noted. "You must be a remarkable man, Father Athanasios, to get Élla to do something she didn't really want to do. Why, the last person to accomplish that little trick was...."

"Just never you mind, Quayne!" Arizélla snapped. "Not a

word!"

"Oh, all right," Brisquayne agreed. "But I don't think Rhie has heard that story."

"And she *won't*, either," Élla emphasized.

"So, why *are* you here?" the queen continued.

Arrhiána caught Élla's eye and shook her head.

"It appears I'm not allowed to say," Arizélla said.

"That bad, huh?" Brisquayne commented. "Well, it must have something to do with the war. Things must be going very poorly indeed to bring you all the way back to Paltyrrha, when you obviously didn't want to come. Someone must have died. I know, I'm not supposed to say anything, and I won't. I'm just an old gossip, you know. By the way, Élla, did you know Princess Mösza when she was at court?"

"Mösza? Now *that's* a name I haven't heard in a long, long time," Arizélla noted. "No, I didn't know her except in passing. I was about thirteen when she disappeared. I think Dowager Hereditary Princess Zubayda felt sorry for me after Papá was killed. A month or two later, when the funerals were over and we were getting ready to go back home, Zee told me I could go through Mösza's things and pick out whatever I wanted from her wardrobe, but only if I'd take them to Dnéprov with me. There was also some jewelry, a couple of miniatures, things like that. I just helped myself. I asked Zee when Mösza was coming home, and got a one-word response: 'Never!' She wouldn't say why, wouldn't even talk about her after that."

"Do you know why she left court?" Father Athanasios interjected.

The woman looked at him in great surprise.

"Not really," Élla responded slowly. "I wasn't that close to her. After all, she was a grown woman, and I was still a girl. I don't even know for sure when she left. The last time I saw her was in May, when some of the womenfolk went to Kórynthály for a *fête* sponsored by Zubayda. King Makáry and his sons were there, but Papá and Grandpapá were in Pommerelia. I remember that Mösza had had too much wine to drink, and she was laughing and carrying on with some of the men. Being only thirteen, I was fascinated with it all, of course. It's strange. Although I stayed in Paltyrrha till fall, I never saw her in public again."

"Well, ladies," Father Athanasios said, "I probably should get back to the abbey." He bowed. "It's been a pleasure."

"I expect it *was*," Brisquayne agreed.

The women all laughed. Athanasios just grimaced, and then departed.

CHAPTER SEVEN
"KILL HER, BEZARDUARDAKUS!"

Late that evening, Mösza confronted the *ifrit* in her home in the Jabal Khaibár. The creature now had the appearance of a hunchbacked little man about a foot in height. Its skin was black and covered with small bumps and protrusions. Its ebon hair was wound 'round its head into a turban-shaped mass, and held in place by two stubby horns, also black.

"Mithrethth," it lisped in its high, squeaky voice, bowing very low, "Bezarduardakuth hath failed."

"So it would appear," Mösza agreed. "How did this happen?"

"The witch Brithquayne," it responded. "Thomehow the woman knew."

"Yesss," she mused, "Brisquayne. She's becoming a real nuisance, my little friend."

Then she turned back again to the *ifrit*. "You know the price of failure?" she asked.

"Not my fault, mithtrethth!" the creature whined. "Merthy," it pleaded, raising two little clawed hands in supplication.

"You're very fortunate that I've had a good day today," Mösza stated. "*Verry* lucky. So, you want another chance, do you? Oh, all right." She idly waved her hand. "Kill Brisquayne."

"Mithtrethth," the miniature beast squeaked, "it ith forbidden."

The woman said nothing in reply, but walked over to a shelf. There she looked at the receptacles carefully, and chose one that had a little red pip in it. It was stoppered with a lead seal embossed with the sigil of Solomon. This container she carried over to her work table, where a large candle was standing. She lit the wick with the ring on her finger, and began roasting the *ifrit*'s heart over the flame. She hummed a little ditty as she worked: "Alas, my love...."

"Wait!" the creature screamed.

Mösza looked around, but did not move her hand even an iota.

"Bezarduardakuth will do it!" the *ifrit* squealed.

She waited a half-moment more before finally removing the flask from the candle flame.

"A little singed, perhaps, but still beating, eh?" she smiled. "I'm really glad we had this heart-to-heart. It's just too bad that the course of true love never did run straight. Still, how nice that even a creature as debased as yourself can see the sweet light of reason. Why, it's enough to give a poor woman hope. Perhaps I'll even meet an honest man one day."

She put the container back in its place on the shelf, and muttered a few words.

"There, nice and safe again," she crooned. "We wouldn't want our things disturbed, now, would we? Kill her, Bezarduardakus! Please do it soon."

"Yeth, mithtrethth," the thing said, touching its head to the table. With an audible "pop," it vanished.

"Now, where are my sweetums?" she murmured, looking about the room. "Doggiewogs! Would my little doggums like some treaties?"

CHAPTER EIGHT
"ANY OLD FOOL CAN BECOME A KING"

The next morning, on the Feast of Saints Peter and Paul, King Kipriyán and his two sons, with Lord Gorázd, Melanthrix, and Siméon, together with their bodyguards and entourage, rode out from Castle Karkára into Westmark in Kórynthia. After several weeks of unremitting heat and humidity, the weather had finally eased. The skies were overcast, and a light drizzle was falling as they exited the Szamár Gate.

They continued down the Gálla Pass all morning, finally reaching the plain around midday. The sun now appeared from behind feathery clouds, but the air remained cool and clear, a refreshing change from Pommerelia's stifling heat.

"It's good to be back on our own soil again," Prince Kiríll noted.

The road was broad and well-kept, marked at regular intervals with granite milestones.

For the first time since Killingford, the king showed some interest in his surroundings.

"Prince Mikíta had a summer retreat near here," he muttered, seemingly to no one.

"Indeed, majesty," Prince Arkády responded, "did you ever stay there?"

"In my youth," Kipriyán stated. "Great-Uncle Víktor brought me here every summer after Papá died, until I came of age." He sighed. "Then...."

He was silent again for several hours.

When they came within sight of the great ecclesiastical city of Podébrad later in the afternoon, he bestirred himself once more.

"While Víktor was alive, he ruled this place as a direct fief of the crown," Kipriyán noted. "All of Westmark was his. He never wanted to be Regent of Kórynthia, and he returned here whenever he could. I remember that he sat me down once right across from him, not long before I attained my majority, and looked me straight in the eye.

"'Kyp,' Víktor said, 'any old fool can become a king. It's just an accident of birth. *This is especially true in your case.* Don't ever forget that God passed over several of your kin to pick *you* instead. You're special. And it's a great responsibility that He's given you. Every time you make a decision, you affect someone else's life. God will hold you accountable for that.

"'Your grandmother and I have done the best we could for you, but in the end, you have to make your own decisions. Not all of them will be easy, and you'll have your share of mistakes. You'll learn to live with those, or they'll eat you up from the inside out. I'm not proud of everything I've done as Regent, but at least I can say that I haven't sent too many men to their deaths. Maybe God will forgive me my other errors. You're young, my boy, you'll have a long reign. When you get to the end of it, I hope you can still look at yourself in the mirror. I hope you can forgive yourself.'"

Then he began to cry. Arkády and Kiríll looked at each other in bewilderment, but when Melanthrix started to move his horse closer, Arkády shooed him back with a sweep of his hand.

Later than evening they transited back to Paltyrrha.

CHAPTER NINE
"YOU'RE LEGALLY REGENT"

The last day of June was a Sunday, the Feast of Saint Iórikos. The appearance of the royal family at the mass held at *tritê* in Saint Konstantín's Cathedral was a *cause célèbre* in Paltyrrha, for only a handful of individuals had been aware of their return. The absence of the Princes Nikolaí and Zakháry and the Forellës was noted by the more astute, as was the presence of Princess Arizélla, and the haggard appearance of the king was considered a matter of great concern by the surviving elder statesmen. When the rising buzz of conversation threatened to disrupt the celebration of the Eucharist, the Hereditary Prince stepped forward and begged forgiveness of the *Locum Tenens* for this breach of etiquette.

"My lords and ladies," he intoned, "do not allow any words of disrespect to be voiced here in this holy place, lest ye be judged by a Higher Authority. The king will preside at a formal session of court in the morning, and will make an announcement at that time. Now, please, allow Metropolitan Timotheos to resume the service uninterrupted."

This was sufficient to quiet most of the talk, and the mass continued. In his homily, the acting head of the church of Kórynthia spoke to the parable of the prodigal son, and how good it was for long-absent members of the flock to be welcomed back into the fold once again. His meaning was not lost on King Kipriyán, who glared back at him from where he was standing in the front row.

After the service was completed, scores of the nobility crowded around the royal family, looking for news of their sons and brothers and husbands, but Prince Arkády again begged for silence, and put off any responses until the following morning. Then, with the permission of the metropolitan, the prince quickly ushered his family back through the sacristy, and into the alcove there, and they used the *viridaurum* to transit to the palace.

The king was bundled off to a well-deserved rest in his apartments, where Polyxena was waiting for him, while Arkády and Kiríll conferred with Princess-Regent Arrhiána.

"Who's stationed at Katonaí Field?" Arkády inquired.

"The Velyaminóli Brigade arrived last week, and we held them there pending further orders," Arrhiána responded.

"Since you're legally regent until tomorrow morning, when the king officially resumes the throne," the prince continued, "I would suggest that you send an order to the commander at Katonaí, putting him on full alert, just in case the news is not what the crowd in Paltyrrha is expecting. They may decide to do something about it, and I don't think either of us would like to see a riot erupt.

"Kir," he ordered, turning to his brother, "tomorrow I'd like you to position yourself at court so that you can ride quickly to Katonaí and take command of the Velyaminólis, if necessary."

"Do you really think all of this is needed?" Kiríll asked.

"Perhaps not," his brother replied, "but better to be prepared."

"I agree," Arrhiána said. "The mood in the capital isn't good. There's much grumbling about the rationing of foodstuffs, and about the prolonged absence of the menfolk. I think we have to be careful. And in the country, the farmers are upset because so much of their reserve has been confiscated, and because of the lack of help in planting new crops. Many of their women have had to go into the fields to assist.

"What about tomorrow?" she continued. "Can father still function?"

"I don't know, Rhie," Arkády stated. "He does seem a little

better these past two days, but I can't predict what he'll say when put on center stage. All we can do is hope his better instincts reassert themselves and carry him through. He *has* to be seen and heard by the public. People will simply not wait any longer for news. But what he'll actually do...."

CHAPTER TEN
"IT ITH FORBIDDEN!"

In another realm of existence entirely, one which cannot even be precisely described or delineated, the *ifrit* called Bezarduardakus was complaining quite vociferously to the King of the *Ifrits*, one Razafandrianavalonamerina, about its present assignment.

"It ith forbidden!" it emphasized.

"And how dost thou find thyself in thy present predicament?" the king inquired.

"Not my fault!" it replied. "The witch thtole heart of Bezarduardakuth."

"Thou art a fool," the king spat. "Thou knowest the trickery of these humans, and yet thou allowest one to entrap thee. Still, thou art right about the law. Who *is* this mortal?"

"Möthza offthpring of Karlomán," it squealed.

"The name signifieth nothing," the king noted. "What is its *cognomen*?"

"Not know," Bezarduardakus admitted.

"Ssst," the king hissed.

The little *ifrit* shrank back from its monarch, utterly terrified, but it wasn't quick enough, for the king grabbed it around the waist and began to squeeze, turning it upside down over its own great mouth.

A drop of green fluid oozed from the creature's little head, and dribbled down onto the king's black, forkèd tongue. The monarch's huge mandible moved back and forth in obvious relish.

"We know that flavor," Razafandrianavalonamerina hissed. "We shall honor thy request. Thou art released from that one's service. In recompense whereof, thou art deprived of thy separate existence for ten thousand years."

Then the monarch popped the little toad into its gullet, and crunched down on the tasty ort. It burped. It was good to be a king.

CHAPTER ELEVEN
"ALL HAIL, KING KIPRIYÁN"

On the first day of July, which is the Feast of Saint Ioulios the Martyr, the best-attended court in years was held in the Great Hall of Tighrishály Palace. Promptly at *tritê*, the new Hankyárar, Lord Frigyes Zsitvay, called the assembly to order, and the king marched to his throne in procession, flanked by Prince Arkády, Prince Kiríll, Prince Zakháry (who had arrived via *viridaurum* from Mylάßgorod the previous evening), plus Prince-Regent Andruin and Princess-Regent Arrhiána.

King Kyprianos III was magnificently cloaked in his best finery, covered with an ochre-and-black linen tunic and *shalvar*, its only decoration an embroidered Tighrishi tiger. A black silk sash was wrapped tightly about his waist. In his manner and bearing, he was the embodiment of the Kórynthi monarchy.

"All hail, King Kipriyán," intoned the Hankyárar.

"Hail, King Kipriyán!" came the unanimous response from the throng.

Then the king rose from his throne, and held his hand high for silence.

"My lords and ladies," the great voice boomed, but was drowned out in continuing huzzahs.

"My lords and ladies," Kipriyán began again, "I have the honor to announce a grand victory at the Schilling-Ford...."

"What?" mouthed Prince Zakháry to his brother Kiríll.

"...We have met the Walküre," the king continued, "and he is ours. King Barnim is dead!"

His words were whelmed by cheers.

"His son, King Walther, will soon be dead!"

The rafters shook with thunder, while Princess Arrhiána shrugged her shoulders at Prince Arkády, as if to say, "What's he doing?"

The king motioned for silence.

"Our great victory did not come without a price," he said, bowing his head. "My brave boy Nikolaí died fighting the good fight."

Groans replaced the cheers.

"King Humfried, Prince Ezzö, Prince Pankratz, Prince Norbert," he added, "they were all destroyed by the evil workings of the Dark-Haired Man."

Now women and old men at court could be seen weeping openly. Princess Teréza collapsed and fainted where she stood. Princess Arizélla rushed over to comfort her, together with a physician.

"The Thrice Holy Patriarch Avraäm perished from a stytche in his heart," the king stated.

"And sad to say," the old monarch continued, "there were many other brave men who perished at the Schilling-Ford while fighting for king and country."

"Who?" called some.

"How many?" questioned others.

More cries of anguish filled the court.

"But," he noted, "their sacrifice shall not be in vain. We withdrew from Balíxira to save our men's lives. Many had been injured by the wicked spells and trickery of the papist-loving Walküri. But we shall soon return. We shall always return, until the persecutors of the True Church have been rousted from the earth."

Kipriyán looked for Arrhiána and Andruin among the throng.

"Son and daughter, you have done well," he commended. "I do now resume the throne of my fathers. You are relieved of your service, Prince-Regent Andruin and Princess-Regent Arrhiána," he noted, repeating the official formula.

"This court is adjourned."

They quickly led him to an antechamber, where he collapsed from the strain, and was tended by Doctor Melanthrix.

CHAPTER TWELVE
"ARIZÉLLA,
DAUGHTER OF KAZIMIR"

Early that afternoon, in his cell at the Abbey of Saint Theophanês, the Archpriest Athanasios finally found time to examine the two torcs in detail. One had been his birthright, part of his possessions from his earliest days, and the other had been a gift to him from Princess Arizélla, having originally been presented to her by Dowager Hereditary Princess Zubayda as a memorial to Arizélla's deceased father four decades before. He also knew from Arizélla's testimony that many other torcs had once existed, and might still exist, if he could but locate them.

He turned the bronze rings over in his hand. Clearly, they had been forged by the same craftsman. Although tarnished now, they had once been fashioned of some shiny copper alloy. A wreath of victory circled the torc, intertwined with an *ouroboros*, the symbol of immortality. Cut into the interior surface of each ring was an incuse cuneiform inscription.

He held both torcs to the light and closely compared the lettering. Much to his disappointment, he could find nothing in common between them. The single vertical wedge at the beginning of each inscription must be a name determinant; it was repeated again about halfway through each line. He knew from what Arizélla had indicated that her torc supposedly read, "Arizélla, daughter of Kazimir." Presumably his ring followed the same pattern. So there were two names indicated on each torc, each preceded by the upright wedge. There also appeared to be another, single-character determinant between each wedge and the following name, slightly different but obviously similar, perhaps indicating "Prince" or "Princess" or "Royal," possibly with a sexual differentiation.

However, there was no correspondence whatever between the single word connecting the two names on Arizélla's torc and the word in the same position on his. Unfortunately, the script was not apparently alphabetical. The cuneiform signs must either be syllabic in nature, or somehow stand for an entire component of each word or name.

The pattern on Arizélla's ring was:

[wedge] [royal?] [?-?-?-?-?]
[daughter of?]
[wedge] [royal?] [?-?-?-?]

or fourteen signs in all. On his torc, the pattern was:

[wedge] [royal?] [?-?-?-?]
[son of?]
[wedge] [royal?] [?-?-?-?]

or thirteen signs altogether. Perhaps Arizélla's torc read something like this:

[name determinant] [royal #1] [Ar-ri-ze-el-la]
[daughter of]
[name determinant] [royal #2] [Ka-zi-mi-ir].

Alas, there were no correspondences between Arizélla's name and Kazimir's name. Then he compared the inscription incised on his own torc:

[name determinant] [royal #3] [?-?-?-la]
[son of?]
[name determinant] [royal #2] [?-?-?-?].

One symbol had been carried over from Arizélla's torc to his ring! Also, there were three slightly different determinants indicating royal status. This didn't help much.

He scratched his beard. *His* torc just didn't fit the pattern. He obviously needed more examples, and he needed to know the names of the recipients of each. But where to find them? He cast his mind back, and made a mental list of the surviving members of both royal houses in 1164. Kazimir had been killed in that year, but his father, Ezzö the Elder, had lived on until the following summer, with Kazimir's eldest son, Ezzö the Younger, succeeding the grandfather in his pretensions. Kazimir had also been survived by a widow, Princess Mariámně, and two daughters, Princess Arizélla, whose ring was accounted for, and Princess Ezzölla. Five memorial torcs could have been distributed to Kazimir's family, and more might have been prepared after King Ezzö's death in 1165.

King Makáry had been killed at Dürkheim, leaving a widow, Brisquayne. Makáry had sired seven surviving children by his two wives: Hereditary Prince Néstor, who had been killed with his father; King Karlomán, who had died shortly thereafter of his wounds; Teréza, now the recently widowed consort of Prince Ezzö the Younger; Genthia, who had married Rufín Count of Arrhéně; and Brisquayne's two daughters, Adèle and Sinthe, who had been infants at the time of their father's death. Néstor had been married briefly before his untimely passing, but had left no children.

Zubayda might also have had torcs prepared for her own surviving children: Khydeón, later Markos VI Patriarch of Paltyrrha; Maríssa, wife of Chingíz Sultan of Juma'a; Margitélla, wife of Hardin King of Bremenburg; Mikhailína, wife of Dêmokritos Graf von Achaika; and Princess Mösza. Two other adult sons, Matvéy Count of Susafön and Menándr

Count of Arkádiya, had died before their brother, Makáry. Memorial rings were probably also fashioned for Princess Zubayda herself and for her co-regent, Prince-Bishop Víktor. *In toto*, thirteen torcs could have been prepared for King Makáry's family, although he admitted to himself that there could have been more.

Some had undoubtedly been taken out of the country by their owners; others might have been lost in the four-decade interval since they were issued. But he would bet that Dowager Queen Brisquayne still had hers, and also knew where her daughters' pair might be.

He would pursue this with Brisquayne as soon as possible. In the meantime, he had a class to teach on "Spirit Taming" at the *Scholê*, and would be late unless he hurried.

Athanasios whistled as he headed down the hall. There was nothing he enjoyed more than doing a little research, particularly when it dealt with his own possible past.

CHAPTER THIRTEEN
"I LOVE MY PAIN"

At the palace, Queen Polyxena was trying to calm Princess Teréza.

"They're all gone, Xena," the princess kept saying, "and they're calling me to join them. I've dreamt about them for the last several nights. Even before the news came, I knew they were dead, all of them. They beckon to me in my dreams."

"Tréssa," the queen begged, "let me take away some of the pain. Let me blur your memories...."

"No!" the princess screamed. "*No!* I love my pain. I want to feel every lucid moment of my pain. Don't you understand? It's all I have left. I can't even cry anymore. My tears have all dried up. My husband, dead. My sons, dead. My grandsons, dead. My only great-grandson, dead. Only sweet little Tína left alive, and I'll never, *ever* see her again. The Walküri won't let her go. They'll marry her off to someone they can control.

"Kipriyán understands. That's why he brought Élla back to court. They've already written my granddaughter out of the succession. *Don't you think I know all this!*" she shouted.

"Maybe I'm not as quick as Arrhiána or as adept as Sachette," she continued, "but I still know what's going on. So what do I have left now? Pity, that's all. Everyone looks at me like I'm some kind of wounded animal. I'm no longer the 'Queen' or even the 'King's mother,' I'm that most embarrassing appendage, the *royal widow*, the *pretender's wife*. Look at how they've treated Brisquayne all these years, how she's had to become a self-effacing nobody. She can't risk offending anyone, for fear that her little estate might be taken away from her. I don't want that.

"All of our sins, we're paying for all of our sins," she wailed. "Generations of sins. How many tens of thousands of innocent men, women, and children have died because of our ambition? How many, Xena? And all so we could save the poor, benighted Pommerelians from themselves.

"We're all hypocrites," Teréza continued. "We say we want peace, and we spend the last thirty years at war. We say we love Pommerelia, and we spend hundreds of years trying to destroy it. We say we're kings and queens, and the people just laugh at us. It's all a lie. *We're* a lie. And now we've received God's judgment on our *hubris*. The House of Forellë has been rendered extinct in the male line, yea, even unto the fourth generation. Let it end here. Let *us* end here."

Then she ran off, and no further entreaties by Queen Polyxena would bring her back again.

CHAPTER FOURTEEN
"O COME TO ME"

Later that day, the Princess Rÿna was playing house with her dolls in the Hanging Garden. The weather was perfect, the air warm and clear, with a breeze wafting through the trees, just strong enough to keep the earth from becoming overheated. She had seated her many playmates in three rows, all looking up at the central keep of Tighrishály Palace.

"It's almost time," she noted, and took her own seat of honor among them.

She gazed up at the Tower of Glass, so called because several of the windows at the top featured colored panes, a rarity in such structures. Rÿna had visited the tower a number of times in recent years, making the long, winding climb to the top to see the Silver Bird, a robin sculpted by the great artist Rüssadir as if it was about to take flight. Why he had used the image of a robin, and for what purpose the image had been commissioned, and why it was posed in that position, no one really knew. He was known to have created many enigmatic works of art, and to have left them scattered at many different locations for the *hoi polloi* to admire.

At the very top of the tower was an open platform from which one could observe the sights of the city, especially at night. Now there appeared a woman dressed all in white, her pale face lifted up to the faint daytime image of the crescent moon. She climbed onto the lip of the low stone railing, and danced around the edge, singing merrily of youth and lost love and the tragedy of life. At one point she stopped, stripped off her shift, and let it drop over the edge. It twisted and turned in gay abandon as it drifted ever lower, a sprite upon the wind, like a ghost suddenly becoming visible where none had been before.

The woman's naked body gleamed brightly in the late afternoon sunlight. Rÿna thought she saw an aura of gold developing around it. She knew suddenly how to reach out with her own mind, and she touched the woman's pretty eyes and face. The gold ring on her finger glowed red.

"Come to me," the girl whispered, gently blowing the words one at a time into the air.

"O come to me," she said, watching them drift away on the wind.

And still the woman danced, ever faster, ever more frenzied, 'round and 'round the lip of the tower, until she abruptly twirled to a stop, right on the edge, shaking with laughter, her glorious hair a-tousle, just above the point where Rÿna and her friends watched.

"You are my chorus!" the woman cried. "You are my jury! You are my glory!"

"O whistle, and I'll come to you, my lass," she added.

"Come to me," Rÿna said, putting her lips together and blowing.

And so she did.

CHAPTER FIFTEEN
"FEASTING OFF THE DEAD"

Four days later, on the Feast of Saint Noumérianos, a state funeral was held at Saint Konstantín's Cathedral in Paltyrrha for the repose of the souls of the patriarch and the great lords of Kórynthia who had perished in the recent war. The returning Kórynthi army had finally reached Borgösha two days before, and the pickled bodies of the royals had been rushed to Myláßgorod, and then transited straight to the church in Paltyrrha. The service was presided over by Metropolitan Timotheos, acting in his capacity as *Locum Tenens* of the Holy Church.

Each of those being mourned was solemnly blessed in turn, his place in paradise being officially assured, beginning with the old Patriarch, Avraäm IV, as well as the deceased members of the Holy Synod, and continuing with Prince Nikolaí, King Humfried, Prince Ezzö, and Prince Pankratz. The body of Prince Norbert had not been recovered, having been ritually disemboweled and quartered, the parts being sent to all the major cities of Pommerelia for display, but a symbolic casket had been set out for him, and it would be interred with the rest of his family. A second funeral mass would be held for the deceased Forellës in Bolémia on the following day.

The Dowager Queen Brisquayne, standing in the second row next to Princess Arizélla, spoke quietly into her ear.

"Where's Teréza's bier?" she asked.

The princess glanced quickly around, then spoke out of one

corner of her mouth: "The synod's divided over burying her in consecrated ground. Some of the old fussbudgets are calling her a suicide, and Timotheos isn't willing to fight them until an election is held."

"Don't they understand she was mad with grief?" the queen whispered.

"All they know is that she was dancing bare-assed on top of the Tower of Glass, and then splattered herself all over the pavement down below, in full view of an impressionable little girl." Arizélla shook her head slightly. "I expect they'll bury her quietly up in Bolémia."

"Well, I for one want to be there," Brisquayne stated.

"So do I," the princess agreed.

Someone behind them whispered "Shhhh!" although when Arizélla turned around, no one would catch her eye.

Afterwards, the congregation would normally have been led forward to view the bodies, but given the rather charred state of the Forellës, the *Locum Tenens* had decreed that all the caskets be left closed. Instead, the celebrants were paraded past a small memorial to all the dead, and asked to donate funds towards the construction of a much larger structure celebrating the deceased of Killingford. Over a thousand staters were collected that day.

Then all of the survivors trooped back to Tighrishály Palace, where a feast was held on the broad green lawn behind the structure. Everywhere signs of normalcy were displayed: a musical group, mounds of fresh food, servants, entertainers, and nervous laughter.

Princess Arizélla nudged Dowager Queen Brisquayne in the ribs.

"I should have stayed in Dnéprov," she said. "Look at them, trying to pretend nothing has happened, while discontent breeds among the masses in the streets like maggots swarming in piles of offal. *This* is civilization?"

They saw Princess Ezzölla laughing uproariously at some-one's half-baked attempt at a joke. King Kipriyán was also smiling, clearly enjoying himself for the first time since

Killingford. In his massive hand was a huge flagon of ale. Already he was flushed with good humor and alcohol.

"They're like ghouls," the princess continued, "feasting off the dead. Don't they understand that tens of thousands have perished from their follies?"

Brisquayne's mouth was a thin red line.

"They don't want to remember, Élla," she said. "They might have to deal with reality then. And they'll be right back at it as soon as they can get another army together."

The old queen snorted. "I'm afraid I find all of this somewhat distasteful. I wonder if two middle-aged ladies might have more fun dunking their feet in a muddy pond out back of my Tamásház, while sipping glasses of white wine."

"I wonder," Élla replied, suddenly grinning for the first time. This was like the old days.

They were just turning to leave together when the king spotted them, and came over, his face breaking into a smile.

"*Cousine*," he yelled, "*cousine*, please stop."

Kipriyán dragged Arizélla over to a small dais near the back of the Palace, and called for attention from the crowd.

Then he motioned to Gorázd Lord Aboéty, who pulled from his sleeve a rolled-up scroll. Unfolding the parchment, the Grand Vizier read:

> "Kyprianos III King of Kórynthia, Overlord of Pommerelia, Mährenia, Morënë, and Nisyria, doth hereby proclaim the following:
>
> Whereas Humfried V King of Pommerelia did perish most bravely on the battlefield of the Schilling-Ford on the xvii[th] day of June in this, his accession year;
>
> And, Whereas his son and successor, King Norbert I, was foully captured by trickery and executed on the xxiv[th] day of June in this, his accession year;

And, Whereas said Norbert left no other relations in the male line, but only a half-sister, whose rights of succession to the throne have been disallowed;

Therefore we, Kyprianos III, do endorse the succession to the Throne of Pommerelia of the Princess Arizélla, eldest daughter of His Highness Kazimir, late Hereditary Prince of Pommerelia, and do acknowledge her as a fellow sovereign.

Given on the vth day of July in the XLIst year of our reign.

Kyprianos Vasileus

"My lords and ladies," he boomed in his commanding voice, "I give you Arizélla I, the new Queen of Pommerelia!"

There was some scattered applause and huzzahs from several quarters.

"Wait," Arizélla sputtered, clearly not expecting this. "I...."

But before she could say anything else, Kipriyán embraced her with his bear hug, and kissed her soundly on both cheeks. Then he presented her once more to the multitude.

"Again, I give you Arizélla Queen of Pommerelia!" he roared.

He glared around at the party-goers, daring them not to clap. Slowly, carefully, the applause grew. Then the king motioned to the group of musicians to strike up *La Marche Forellée*, and led the new queen unwillingly around in a circle, almost like a dance, introducing her to this or that noble, or this or that widow thereof.

Queen Arizélla grew increasingly angry as the promenade continued, but felt trapped by circumstances. She caught Brisquayne's eye at a distance, but the dowager queen just shrugged her shoulders. There was nothing *she* could do to help her friend.

The new monarch was forced to remain at the celebration for another two hours, smiling at and pandering to her newly-found supporters, and getting steadily drunker as the afternoon progressed.

At least some *of the time was put to good use*, she thought to herself.

Then, when she was good and soused, she managed very prettily to vomit the day's leavings all over the elegant gown of some count's wife, and daintily made her exit, still smiling.

CHAPTER SIXTEEN
"DO YOU ACCEPT
THIS ELECTION?"

On the next morning, the Feast of Saint Monenna, the Holy Synod of the Church of Kórynthia met in solemn prayer in the Chapel of Saint Hyakinthos, an adjunct to the Cathedral of Saint Konstantín, to elect a successor to Avraäm IV, late Archbishop of Paltyrrha and Patriarch of All Kórynthia.

Only six members of the synod had survived Killingford: Timotheos, Metropolitan of Örtenburg and All Nördmark and *Locum Tenens* of Kórynthia; Mêtrophanês, Metropolitan of Aszkán and All Arrhénë; Konôn, Metropolitan of Sevyerovínsk and All Zándrich; Kyriakos, Metropolitan of Podébrad and All Westmark; Eudoxios, Metropolitan of Susafön and All Susaföniya; and Zôïlos, Archbishop of Veszprém and All Velyaminó. Bishop Varlaám sat with the Synod as a non-voting secretary.

Metropolitan Timotheos gave the simple invocation.

"Lord," he said, "we pray to Thee most humbly, that Thou wilt give us a sign. Impart unto Thy humble servants Mêtrophanês, Timotheos, Konôn, Kyriakos, Eudoxios, and Zôïlos the wisdom and clarity to choose well the next shepherd of Thy flock. Amen."

"Amen," they repeated.

Then Archbishop Zôïlos nominated Metropolitan Mêtrophanês for patriarch, and Metropolitan Konôn proposed Metropolitan Timotheos. The *Locum Tenens* asked if there were any further nominations, and when he received none, directed that the election proceed, with Varlaám appointed to count the ballots.

Timotheos put six consecrated hosts into a bejeweled chalice, and covered it with its silken veil.

"Bishop Varlaám, please read the rule," the *Locum Tenens* ordered.

Varlaám pulled out a small book, opened it about a third of the way through, and intoned:

> "8.ιv.α. To elect a Patriarch, each Psairothi Metropolitan shall vote by impressing the chosen symbol of his candidate upon one of the consecrated hosts in the covered chalice.
>
> "8.ιv.ß. The votes of two-thirds of the Holy Synod shall be necessary to validate an election, together with the acceptance of the duly-elected candidate."

"Very well," Timotheos stated. "You may begin."

One by one the hierarchs came forward, knelt to the chalice and prayed, and then touched the receptacle with the ring of his index finger. Then each prayed again, and returned to his place.

When five votes had been cast, Timotheos himself came forward, and bowed in humble prayer. After letting forth an audible sigh, he also tapped the chalice.

Then Varlaám placed two smaller silver chalices next to the ornate gold one, and carefully and reverently held up each host to the light so that it could be seen by all before putting it in its proper place. Three of the hosts were marked with the fox of Mêtrophanês, and two with the owl of Timotheos; one was blank.

"We do not have an election," the *Locum Tenens* intoned.

They then consumed the hosts, and returned to their cells.

Two hours later, before the midday meal, they balloted a second time. The result this time was two votes for Mêtrophanês and three for Timotheos, with one blank.

In early afternoon, they tried again, with the same result, and retired for two more hours.

During that interval of prayer and contemplation, the Metropolitan Konôn privily sought out his old friend.

"Arik Rufímovich," he said, "I fear we are deadlocked, unless the sixth member of our group can be persuaded to vote. I know that the abstainer is you, and I understand why you do not want to be chosen on the basis of your own vote. I respect your humility, old friend, but I must tell you quite plainly that the future of the church is at stake. Avraäm wanted this, and a majority of the synod now desires it. You *must* make up the difference."

Timotheos looked up at the icon of his patron, Saint Timotheos the disciple of Saint Paulos, tacked to the wall of his small cell, and crossed himself.

"Ah, Sávva Marínovich, we had good times together at Saint Svyatosláv's, didn't we?" Timotheos reminisced. "I would like very much to do as you request, but I can't in good conscience promote my own ambitions, even if, as you say, the future of the Church is at stake. It is *always* at stake, no matter what we do. This is in God's hands now. If it is His will that I assume this burden, then I will accept it. That is as much as I can do, my brother."

An hour later the six returned to the chapel to conduct the fourth ballot. Varlaám's resigned face tolled off the votes in order: "Mêtrophanês, Timotheos, Mêtrophanês, Timotheos, Timotheos."

Then he pulled out the final ballot, and held it to the light. He stopped, and looked again. They all did. An owl was clearly impressed onto the center of the host.

"Timotheos!" he managed to blurt out. "The vote is four to two."

The *Locum Tenens* sat there, stunned by the outcome. *He had not voted!* Metropolitan Mêtrophanês, senior among them, went through the ritual.

"Timotheos, Metropolitan of Örtenburg and All Nördmark,"

he softly spoke, "you have been duly elected Patriarch of Paltyrrha and All Kórynthia by a lawful ballot of your peers. How say you: do you accept this election?"

Timotheos could not speak. His entire life had been leading him to this one crucial decision. Every fiber of his being was saying "No!" He absolutely did not want the responsibility of rebuilding the church during this period of devastation. So he forthrightly gave the synod his decision.

"Apodekhomai," he said, "I accept."

CHAPTER SEVENTEEN
"THRICE HOLY ART THOU"

The following morning, which was Sunday and the Feast of Saint Palladios, the Patriarch Timotheos III was consecrated and enthroned at a solemn service held in Saint Konstantín's Cathedral. Wearing only a homespun monk's robe and rough sandals, the metropolitan prostrated himself face down before the altar of God, in a simple ritual that had not changed substantially in five hundred years.

"Arik Rufímovich," Metropolitan Mêtrophanês intoned, "wilt thou accept this burden with an open heart and a fullness of faith?"

"I will," he replied.

"Wilt thou be consecrated to the service of the Lord, and place no other wish before His?"

"I will," came the response.

"Wilt thou preserve and increase His church, and defend it against all challenges, external and internal?"

"I will."

"Remember, Arik Rufímovich, that thou art a man. Even as thou art given the power and the glory and the trappings of a king, so wilt thou be held accountable to a higher standard when thou meetest thy Maker. Dost thou accept this responsibility?"

"I do."

Then the five surviving metropolitans laid their hands on the new patriarch, their combined rings flaring and overlaying one another with their auras, as the power surged through their hands. Each individual displayed a slightly different tint—pink, light blue, pale yellow, weak gray, yellow-green—but when they merged into the body of Timotheos, they became pure white.

"Thou art holy," Mêtrophanês continued, "for thou representest the Father on earth.

"Thou art holy, for thou representest the Son on earth.

"Thou art holy, for thou representest the Spirit on earth.

"Thrice holy art thou. Therefore, do we consecrate thee to this sanctified office. Rise, oh patriarch!"

Then the five raised Timotheos to his feet, and began to dress him, first as a priest, then as a bishop, then as an archbishop, then as a metropolitan, and finally as patriarch.

The dean of the Holy Synod, the Metropolitan Mêtrophanês, placed upon their new leader's right hand his golden ring of office, then turned to the congregation, and formally announced their new leader:

"Kos Kos Patriarkhês Timotheos!"

One by one the metropolitans made their submission in order of seniority, kissing the new patriarch's ring, and they were followed by all of the attending clergy, including Father Athanasios, and then the secular world, represented by King Kipriyán and his family, and by the chief counselors of state.

Then the patriarch celebrated his first mass as leader of the church. All of the Psairothi present could see his body glow with joy as he raised the Body and Blood of our Lord Jesus Christ on high. Many of the celebrants wiped tears from their eyes as they accepted the bread and wine from his hands.

After mass, Patriarch Timotheos gave his special homily of inauguration.

"Most holy metropolitans, archbishops and bishops, most noble king, princes and princesses, my lords and ladies, people of Paltyrrha," he began. "I come before you humbly as the new shepherd of the Church of Kórynthia. I am not worthy of this high honor, but I have accepted it with reluctance, knowing full well the arduous task that we face before us.

"My predecessor, the Patriarch Avraäm, blessèd be his name, was a great teacher and philosopher, an accomplished Psairothi who will be remembered long after the rest of us are gone. He once told me that the hardest thing for him about being patriarch was reminding himself each day *why* he was elected. It is far too easy, he said, to immerse oneself into the day-to-day details of running an administration, into the meetings with king and synod, into the ceremonials and pageantry of this holy office.

"'I was not elected,' he told me, 'to do those things, however worthy they might be, but to minister to the people. Never forget,' he added, 'that the people are the church.'

"I shall try, my people, to learn from his saintly example. This is a time for reconciliation and rebuilding. Too long have we spent waging war on the nations around us. Too many innocent lives have been lost in our fruitless struggles to conquer other peoples. Let us come together. Let us mend our differences. Let us learn from the example of Jesus Christ to turn the other cheek. Let us love our brothers, whomever they may be. Let us...."

"Heretic! Traitor!" yelled King Kipriyán, pointing at the new patriarch. "He's the Dark-Haired Man!" he shouted. "He's a tool of the devil! He's the Anti-Christ! Fake! Cæsarist!"

Patriarch Timotheos was taken aback by this outburst, but declined to respond. He blessed the congregation, trying to make himself heard over the king, and then turned his back and retreated to the sacristy, followed in order by the assembled metropolitans and churchmen.

A buzz of conversation swept through the cathedral:

"Appalling!"

"Madness!"

"Can this be true?"

Everyone was trying to observe the monarch and his family and what they would do.

Suddenly the Princess Arizélla was seen standing by herself just below the altar.

"How dare you!" she shouted, pointing her *psai*-ring right at the king. It glowed bright red. "How dare you accuse this holy priest of God! You've just slaughtered forty thousand men for no good reason than the furtherance of your own ambition. I'm ashamed to be accounted a Forellë. I'm ashamed to be connected to the House of Tighris. Someone in our family must finally say 'no!' to all this madness, to all this killing.

"I renounce my name. I renounce my house. I renounce *you*, Kipriyán the Cruel. I will spend the rest of my days begging God Almighty to forgive us for our *hubris*, trying to make restitution for what we have done to the poor people of Pommerelia. Go play your silly games, if you choose, but play them without *me*, o king."

Then Arizélla disappeared into the crowd, and the king began shouting for his guards.

"Arrest her!" he screamed. "Stop that bitch!"

But the congregation surged into the aisles, and the guards could make no headway without violating the sanctity of the church.

By the time order was restored and the crowds began leaving, the princess was nowhere to be found.

The Archpriest Athanasios had been watching the entire scene from the sacristy with a growing sense of horror, and he immediately grabbed Arizélla, yanking her into a little-known side altar before she could be apprehended.

"Whatever possessed you?" he breathed, hurrying them both along a passageway. "He'll kill you if he can."

She stopped him then, grabbed him by the elbows, and looked him straight in the face.

"What difference does one more life make?" she asked. "He's mad, Athy. He'll lead this nation into an orgy of self-destruction if he continues down this path. Someone has to stop him. Someone has got to speak out."

"And do you really think that he'll change his mind because you want him to?" Athanasios asked.

Then the priest caught himself, ashamed of his harshness.

"I'm sorry," he said, "that's not a fair question. I admire the courage in others that I can't seem to find in myself. But now we have to get you out of here. If you're caught loitering in this area, where women are forbidden, it will only be worse for you."

He locked her in a closet off the corridor, and then went to a small vestment room used by some of the acolytes. He quietly grabbed a clean robe and hood and sandals off the shelf. Everyone was far too busy commenting about the turn of events to pay much attention to him. He flattened himself to the wall as a guard rushed by.

Athanasios went back to the closet, and thrust the garments inside, saying: "Take off your dress and shoes, and put these on instead."

When she was ready, he joined her inside the confined space, lit a ring-flame, and carefully looked her over.

"You're still too pretty," he commented, wiping off some of the color from her face with a corner of her dress. The close presence of an attractive woman threatened to overwhelm his control.

"You like me, don't you, little priest?" she noted. "You're very sweet," she added, kissing him lightly on the cheek.

When he jumped back, she giggled.

"Don't worry," she said, "I'm not going to spoil your vows. But thank you, father, for having the courage—yes, *courage!*— to risk your life for me."

He didn't respond, afraid of what he might say, but looked her up and down again quite carefully, trying to avoid those parts that might inflame his blood.

"Keep your head down and your hood up," he ordered. "Say nothing. You're Brother Trayán. You're mute and submissive. Follow my lead in all things."

Then he took the dress, balled it up in his hand, and flung it to the ceiling of the closet, sticking it there with his power. The shoes he disguised temporarily as chamber pots. They would revert back to their original shape in a day or two, long after Arizélla had left the place.

He ordered her to "Stay put!" for a moment, and went off to the abbey to locate the new patriarch. He found him surrounded by well-wishers.

"May I see you for a moment, holiness?" he interjected.

Timotheos made his excuses, and Athanasios pulled him over to a private corner.

"I request permission to take a day's leave from the *Scholê*," the priest said.

"Indeed. And should I inquire why?" the patriarch asked, raising one bushy gray eyebrow. There was a suspicious smudge of color on Athy's cheek.

"Probably not," Athanasios replied.

Timotheos smiled slightly.

"You have my leave," he responded. "Just be careful, Athy. I wouldn't want you to suffer an untimely accident."

"Nor would I," his friend noted. "I'll be back on Tuesday. Please give me your blessing before I go, Arik."

The archpriest knelt before the new patriarch, who placed one hand on the younger man's head, and made the sign of the cross with the other.

"Thank you, holiness," Athanasios said, kissing his mentor's *nomen*-ring with respect. He then headed back to Arizélla.

Very carefully and quietly, the pair made their way to a little-used alcove near the kitchen of the abbey, which directly adjoined the cathedral. Although they saw several other monks, no one paid them much attention or even spoke a word to them.

"Where do you want to go?" the priest asked.

"Home!" said Arizélla, and twisted the leys to carry them back to her *dacha* in Dnéprov.

CHAPTER EIGHTEEN
"IT NIPPED ME"

"I probably have a day before they'll think to send someone out here from Dneprόvgorod," she continued, "so I'll pack what I can and leave the rest. If there are any of these pieces you particularly want to keep, by all means take them, Athy."

She changed into a plain striped shift over her undergarments, and began gathering her clothes together into bags.

"Where will you go?" he inquired.

"Pommerelia," she said, turning to face him. Her face was grim. "I wasn't just blowing air out of my mouth back there. I must do something to redress what my family has done to the people of that country. I'll go to the new king, and beg his leave to establish a charity to aid the homeless refugees. Or anything else that might help."

"He might well kill you," the monk replied.

"Every day we spend on earth involves risk," she noted, pursing her lips into a slight frown. "*Every day*, Athy. Why did the Lord take my daughter from me, my dear little Tamára? *Why?* She was just an innocent child, and I loved her so very much. I would gladly have gone in her place, father. But I wasn't given that choice, and I can't ever replace her. She was my only girl.

"No. My previous life of self-distraction is over, father. Even if I hadn't said what I said, I still couldn't return here. I must do something to restore the balance. Maybe God will eventually understand. I certainly don't."

"God always understands," the priest stated, "and so do I, Lady Élla. Do whatever you must to save your spirit, with all of my blessing."

Then Athanasios took a moment to walk about her cottage for one last time. He spotted what was obviously a small self-portrait done in color ten or fifteen years earlier, and held it up to the light.

"If you don't mind terribly, I'd like this," he stated.

She smiled, transforming her entire face into a vision of love-liness, the lines around her eyes and mouth briefly wiped away.

"I'm touched that you think it worthy of your consideration. But what will your superiors say?" she asked.

"Well," he noted, "I won't tell them. I'll have it framed like the icon of a well-known saint, and put down a candle or two in front of it, and they won't give it another thought."

She laughed out loud, and smiled broadly, grasping his right hand.

"If I'd known you ten years ago, father, you wouldn't have escaped so easily," she said.

He blushed and ducked his head in embarrassment. Although he would never experience a traditional male-female relation-ship, he thought he understood a little better now just what he could have had if he hadn't been sent to Saint Svyatosláv's as a child. Out of the corner of his eye, he spotted several small paintings on a bottom shelf of the main room.

"Did you also do these?" he asked.

She bent down to look.

"No," she indicated, "someone gave them to me years ago."

"I recognize King Makáry," the priest stated. "Who are the other two?"

"The bearded one on the left's Hereditary Prince Néstor, and the other's his mustachioed brother, King Karlomán. Both were killed in the last war."

She idly picked them up and handed them to Athanasios.

"Take these, too," she ordered. "I don't want them."

"But, I...."

Not wanting to offend her, he reluctantly agreed.

Finally, she finished putting together the few possessions she thought necessary. Then she fixed them a luncheon of fruit and cheese. They went out on the terrace behind her house to eat.

"How I shall miss this view," she said, sighing. "Oh dear Athy, I've danced a pavane with candor once too often this time, haven't I? I don't think they'll ever let me return."

They watched the boats sailing back and forth on Dnepróvsky Sound for half an hour, before she finally broke the spell.

"There's something else I must do," she noted.

She went back into the *dacha*, and some moments later came back with a sheaf of papers tied together into a bundle and wrapped in hard leather.

"Give the top sheet to your patriarch," she requested. "It's a deed signing all of my possessions over to the church. I doubt that even King 'Crabian' will be able to challenge it. I've dated it last Friday, when I was still legally acknowledged as queen.

"This second document is a letter to my sister. Please see that she gets it, not that she'll really want to read the thing.

"The third paper is a letter to Queen Brisquayne. Please give her my love.

"And this fourth letter is my official abdication as Queen of Pommerelia and Countess of Bolémia, in favor of my only surviving sister, Princess Ezzölla. I've had this prepared for over a week.

"I just wish I could give you something else in return for your friendship." She sighed. "If wishes were horses...."

Then she saw a movement out of the side of one eye.

"There is this, Athy," she said. "Please take care of my kitties, Sybélla and Buténky. They're good little mousers, and no trouble at all, really. Especially Bella. There's something of me in her, I think."

She picked the coal black cat off the floor, and handed her to him. He'd never had a pet before, but when it started to purr, he was immediately captivated.

She laughed again.

"See, she likes priests too," she said.

Athanasios fumbled in his robes, and produced a curious green stone that had been part of his possessions since before he could remember. It was mounted in an electrum ringband.

"I'd like you to have this," he stated, handing it over. "I don't know what it means, or why it's important, only that it is somehow. Perhaps you can do more with it than I've ever been able to."

"Why, Athy!" she exclaimed, clearly pleased.

She held the milky emerald up to the light, watching the colors swirl and eddy within. There was a glow emanating from the interior, as if the stone itself were alive.

"It's beautiful," she said. "I'll wear it hanging next to my heart.

"Now we must go," she emphasized, "before the *gendarmes* arrive. Come with me, and I'll show you a place that you can use as a refuge if you ever need one. But first, memorize the details of my *albaurum* in case you ever want to come here. You'll be the only other person who knows about the thing, and it's very different from the usual kind. I'll set a trap so that only you and I can ever employ it."

"Albaurum?" Athanasios inquired. "I've heard of them, of course, but I didn't realize what it was when we originally transited through. Your alcove is sufficiently recessed to keep it dark most of the time, and you led me into the leys yourself."

"It's a very rare and unusual artifact," she noted, "dating back, I think, even before the days of the great Julian I, to a period when the empire ruled the civilized world. I've never seen or heard of another exactly like it, although perhaps the Holy Roman Cæsar has one locked away in his vaults in Ravenna."

"Even if he has," the monk replied, chuckling, "I doubt very much whether old Marcus Ætherius III has any idea of what it might do for him. The few *albaura* that I've encountered have all been much smaller implements, and usually round in shape."

"As is this one, although I've disguised the fact," she said.

Élla took him by the hand and dragged him across the room

to the recess where the mirror lived, placing his palm right over the shiny metal at its heart.

"Feel it!" she commanded. "Subsume it. Remember the beat within. Allow it to accept your spirit."

"It has a warmth to it unlike a *viridaurum*," he mused.

Then he jumped and abruptly pulled back.

"It, it nipped me," Athanasios said, looking at the red circle of dots embedded on his open palm.

"Had it rejected you," the princess replied, "you would not be standing there so complacently, I think. An *albaurum* has a mind of its own.

"Now, give me your hand again," she continued, clasping his stained palm. He jumped a second time. "We're going to a hermitage once used by the Nathanites in Axium. And don't give me *that* look. You have to trust me, little priest. I came across it years and years ago, when an old friend of mine...."

She twisted the leys and they vanished, just like that. The king's agents didn't arrive for two more days, and then they found nothing to indicate where the Princess Arizélla had gone. When one of them tried to employ the *albaurum*, he never returned from wherever it was he was sent, although somehow they could still hear his cries for help, if they listened carefully. Then they sealed and posted the dwelling with a *sigillum* of power, forbidding entry or exit to all, on pain of death.

After they had departed, however, the *albaurum* reached out and adjusted the working so that it only operated in one direction. Buténky checked the implement's reshaping for its taste and structure, and then turned and walked straight through the great whitegold mirror, looking neither to the left nor the right. It was time for him to move on.

CHAPTER NINETEEN
"THEY MUST PAY!"

The evening that Arizélla left home, Mösza called together the first session of the Covenant of Christian Mages in almost six months. Just five of the members, including herself, appeared in the great domed chamber. Count Zhertán and Prince Arkády did not attend, because they had not been invited, although the other four attendees did not know this.

Finally, Mösza rapped the meeting to order.

"It appears that the war still divides us," she said, "so perhaps it is time to consider appointing replacements for our long-missing members."

"I am not sure of this, beautiful lady," Nur ad-Din replied. "I think that perhaps we should consult these individuals first, before making some attempt to remove them."

"I don't," said Kulmann Graf von Einschlag, who had been slightly wounded at the Kleine, while acting as an observer for the King of Franconia. "Let's get on with it."

"I nominate Widdekin, Hereditary Count of Körvö, to replace his father," said Aurora Lady Estavaye, a native of that place.

"Seconded!" Count Kulmann agreed.

"Any objections?" Mösza asked. "Hearing none, he is elected. Who else?"

"I don't want another Kórynthi taking Prince Arkády's place," Kulmann insisted.

"Then I propose Arslan Tash, a native of Ras ash-Shamra," Mösza stated.

"Does anyone else here know him?" Aurora inquired.

"I'll vouch for him," interjected Prince Philodème of Neustria.

"Any objections?" asked Mösza. "Very well then, hearing none, I'll consider him enrolled. I will now accept nominations for a new chair."

"I nominate Mösza, Countess of Rábassy," offered Philodème.

"Any others?" Mösza asked of the group. "Hearing no objection, I declare myself duly elected. I will notify the nominees, and also those missing from our *soirée* today. I'll call another meeting as soon as we're ready to seat the new members. Thank you, all."

When the rest had transited home, the old countess walked back into the council chamber, and looked around at the great windows.

"Oh, you fools!" Mösza screamed, laughing and crying all at the same time. She climbed onto the great round table and twirled about in a grotesque parody of a dance. Outside the window an owl hooted at her.

"Oh, I'm so looking forward to playing with you," she added.

Suddenly she saw a movement near the door, and fell backwards onto the center of the table.

"Who the Hadês are *you*!?" she demanded, propping herself up on her elbows.

She peered over her nose, trying to make out the dim figure standing there. It appeared to be a woman wearing a peasant's robe.

"I said, *who are you*?" she yelled.

"Just a friend to those in need," came a soft voice in response.

"I have no friends!" Mösza replied. "I have no needs."

"How very sad for you," the shadow commisserated. "Have you nothing worth living for?"

"My pain," the countess blurted out, putting her hand to her mouth when she realized what she had said.

"And your hate," the stranger noted. "Yes, I can see that. Why do you hate?"

"I was wronged," Mösza responded, unable to stop herself.

"So you were," the visitor agreed, "but is that any reason to chastise the innocent?"

"They must pay!" she emphasized.

"They are all dead," the figure said. "They have already been judged by Almighty God for what they did or did not do, just as you will be. Come along with me now. Let me show you another way, the way of light and peace. It's still not too late."

"No!" came the retort. "They must pay! They must *all* pay!"

"And so they shall, dear Mösza," said the fading voice. "But you shall pay the most of all."

And then she was gone.

CHAPTER TWENTY
"MADNESS"

Several days later, on the Feast of the Seven Brothers of Kybolla, the first full council meeting was held since the king's return to Kórynthia. Princess Arizélla's abdication was presented, read into the record, and accepted by the king. He added several choice remarks about the woman, grinning knowingly at the councilmen.

"The throne of Pommerelia being vacant," he continued, "we hereby declare that the Princess Ezzölla, second daughter of Kazimir late Hereditary Prince of Pommerelia, has succeeded to the Crown of Pommerelia and County of Bolémia under the title Ezzölla I, effective this date. Gorázd, prepare the proclamation."

The king's face suddenly flushed red when he recalled the humiliation visited upon him at the church.

"Further," he continued, "we do declare the Princess Arizélla, late Queen of Pommerelia and Countess of Bolémia, as outlaw and renegade, she having fled our jurisdiction without our authorization, and banish her from our realm for life, under pain of death. Record this, Gorázd," he ordered, pointing down at the register, and hitting it several times with his index finger. "Do it now."

"Further," he added, staring coldly across the table at the primate, "we hereby withdraw our recognition from Timotheos Patriarch of Paltyrrha and All Kórynthia, and declare him deposed from that office, effective immediately."

"What?" came the reaction from around the room, for Timotheos had been a popular choice, both among the clergy and the councilmen.

"Father?" said Prince Arkády, but the king continued without interruption.

"...The Bishop Varlaám Njégosh, Secretary of the Holy Synod," the king stated, "is nominated *Locum Tenens*. We would also not be at all displeased were he elected patriarch. Record this," he sputtered, waving at Gorázd, who continued writing as fast as he could go.

"The Patriarch Timotheos having been dethroned, he is ordered to depart this council forthwith," Kipriyán declared, glaring across at Timotheos.

"Guards, escort him from the room!" he yelled.

"I will leave on my own two feet, thank you," Timotheos said, standing up. "Sire, although I respect your office, you may not interfere with mine, which came to me from God Himself. Until such time as I am restored to office, I declare you excommunicated, and I order the Holy Synod to proclaim my decree, publish it throughout Kórynthia, and enforce it to the letter. You shall not take the sacraments or attend mass in this kingdom until you relent. You are condemned to everlasting Hell until you seek repentance. No man, not even the king, is above God."

King Kipriyán sputtered and jumped to his feet, almost pulling his sword. He stopped himself with his weapon halfway out of its scabbard. Then he pointed at the patriarch.

"Arrest that man," he ordered the guards, "and throw him in the 'Hole.' He will be bound over for trial one week hence."

When they hesitated, he screamed, *"Do it!"*

Before the soldiers could grab him, Patriarch Timotheos smiled serenely and said: "He who touches me is excommunicated. I place the Kingdom of Kórynthia under interdict. No masses shall be said, no sacraments given, no weddings held, no dead buried, until I am released, and until the king humbles himself before God. I forbid any of the clergy to continue in your service. He who raises his hand against the patriarch, raises it against the Church; he who raises it against the Church, raises it also against God."

Then he turned to the two guards, and said: "I forgive you, my sons. Lead me to my prison cell, and I will gladly follow."

His dignity intact, he meekly left the room, and was dutifully trailed by both the Archpriest Athanasios and the Bishop Varlaám.

"Stop them!" ordered the king, but no one moved to obey.

He looked wildly around the room.

"What is the matter with all of you!" Kipriyán raved. "Are you all possessed by the Dark-Haired Man?"

"Sire," said Prince Arkády, "there is no Dark-Haired Man."

"Oh, I see," the king sneered, "now that you've tasted some of my power, you want it all. Well, my boy, we'll see about that."

He turned to the grand vizier.

"I order Prince Arkády and his children removed from the register of succession," he stated, very calm now. "List them all, one by one. I hereby declare my second son, Prince Nikolaí, the new Hereditary Prince of Kórynthia."

Lord Gorázd looked very strangely at his king.

"But, sire," he said, "Prince Nikolaí is dead. He perished at Killingford."

"Killingford?" Kipriyán responded, "I forbid the use of that name. It bespeaks an attitude of defeatism. The proper name is the Schilling-Ford, and it was a great victory for Kórynthia. Have I not said so? Kipriyán the Conqueror does not lose battles, and he does not lie. Ever. *Record it!"* he yelled at Gorázd, pounding the table.

"Record it or be damned," he added in a softer, even more sinister voice.

"It is so recorded, majesty," Gorázd emphasized.

"Very well. Nikolaí, what is our military status?" he inquired.

"Uh, Prince Nikolaí is regretably absent, sire," Lord Gorázd noted.

"Then, uh, Kiríll, *tell me what I need to know!"* the king blurted out.

"Yes, sire," Prince Kiríll said carefully, rising from his seat, and glancing at his older brothers.

Arkády inclined his head ever so slightly.

"As you've heard," Kiríll continued, "Prince Walther has apparently become King of Pommerelia under somewhat mysterious circumstances. There are so many different rumors being circulated in Balíxira about the passing of old King Barnim that they are impossible to fathom.

"Secondly, we have evacuated all of our armies from Pommerelia except for the forces occupying the three fortresses of Lockenlöd, Karkára, and Borgösha...."

"*What!* On whose orders?" the king interrupted.

"Prince Arkády's, sire," his son replied. "You were, uh, somewhat incapacitated after the great battle...."

"*I was not!*" he shouted. "I was just fine. But you refused to listen to me. Sit down!" he added.

"Zakháry," he continued, "what is our battle readiness?"

"Sire, the army has mostly gone home," Prince Zakháry reported. "We still have a few thousand men in the citadels, as already reported, but the rest are...."

"Traitors! You're all traitors and whiners," the king said. "I can't trust any of you anymore."

Kipriyán turned to the army commander, who was present at this meeting both as a courtesy and also to provide additional information on matters military.

"General Lord Rónai," Kipriyán ordered, "I want you to hold those castles at all costs."

"Yes, sire," the officer replied, saluting crisply.

"How soon can we call up the reserves?" Kipriyán inquired.

"Well, highness, I don't know," Rónai stated. "Perhaps a month or six weeks."

"Order it done," the king commanded. "I want to mount a second expedition as soon as possible. And get those damned Arrhénis back. We wouldn't have had these problems in the first place if Sándor had been doing his job. In the meantime, I want to reoccupy the Valley of the Spargö as a staging area. Can you do that with the men we have available there?"

"Possibly," the general responded. "Just barely. But we'd be subject to constant attacks by the irregulars."

"Then kill them. Burn them out. For every attack on our troops, execute a hundred farmers. Are there any questions?" the king asked, glaring around at his councilors, who sat in absolute silence.

"We'll reassemble here in a few days," he added. "And then I want some answers from all of you.

"Finally," Kipriyán noted, "I see that we're short several councilors. Therefore, I do appoint General Lord Rónai, General Lord Reményi, and Doctor Melanthrix to the Royal Council, effective with our next session. This meeting is adjourned."

The king stomped out of the room, clearly displeased with the entire proceeding.

Arkády remained in his chair, covering his face with his hands.

"Lord God," he said to no one in particular, "what have we ever done to deserve this?"

The other councilors were equally stunned. They murmured back and forth to each other in barely audible tones as they slowly exited the room.

"Madness," Arkády heard from several quarters. "He's gone mad."

The prince could only agree.

CHAPTER TWENTY-ONE
"WE'VE HAD ENOUGH KILLING FOR ONE YEAR"

An hour later Prince Arkády met secretly with his sister, Princess Arrhiána, in Kórynthály. Each of them had transited there separately, and then walked slowly to the back of the tomb of King Makáry, their grandsire, checking carefully to make certain that no one had followed them.

"I can't believe what I just heard," Arrhiána said. "I don't understand what Papá is doing, or why."

"Nor can I, sister," Arkády replied. "But he did it nonetheless, and I'm very worried about his frame of mind. Where do we go from here? I don't think the country can survive a second war this year. We lost so many soldiers in Pommerelia that we don't have enough men even to bring in the crops.

"I don't think father understands the level of unrest out there. Either that, or he just doesn't care. I don't know which is worse. But I can't sit idly by while we rush headlong into another conflict. I do hope you'll attend the next council meeting on Saturday, sister."

"Oh, I'll be there, Kásha," she indicated. "We've had enough killing for one year. I'm already tired of celebrating memorial masses for the people I love."

"I don't know what we're going to do," the prince said. "We can't continue in this direction for very long: we'll have insurrection in the streets, possibly even civil war. What's happened to the strong, fair, gracious leader we once knew? Father seems to have lost all of the finer virtues. All he has left now is his naked authority."

Arkády glanced up at the massive structure of the tomb of their grandsire looming over them.

"Do you remember, sister, when we found Papá wandering here last March?" the prince asked.

"How could I forget," Arrhiána responded. "All that nonsense about the Dark-Haired Man."

"I'm more interested," he continued, "in what father was saying about the two regents, Dowager Princess Zubayda and Prince-Bishop Víktor, and about King Makáry. Something untoward obviously happened during the Great War, something out of the ordinary, something that was later hidden away."

Princess Arrhiána clasped her hands together for a moment, and then looked down at the interlocking fingers, one laid over another.

"According to Brisquayne," she said, "Mösza may have been involved in a scandal at court during the year 1164, an incident so abhorrent to the regents that they packed her off somewhere out of the country, never allowing her to return. Papá might have known about it in general, without being aware of any of the particulars."

"What kind of scandal?" her brother inquired.

"An *affaire d'amour*, perhaps," the princess replied, "or maybe something more. Brisquayne overheard a conversation during that period that would indicate the possibility of Mösza having borne a natural child. But Brisquayne also said that Mösza was essentially an innocent, even at the ripe age of twenty-four, and that she couldn't have instigated such a *liaison*."

"But what *difference* would it have made?" Arkády mused. "There have been plenty of illegitimate members of our family sired over the years, and nobody has ever paid much attention to any of them."

"Well, Víktor was a churchman and Zubayda originally derived from Tôrtous," Arrhiána noted. "Perhaps the idea of a supposedly virginal princess bearing a child out of wedlock was anathema to them."

"I still think there has to be more to it than that," Arkády speculated. "I sense that we're missing something vital here. I repeat my earlier question: however scandalous the situation might have seemed to the old regents, what difference would the child have made to any of them? Why not just pack the infant off to the local monastery, and marry the girl to some foreign monarch? Why would Kipriyán have been told by his guardians to be so very careful about this particular situation?"

"Hmmm," the princess pondered. "If we look at the history of the time, at the end of 1164 Papá was the last surviving male descendant of King Makáry. Had he died before producing an heir to the throne, his uncle, Patriarch Markos, Makáry's next youngest brother, would have succeeded, except that as a high-ranking churchman, he might have ruled himself ineligible.

"Grandpapá had no other surviving brothers at the time of his death, and they themselves had all died young without producing male issue. However, several elderly great-uncles, the Princes Ysídor, Siegfried, and Víktor, were still living then. Two of them had sired both children and grandchildren by that time, but the law of succession allows the throne to pass through female lines when more than two generations have intervened. Thus, a strong claim to the crown might have been made under such circumstances for the sons of Papá's eldest surviving sister."

"The Forellës!" Arkády exclaimed.

"Yes," his sister agreed, "Teréza's future children were potentially the next heirs to the throne, followed by the Arrhéni offspring of Princess Genthia, unless another, relatively unfettered, senior male heir could have been produced, from offstage, so to speak."

"Mösza's child," the prince stated.

"Possibly," she affirmed. "Of course, this is all speculation, but the child, if he were a boy, would have had an equal right under law to the throne after the deaths without children of Kipriyán and Patriarch Markos, and a better right by age and seniority to any sons of Teréza and Genthia, who weren't born in any case until somewhat later. Or so I believe.

"*I* think that they prudently arranged to have the child sequestered away somewhere, under very tight control, just in case they eventually needed him. Then, when Kipriyán began producing heirs of his own, they quietly disposed of the lad."

"That would explain some of it," her brother acknowledged, "but I still think there's something missing from our little drama."

She cocked her head, and smiled her sly, slanting smile.

"Have you never considered, brother, that maybe they just didn't get along very well?"

He grimaced, and gave her a mock blow across the back of her head.

"Just like you and I, huh?" Arkády intimated.

"I knew you'd understand," she laughed in return.

CHAPTER TWENTY-TWO
"I NEED TO MAKE A FEW THINGS DEAD"

At the same time, Prince Kiríll was meeting with his elder brother, Prince Zakháry, at their hunting lodge in the Börzsö Forest.

"We have to do something, Kir," Zakháry was insisting. "Now that he's appointed that quack to the council, God knows what else he'll do before he's done. I'm absolutely convinced Melanthrix is behind all of this. If we get rid of him, we cure father, it's as simple as that. How does he expect us to fight another war without men and supplies?"

"I don't know, brother," Kiríll responded, "but again I have to urge caution. You saw what father was like today. It wouldn't take much to push him over the edge, and then any of us could quickly become expendable. Extra royal princes are always somewhat of a nuisance anyway. Whatever we decide to do, we mustn't give anything away. You especially. Learn to bow and simper with the best of them. I know it's not in your nature, Zack, but better that than seeing you brought to the block. This is a very dangerous time for all of us. Be careful."

"'Careful' is my hallmark," Zakháry snorted. "Now, I need to work some of this aggression out of my system. Let's grab some bows and see what game we can scare up out of the brush. I need to make a few things dead."

"I'm for that," his brother concurred, eager to be killing in the fields. "Come along," he said, hurrying out the door.

CHAPTER TWENTY-THREE
"MOST BUFONIOUSLY WARTY"

In her home in the Jabal Khaibár, the Countess Mösza was wondering at the prolonged absence of her little friend, the *ifrit*, and the equal omission of any recent obituaries from Kórynthály. She suspected a fly floating in the broth, and so she was taking steps to discover just what had happened to her unwilling helpmate.

She had in her possession an old blanket woven from the fur of a very special cat, one capable of housing an entity such as herself. This shroud had belonged to one of the ancient mages, perhaps Rÿah or Tsrükh or MassáttLlán. She wasn't really sure. The artifact was very rare, very potent when used in the proper fashion, carrying within it the fragmentary essences of makers and makings unusual and undivine.

Mösza activated her *psaiaura*, which were built into the very structure of her house, and laid the cloth flat on a worktable, fastening it with pins already set in place for that purpose. She sprinkled holy water over the blanket, mixed with the blood from an unbaptized babe, and spoke a few words in the old tongue.

Then she raised up her hands and twisted the æther with her two wills, and called up the dæmon Vörshchkelidôg.

A faint image of a miniature gargoyle formed over the cloth.

"Who disturbs the *sphygmos?*" a rough voice issued from the mouth of the grotesque being.

"I have an *ifrit* gone missing," Mösza complained. "I sent

Bezarduardakus on an errand, and he never returned. I want an accounting."

"This entity will check," replied the warty one, and his entire body vanished and reappeared in just an instant.

"*Ifrit* claimed unlawful compulsion," the dæmon continued. "Petition made to king of *ifrits*, who upheld its appeal, voided the indenture, and enslaved said entity for ten thousand years."

"I claim recompense," she noted, "under the law of unfair employment of magical assistance."

"Granted," it said. "What is thy wish?"

"The death of a human," she demanded.

"Inappropriate use of an *ifrit*," the dæmon noted.

"Then use another, damn you!" Mösza cried.

"This entity is already damned, by definition, and cannot be redamned," it responded.

It paused for a moment, lost in thought.

"Cost is 6.66 souls," it added.

"Oh, very well," she agreed.

"One attempt only will be made," the dæmon indicated. "No further assistance shall be provided thereafter."

"Just get it done!" she ordered, and closed down the æthernet.

From the corner of the room Sadyris had watched the entire drama out from one half-lidded eye, while pretending to be asleep, and now she took herself to her little box, where she stretched her tail into a rigid line and thereby touched another.

Thus it was that the dæmon Vörshchkelidôg, upon further reflection, grew less and less satisfied with its transaction, and finally approached its superior being, with some trepidation.

"This entity has a difficulty," it stated, explaining the situation.

Then it listened to a very lengthy response and a question.

"No," the dæmon responded to its better, "no time specified."

There was some further conversation, before Vörshchkelidôg finally grinned.

"Most satisfactory," it said, working its tusks together. "Most bufoniously warty."

CHAPTER TWENTY-FOUR

"I CAN'T WAIT TO
GO TO WAR AGAIN"

Three days later, on the Feast of Saint Silas the Silent, another council meeting was held. The first order of business was to swear in the three new members, the Generals and Lords Rónai and Reményi, and Doctor Melanthrix.

The first two ceremonies proceeded without opposition, but when Melanthrix stepped forward, his silver chains jangling, Prince Zakháry immediately raised an objection.

"I accuse the sorcerer Melanthrix of treason," he stated, "for disrupting the working at the Schilling-Ford. He is unfit to join this council."

"Absurd!" the king responded. "I won't hear of it. Doctor Melanthrix has been my friend and *confidant* for almost three decades. During that period he has treated me for many different afflictions, each time successfully. His loyalty is without question. The charges are dismissed with prejudice. This matter will not be raised again. Understood?"

Kipriyán glared down at his son, who abruptly sat back down in his chair, not willing to challenge his father directly.

"Agreed!?" he demanded again.

"Agreed," Zakháry said, looking down at the patterns on the table.

"Very well," the king added, "let's proceed with the real business of this meeting. General Lord Rónai, what's the status of our forces?"

The new council member rose in his place, and pulled out a sheaf of notes.

"Well," he stated, "I was able to stop the decommisioning of the Arrhéni and Velyaminóli Brigades, and they're now on their way back to Myláßgorod. I expect them to arrive there in about a week. The king's summons has also gone out to the provinces, and we're just now beginning to get the responses. We should have about ten thousand troops ready to march by mid-August. Most will have received only the minimum of military training, but the enemy will have no better. They will not be expecting our return."

"Good," said Kipriyán. "What about the situation in Pommerelia? What are we doing to re-establish ourselves there?"

"We have moved our perimeter lines out from Borgösha and Karkára," Rónai continued, "using the rivers there as natural defenses against the partisans. We have also reinstated regular patrols up and down the valley.

"However, the small garrison at Lockenlöd Castle is under siege by the new Count of Einwegflasche, Lord Kortis, and while they're in no immediate danger of falling, neither can they do anything to expand their sector of influence to the south. We need to reinforce them within a month, or at the most six weeks, or we face the real threat of losing that fortress."

"Thank you, general," the king commended. "It's good to have someone on this council who can think more positively."

Turning to the grand vizier, he inquired: "How are the people taking all of this?"

Gorázd Lord Aboéty nervously clutched at his throat, ostensibly scratching at his beard. He sipped a cup of water before responding.

"There, uh, may be some discontent among certain quarters, sire," he indicated. "I...that is, I believe it would be wise for your highness to consider a possible reconciliation with the church before we embark on this new expedition. Tomorrow is Sunday, and no masses will be said anywhere in the country. This will be the first time most of the people will have noticed the inter-dict. I do not think they will be happy."

"Don't you, now?" Kipriyán scoffed. "Grand Vizier, you are relieved of your position. Please hand over the chain of office."

Gorázd went completely pale.

"But sire," he said, "I have always been loyal, *always!* I have been *your* man, yours alone, for twenty-eight years. What have I ever done to deserve such treatment?"

"What have you *not* done, you incompetent ingrate?" the king yelled. "You dare to speak such insolence to *me*? You've obviously consorted with the Dark-Haired Man! Be glad that I don't take your life as well."

"Yes, highness," Gorázd meekly replied, sitting back down and removing the great gold seal hanging 'round his neck. He passed it down the table to the monarch.

King Kipriyán looked pointedly around the room.

"If there is anyone else here who's disloyal or disrespectful," he boomed, "be advised that my leniency has its limits. I am the king, and I will have no other kings before me. Is that under-stood?"

He beckoned to Melanthrix, who walked around the table to approach him. The king grabbed the philosopher's arm, turned him around, embraced him, and then placed the chain of office over his neck.

"I give you the new Grand Vizier of Kórynthia," he intoned. "Gorázd, turn the pen and register over to him," he ordered.

Gorázd looked ill, but he did as he was ordered.

"I further declare that all of my councilors shall henceforward be tested weekly for mental aberrations by Doctor Melanthrix," Kipriyán stated. "Anyone who refuses to be tested shall be sent to the 'Hole' until he recants. Anyone who is tested and found disloyal shall be tried for treason and executed immediately. Record it!" he ordered Melanthrix.

"As you wish, sire," the philosopher stated, and began scrib-bling in the black book.

"I must object!" Prince Arkády declared, jumping to his

feet. "Sire, this is unbecoming a monarch of your stature. These brave men have followed you through the gravest tests anyone could ever have faced, through battles and dangers and the hazards of war. They have proven themselves steadfast and loyal beyond any possible doubt. To treat them in such a cavalier fashion after all they have done for you and for Kórynthia is at the least ungracious. No one questions your right to make decisions. We will follow you to the ends of the earth, if that is what you command. But don't do this. Please."

King Kipriyán flushed, his Adam's apple working up and down as he digested his eldest son's remarks. Then he sneered at Arkády, in such a blatant fashion that even the seasoned politicians on the council flinched at the sight.

"So, you finally show your true colors," he hissed. "Now that you're no longer hereditary prince, you have no compunctions about turning on your dear old father. Well, I've had quite enough of your insolence, boy. It was *you* who caused our retreat from Pommerelia, when I was abed with indigestion, it was *you* who cost us victory when all we had to do was march on a defenseless Balíxira. God forgive me that I ever sired such a coward and a weasel. You'll be the first one tested by Doctor Melanthrix, oh yes, and you'll like it too, won't you, boy?"

He laughed, throwing his head back.

"I respectfully refuse," Arkády threw back at him.

"Then to the 'Hole' with you and be damned," the king blurted out. "Guards, seize him!"

They moved to comply.

"Perhaps, sire, you should be the first one tested," the prince suggested. "You seem to need it more than the rest of us."

The king just smiled.

"Now you're edging into treason, my dear boy," he declaimed. "You'll be held for trial indefinitely, until I decide what to do with you. Record it, Melanthrix!"

"Yes, highness," the Grand Vizier complied.

"And as for that cripple you call your son," Kipriyán continued, "he is obviously not thriving well where he is. Therefore, I order him to be taken from his family and sent to the cloister, there to be raised as a monk in perpetual service to the church."

The members of the council glanced at each other in amazement, but the king just ignored them, rubbing his beard as if considering some great question of philosophy.

"Yes, I have it!" he added. "We'll send him to that hell-hole, Saint Svyatosláv's Monastery, in northern Zándrich. Let him spin out his life shivering through the long winters there."

"Majesty!" Arkády yelled. "Please don't do this, I pray you. My son isn't strong. He wouldn't survive even *one* winter in Zándrich. If you're upset with my insolence, then punish *me*, not my innocent boy."

"Please, Papá," Princess Arrhiána interjected, "please have mercy. Everyone knows you're a great king. You've not been yourself recently, I know, but...."

"Not myself!" the king shouted. "Not myself?! I'm feeling more like myself every day, daughter. I'm feeling *great!*, better than I've felt in my entire life, now that I can see the traitors so evident in my own family. No wonder we retreated from the field. We had traitors in the field and traitors at home. You can join your brother in the dungeon. Arrest her!" he ordered.

"And take that damned bitch of a blind sister with you as well," the king added, "since you took it upon yourself in the first place to remove her from the convent without my permission.

"Does anyone else want to express an opinion?" he continued, looking around and through each and every one of them.

He grinned again, baring his yellow fangs like an old gray wolf.

"Oh my," he added, "I've having such fun today! I can't wait to go to war again."

CHAPTER TWENTY-FIVE
"I CAME TO SEE THE GHOST"

"Father's gone mad!" Kiríll whispered to Zakháry.

He looked out over the city of Paltyrrha from the rampart at the top of the Tower of Glass. They had ventured here to ensure absolute privacy in their conversation, and even so, kept their voices deliberately, almost reverently low. After all, there had been madness aplenty on the tower recently, too.

"It's Melanthrix," Zakháry replied. "I'm convinced of it. He's poisoning the atmosphere at court. But there's just no way to get rid of him. I've thought and I've thought, Kir, and I can't find a means. When he's here, he floats around father like a bee attracted to honey, so close that the King's Guards protect him just as much as father. And no one knows where he goes outside of Paltyrrha when he disappears. His quarters are closely guarded, within and without, and cannot be accessed by anyone save himself. He doesn't even allow the palace maids to clean his room."

Prince Kiríll pondered the situation for a moment, fingering the statue of the Silver Bird.

"What about ambushing him outside his apartment?" he proposed.

"That was the first thing I considered," Zakháry responded, "but he never enters or exits his door unless there's a guard posted. He has the room directly across from Princess Arrhiána, so there's always a great deal of traffic there, and plenty of *gendarmes*. When the guard is reduced at night, he apparently uses transit mirrors to go directly from one place to another, if he even *remains* in the palace, which I can't tell. There are no open windows in his flat—they've all been boarded up—and he rarely eats or drinks except at formal banquets, and then only what everyone else is eating and drinking. I repeat, there's no way to get to him."

"There's *always* a way, brother," Kiríll pronounced. "Maybe we can hire it done."

"Professional assassins?" Zack scoffed. "Oh come now, are we reduced to *that?* We sound like some displaced, debauched princeling from Köstrzyn or Venicia. No, I won't do that, on general principle. If we can't accomplish it ourselves, perhaps with some help from our friends, then we probably deserve him."

"I won't argue with you," his brother noted. "Of course, if father ever finds out, in his present state he might...."

"Not *might! Would!*" Zakháry stated. "But I still think we have to take the chance. We can't let things continue as they've been going. Sooner or later, there'll be some serious disaffection out there, both among the surviving nobility and in the populace, and *all* of our lives will be at stake. I think father's time is rapidly coming to an end."

He sensed a movement behind him, and whirling around, pulled a wicked dirk from his belt.

"Who's there?" he hissed.

"It's just me!" Princess Grigorÿna declared, stepping from the shadow of the open staircase. "I came to see the ghost, Uncle Zack."

"The ghost?" Kiríll inquired.

"The ghost of Aunt Tréssa," she said quite sweetly, curtsying. "I talk to her sometimes. She tells me things. Things about Melánty."

"What do *you* know about Melanthrix?" Zakháry asked.

"Oh, lots of things," she chirped. "I know more than you do. I know he's been a bad boy, and bad little boys and bad little girls have to be punished. That's what happened to Aunt Tréssa."

"What do you mean?" Zack added.

"*You'll* find out," Rÿna pouted. "I know something you don't know," she sang, "I know something you don't know," and darted back down the stairs.

"That little girl has gotten very strange of late," Kiríll commented, watching her depart.

"However, to get back to the subject at hand, brother," he continued, "I again urge caution."

"You're *always* urging caution," Zakháry noted.

"And I'm always right, aren't I?" his brother replied. "We must watch and wait and be very, very careful while father is in this mood. Let him chase other enemies. Our time will come. And when it does, that damned charlatan will wind up floating down the Paltyrrh River."

Prince Zakháry chuckled at the thought.

"Come on," he said, "let's get back to the family."

As they headed down the open staircase, however, they failed to notice the head of the Silver Bird slowly turning to follow their passage. After they were gone, it opened wide its shining beak, and issued forth a butterfly, which promptly flew away from the castle towards the southeast, at a speed and height that put a lie to its shape.

CHAPTER TWENTY-SIX
"PRAY FOR POOR OLD KÓRYNTHIA"

Early that evening, Queen Polyxena sought a private audience with former Patriarch Timotheos, who in a gesture of conciliation had been released from prison that same day after giving his *parole d'honneur* to appear for trial, and after agreeing to lift the interdict from the Kingdom of Kórynthia. They met in the loft of the Church of Saint Ióv in Kórynthály.

"Holiness," she said, "thank you so much for seeing me on such short notice."

"The pleasure is mine, highness," the patriarch acknowledged.

"I've lost my way, Timotheos," she stated. "I don't know what to do anymore. I feel as if my world is crumbling away beneath me, but I can't seem to stop the erosion. Kipriyán is not himself. He seems almost possessed by the devil. He's changed more and more since this Dark-Haired Man business started late last year.

"And suddenly he's getting worse, much worse, father. He's imprisoned three of our children. How could he do this if he were sane? Another is buried among the tombs out back. Our grandson is being sent to a monastery, and I fear for the safety of the others. You've been illegally removed from office. The grand vizier has been deposed and replaced by a man of questionable morals. Kipriyán has been excommunicated. Is the world coming to an end?"

Tears were running down her white cheeks in the twilight. Nearby, a dozen fruit flies buzzed 'round and 'round in their endless mating circles, lazily catching the last rays of the setting sun shining through the great circular window behind them.

"My queen," the patriarch began, "I am myself reduced to little more than a parish priest in just a week. It's a humbling experience for one who's spent his lifetime in service to the church. Yes, your husband's ill, that much is certain, and if you oppose him directly, you will be subjected to the same unreasoning anger that has been visited upon your children.

"You have, it seems to me, only two choices," he continued. "You can accept who and what he has become, and close your eyes to the injustices that are being perpetrated in his name, or you can respond to your conscience, which is another way of saying to God's word, and take steps to oppose him. Both choices offer potential consequences that are terrible to contemplate.

"As for advice, well, I can only tell you what I would do in your circumstance, and you know what that is. I'm the chosen representative of God on earth, and so I don't have the right to follow any commands save His, or any precepts except those sanctioned by His holy word. That's why I had to do what I did, and that's why I cannot release the king from his state of peril until he truly repents. Other men follow his lead: if they see him successfully challenging the moral authority of the church, then chaos will ultimately result. I won't allow that to happen, even if it means my own death.

"We all have choices," he concluded. "Sometimes the price of doing nothing is greater than that of taking action. You must decide for yourself, however. Trust in God, Queen Polyxena. Take your strength and your wisdom from Him. He will always show you the right way, if you listen to Him. Now, please do me the honor, my queen, of praying with me in this, our shared time of troubles."

He led her then to a side chapel devoted to the memory of Saint Auréa the Martyr, and they each lit a candle as a beacon of hope for the future, and knelt down most humbly in front of the altar of the Lord.

As they quietly prayed, she sensed a movement among the shadows to the right, feeling a presence that reached out gently to soothe her mind. Her eyes opened wide, as she strove to penetrate the growing darkness.

Who are you? she inquired.

Your strength, the shadow replied. *Your courage, Queen of Kórynthia. What is done can be undone. You have more allies than you can know.*

She felt a wave of peace such as she had never experienced wash over her, draining her tensions and giving her back her will. Then whatever it was vanished, as if it had never been. Finally, having no idea of how much time had passed while she had knelt there, she sent a prayer of thankfulness to Saint Auréa, and broke the silence.

"Will you bless me, father?" she asked.

"Most willingly, sister," he replied, giving her his benediction.

She knelt before him and kissed his gold ring. "I now know what I must do," she said. "Pray for me, Timotheos. Pray for my husband." Then she added, almost as an afterthought: "And pray for poor old Kórynthia."

CHAPTER TWENTY-SEVEN
"WHATEVER THE CONSEQUENCES?"

In the keep of Legalsó Vár, popularly called the "Lyuk," which is to say, the "Hole," the Prince Arkády tried to find a comfortable spot on which to rest. All he had was some damp straw to ameliorate the hard, cold stone of the cell. The smell of human waste, the ever-present vermin, the occasional moans of other prisoners in far-distant cells, were depressing enough, but the thought of what his father had become overrode all the rest.

He tried again to establish a link with Princess Arrhiána, forcing the unpleasant conditions out of his mind, and concentrating on reaching her through the solid stone surrounding him. It was another way of riding the leys.

Is that you, Kásha? came the faint reply.

Thank God! he responded, focusing on and strengthening the link, gradually weaving the threads piece by piece until the whole was established.

How far away are you? his sister inquired.

I think they segregate the women from the men here, he indicated, *so you're probably either another level up or down, or in another wing.*

Are your accommodations as fine as mine? he added, putting a hint of laughter into his message.

Oh, this is just like vacationing in Telámô, she noted. *I have my own private room, servants to wait upon my every need, and the finest food and drink that's available in the place. All I lack is the proper companionship.*

Well, he said, *perhaps I can send you a husband from among the guards. You know, there's one burly fellow who looks as if....*

Never you mind! she retorted. *I already have four of them being trained to wait on me hand and foot, and I prefer to do the conditioning myself, thank you.*

I keep thinking about Nicky, he said, *and how much I miss his energy, his sense of joy in life. He took a blow meant for me, Rhie. I should have died at Killingford. He saw the axe coming towards me, and stepped right in front of it. He smiled as he breathed his last, and grabbed my hand. I keep wondering if I could have done something to stop it.*

And if you had died, she replied, *would we be any better off? I don't think so. I miss him just as much as you, but I also know that you're the better man to face this kind of crisis. And it is developing into a crisis. What are we going to do, Kásha?*

Get out of here, for one, he stated. *Keep our sanity, for another. And I really think we are going to have to do something about father, as much as I hate being forced into that position. His mania has reached the point where it's starting to have a serious, even an evil, impact on the nation. So long as we were the only ones affected, the potential harm to the country outweighed any personal considerations. But I truly believe we have crossed the line in the opposite direction. We must take action to save Kórynthia.*

I know, she commiserated. *I've come to the same conclusion. He's been tainted or infected in some way by a hideous disease of the mind or spirit, one that's destroying him—and all of the rest of us—from within. Recently, I think, the process has begun to accelerate. Things are deteriorating very rapidly now. If we don't act soon, there'll be nothing left to save.*

Then what do we do, sister? Arkády asked.

We wait for a while to lull our enemies to sleep, she replied. *And when the opportunity presents itself, we strike!*

Whatever the consequences? he inquired.

Whatever the consequences! she agreed.

CHAPTER TWENTY-EIGHT
"TAKE HIM AWAY"

Another meeting of the council was held on the following Saturday, the Feast of Saint Boulmaros. Doctor Melanthrix continued to preside as grand vizier. Although the patriarch had been released from prison a week earlier, he had not been allowed to return to the council, and the Bishop Varlaám, the king's choice for *Locum Tenens*, sat in his place. Father Athanasios had returned to the council as grammateus.

"Is everyone here?" the king asked. "Very well, let's begin. General Lord Rónai, please provide us with an update of our military situation."

The officer rose in his place and shuffled some papers.

"My lords," he intoned, "the Arrhéni and Velyaminóli Brigades have arrived intact at Myláßgorod, under the joint command of Count Sándor. Count Zygmunt assures me that provisions are adequate, and that the troops will be ready to march whenever we call on them. In the meantime, Sándor has instituted a regimen of intensive training over the next three weeks.

"Seven other brigades are in the process of being formed, using as a nucleus some of the experienced surviving commanders from the previous expedition. We've also secured the services of a brigade of Ras ash-Shamra mercenaries, who are presently sailing to Dnepróv. Our target date for leaving Borgösha is a month from today."

"Thank you, sir, for your excellent presentation. Any questions?" asked Melanthrix. He nodded towards an elderly councilman. "Lord Bunénë?"

"Yes, sire," the gray-bearded baron stated. "I was wondering about your plan of action once we re-enter Pommerelia."

"Good question," Melanthrix responded. "General?"

"Uh," the officer was fumbling again with his notes, "here it is. We propose to occupy the Valley of the Spargö permanently, establishing a line of forts cutting off the County of Körvö at its lower end, and also moving to the southern end of Lake Zhordán, thereby sealing off any threat from Dharmagrigg. To the north we will place a line of forts across the end of the valley from just above Karkára to the top part of the Läuterung Hills, and gradually add Einwegflasche, Mimmäma, and the other northern counties of Pommerelia to our control.

"Eventually," he continued, "the pressure on the Walküri will be so great that they will have no choice but to move against us, and when they do, we'll be waiting for them in our fortified emplacements. Once their main army has broken itself against our line, the road will be open to the Pommerelian heartland, and we'll put Balíxira and Dürkheim under siege."

"A worthy plan!" endorsed the king. "Anything further before we move to our next topic?"

"Yes," said Lord Bunénë, "I wonder...."

But what he might be wondering was lost forever, when he sprawled forward on the table, his forehead hitting the wood with a distinct "thunk."

"What's wrong?" Kipriyán yelled.

"Call a physician!" Prince Kiríll shouted.

Lord Gorázd helped ease the distressed baron back into his seat, then looked up in anguish.

"He's dead!" he announced, then quickly moved back out of the way as Fra Tibor Türdetány rushed in.

The doctor thoroughly examined the old man's body, feeling him all over and poking into his orifices.

Suddenly there was a flash of green light off to one side, and a squawk from the king that turned into a loud gasp for breath.

The attention of the council members immediately swiveled to the end of the table, where Lord Gorázd was sending bolts of energy at close range straight into Kipriyán's body.

The king had been caught completely by surprise, with barely enough time to raise his rings, and he was weakening rapidly under Gorázd's relentless attack. If his strength failed, his mind would be emptied and his body fried.

Father Athanasios, sitting to the king's right, immediately centered himself, activated his own rings, drew his feet up towards his stomach as far as they would go, pressed them firmly against the end of the table, and then shot them out with all of his strength, pushing his solid wood chair directly back into the body of Gorázd, knocking the attacker off his feet and into the wall.

The Princes Kiríll and Zakháry were immediately on top of Gorázd, pouring their combined energies into the prone body of the attacker. He fought back with ferocious strength, singeing Zakháry's shoulder, before a blow from Kiríll's mighty right arm sent him into unconsciousness.

"Fra Tibor," Athanasios called, "sedate the man."

The physician puffed some powder from a phial under the attacker's nose, but was unprepared for the sudden reaction. The former grand vizier first went rigid, then convulsed several times in massive, body-wide spasms, before finally going completely slack.

The doctor checked for a pulse, and looked up in amazement, shaking his head.

"Gone," he said.

King Kipriyán got to his feet. His hands were trembling from exhaustion and in reaction to the aftermath of the attack.

"Tibor," he ordered, when he had regained his composure, "have a necroprobe done as soon as possible on both men. We'll adjourn this meeting until this afternoon, when I want a complete report. Now, I must rest for a few hours."

His sons helped him out of the room, followed slowly by the rest of the stunned councilmen, leaving only Doctor Melanthrix behind.

The philosopher looked around the empty chamber, idly fingering his chain of office. He stooped to pick something from the floor, and secreted it in his purse.

A guard came rushing back through the door.

"Sir," he shouted, "it's the king!"

Melanthrix immediately came to his feet, and hurried towards the exit, brushing aside the soldier.

What is it now? he thought.

He was almost to the exit when some instinct, perhaps the hint of a slight rustling behind him, made him suddenly fling himself sideways to the floor. A short sword or long knife slashed across his back, cutting through his cloak and breaking the skin. He rolled over without thinking, gathered his energies, and sent a bolt of ruby flame straight at the guard.

A high-pitched scream brought the other guards on the run. They entered to find a tower of moving fire, something that had once been a man, trying desperately to find some relief from the all-consuming pain. The old philosopher was sprawled on the floor nearby, his back soaked in blood.

The assassin toppled onto the table, finally removed by death from his misery. Melanthrix staggered shakily to his feet. A few inches deeper, and it would have been *his* death they would be celebrating.

"Take him away," the philosopher gasped, waving at the blackened body, and then limped heavily out of the room.

No one there offered to assist him.

CHAPTER TWENTY-NINE
"HE MUST BE...REDIRECTED"

After putting her husband to bed, Queen Polyxena took her sons Prince Kiríll and Prince Zakháry to one side, and motioned them to join her.

They silently followed her to Princess Arrhiána's quarters, which she entered using a key that Arrhiána had given her.

Across the hall, Doctor Melanthrix lay on his side in his bed, groaning from the pain. He had taken an elixir that would heal his wound within a day or two, but dared not go to any local physician for further assistance. The temporary agony would just have to be endured until it passed.

Someone had actually *tried to kill him!*, he thought, appalled at the very notion. He dreaded even being touched by another being, for good and valid reasons rooted deep within his history, but to be attacked in this way meant that his vulnerability had just increased. No matter that it had failed. Others would soon try again.

Somewhere in his dulled mind he heard the slight commotion across the corridor, but was just too tired and weak and upset to investigate. Later, he would very much regret his present lack of initiative.

Polyxena locked the door behind her, and sat her two sons down in Arrhiána's parlor. They gazed back at her with great concern. This was most unlike their demure mother, who usually remained in the background while the king made all of the decisions.

"My dear boys," she said, "I know that you have been as concerned as I have about your father's recent behavior. He hasn't been himself for some months now. He has this idea that the Dark-Haired Man, whoever he might be, is somehow persecuting him, and this bizarre notion has colored all of his thoughts and activities."

She looked to be on the verge of tears.

"I've tried talking with him," she continued. "I've tried reasoning with him, but on this matter there simply is nothing of reason to be found. It has poisoned our relationship as much as it has changed his relation with his own country.

"Even during the height of the wars with the barbarians, Kipriyán never lost his sense of humor, his good nature, or his strong belief in the king as the ultimate arbiter and guarantor of justice in the land. All of that is gone now. Instead, we see a tyrant sitting upon the throne of Kórynthia, a man who is destroying himself as he destroys the very heart of his nation.

"I cannot allow this to continue. For his own sake, for the sake of Kórynthia, he must be...redirected."

She wiped away two tears now winding their way down her cheeks.

"Tonight I will go to the 'Hole' and free my son and daughters from that awful place, and also release any of those others who have been unjustly imprisoned there these past six months. Will you help me?"

Prince Zakháry grabbed his mother's hands, and pulled her close, feeling the trembling of her body. He felt a great pity in his heart for what she had endured in recent times.

"Of course we will," he murmured.

As he looked over her shoulder, his eyes caught those of his brother, Prince Kiríll, who nodded his head in agreement.

"We've both thought for some time that something has to be done to save father from the machinations of that quack, Melanthrix," he added. "We'll do anything necessary to help return things to normal."

The queen withdrew from him and held him at arms' length.

She looked at him for a long moment before speaking.

"You do understand what I'm saying here?" she asked. "Once we start down this road, there's no going back for any of us. If we're discovered and caught, we'll either wind up in the dungeon ourselves, or God forbid, worse."

"We understand, mother," Kiríll piped in. "But even if we don't act, something similar is apt to happen very soon anyway. If the likes of Arkády and Arrhiána and Patriarch Timotheos can be called 'traitors,' then no one here is safe, you included. We have to root out the evil, even if it means saving father from his own worst tendencies. Then we have to go after that other malignancy. Only when Melanthrix is destroyed will any of us be able to sleep at night again."

"Very well," she stated. "Meet me in the Cathedral Annex at *apodeipnon*. Come armed. I'll have a forged pass to use at the keep, and I hope to persuade several others to join us. Now go! You have to be back at the council meeting this afternoon, and I don't want us seen together before then."

Each of them left separately, Queen Polyxena last of all. Across the hall, the philosopher Melanthrix heard the door close, but assumed it was one of the maids. He rolled over and went back to sleep, but forgot to set his internal clock to wake him as he had planned. His thoughts were muddled by the pain and the drug, and he drifted through a sea of ill dreams, dark and dangerous and drear, and finally awoke—late—to his own screams.

CHAPTER THIRTY
"I WAS NOT THERE"

At the resumption of the council meeting that afternoon, the tardy appearance of Doctor Melanthrix caused quite a stir. He came limping through the door, dressed in an ordinary tunic and holding onto his side.

"What happened to you?" the king inquired, clearly concerned.

"We were attacked in this chamber shortly after the meeting adjourned," the philosopher explained. "We were cut across the back and side and our cloak was destroyed. Fortunately, we survived. Our attacker did not."

Then the guards came forward to corroborate his account.

The king faced the council members, his face set in a grim mask.

"I take an exceedingly dim view of these cowardly assaults," he said. "Whoever is responsible has committed treason against me and Kórynthia. I shall seek out the villain, and I shall take great pleasure in seeing him disemboweled alive."

Then Fra Tibor reported his findings to the king.

"I examined the bodies of Lord Bunénë and Lord Gorázd Aboéty myself," he said. "Bunénë was murdered, probably by Lord Gorázd, being stabbed in the side by a long, narrow needle which punctured his heart and caused almost instantaneous death. The wound was so small that it wasn't obvious until I examined his body more thoroughly. Undoubtedly, he was killed to draw attention away from the attack on the king.

"As for Lord Gorázd," he continued, "his mind was empty, very much like those of the victims that Fra Jánisar and I observed several months ago. I found traces of a strong compulsion planted quite recently in his mind, almost certainly within the last day, and perhaps as recently as this morning."

"How can you be sure?" asked Father Athanasios.

"Obviously, I'm not," the physician retorted. "However, I've examined four of these bodies previously, and Gorázd matches them completely, except that the signs are fresher. Our assassin is back!"

"Who met with Lord Gorázd this morning before the council meeting?" Athanasios pressed.

The former grand vizier's longtime aide, Aloÿs Monck, was called to the chamber.

When he appeared, Kiríll took the initiative.

"You were responsible for maintaining Lord Gorázd's schedule?" the prince inquired.

"Yes, highness," Monck replied, "for the past twenty years."

"With whom did he meet this morning?" Kiríll asked.

"Because of the council meeting, he had only one appointment scheduled for this morning," the servant noted, "with the Bishop Varlaám."

"What!" shouted the prelate, rising in his place. "That's a vicious lie!"

"You see the man standing there," Kiríll stated. "Is that the person you saw enter your master's apartment this morning?"

"Yes, it is, highness," Monck avowed. "I have no doubt whatever."

"Thank you," the prince acknowledged. "You're dismissed."

Then he turned to Varlaám.

"Sir, do you wish to recant your story?" the prince inquired.

"*I was not there,*" the frightened bishop replied. "I don't know what else I can say."

"Then where were you?" Kiríll asked.

"In my cell at Saint Theophanês's," Varlaám responded, "praying and preparing for this meeting."

"Did anyone see you there in the hour prior to *tritê*?" the prince continued.

"I don't believe so," the bishop said.

"Then I order your arrest for the murder of Lord Gorázd and others, subject to confirmation by the king."

He looked at his father, who nodded his acquiescence.

"Guards, seize him!" Kiríll ordered.

"Wait! I didn't do anything," Varlaám frantically pleaded. "Majesty, help me, please!"

"Melanthrix, probe him," the king ordered.

"No! I...," the priest protested, but before he could speak further he was abruptly jabbed with the "*szósz*," a drug that tended to dull the mind and put the recipient into a sound sleep.

Melanthrix's thin white face suddenly loomed over Varlaám's wide, pink one, and the priest's brown eyes seemed to melt and retreat under the cold blue orbs staring down at him. They sucked out his soul from his brain like a yolk being drained through two small holes in an eggshell. One could almost hear the spirit slurp as it deflated.

The prelate's body abruptly went limp, and Melanthrix looked up, his demeanor cool and satisfied.

"We regret to inform you," he stated, "that the Bishop Varlaám is guilty as charged. Alas, that he perished during the interrogation."

"Take him away," Kipriyán ordered the guards, "and bury him in unhallowed ground in the potter's field.

"Grand Vizier," he continued, "whom do you suggest as Varlaám's replacement for the office of *Locum Tenens* of the Holy Church of Kórynthia?"

Doctor Melanthrix paused for a moment, as if to consider carefully the problem.

"Ah," he said, "as to that, we have another churchman resident on this council, and certainly one as worthy as the late Varlaám. We commend the Archpriest Athanasios to your majesty's consideration. Indeed, God Himself showed His approval this morning, when Athanasios saved your majesty's life."

"So he did!" the king agreed, suddenly pounding the priest on the back.

"I agree!" he ordered. "Record it, Melanthrix."

Athanasios was dumbfounded by this turn of events. To have gone from simple priest to acting head of the Church of Kórynthia was beyond anything he had ever anticipated or sought. He thought to protest the appointment, particularly since he was sitting in the place of the true patriarch, but then he recalled the fate of several others who had so recently taken a stand against the king, and decided better of it. He would bide his time, and seek a way to restore his friend Timotheos to his proper place.

"Further," added the king, "I hereby appoint the Grand Vizier, Doctor Melanthrix, to be Lord Governor of the City of Paltyrrha, and on this day I have created him Lord Fértö, with his fief situate in the County of Marrhás."

Kipriyán motioned to Athanasios, who passed along the appropriate decree of appointment and letters patent to the old philosopher.

"Kudos, Lord Fértö!" the king announced, and following his lead, all present thumped their breasts in acclamation.

"This meeting is adjourned!" Kipriyán declared.

Afterwards, Father Athanasios followed Melanthrix out into the hall.

"Congratulations, Melánty," the priest offered. "Are you sure you're all right? You look very tired to me."

"Kudos to you, Athy," Melanthrix replied. "We have, perhaps, been burning the midnight candle too many times. And all this violence, it takes its toll upon every one of us. Soon, we hope, very soon it will all be over, and we can rest again. It seems so long since we've been able to sleep all the night through, and feel refreshed again the next day. But we do appreciate your concern. No one else much cares about us except the Princess Grigorÿna and Prince Arión."

"Surely that's not true," Athanasios said. "You must have other friends."

"You know the answer to that question better than we," the philosopher stated. "We gave up our personal life many years ago to pursue our studies, and when we returned to the real world, we found it very much changed, and ourselves along with it. Now, we have only our purpose left, and those few individuals who seem to appreciate what little we have to offer. But enough of us. We are only an old fool who has not very long to live. Tell us instead what *you* have been doing with yourself."

Athanasios then talked in general terms about his quest for the origins of his existence.

"I've seen some progress," he continued, "but for every twist and turn that I make, for every advance, I either come to some ending that I didn't expect, or what I find makes no sense to me, and leads me nowhere."

"Why is this search so important to you?" Melanthrix inquired. "What possible difference can it make if you discover that you are the son of a king or the son of a sheepshearer? Are you not who you are...inside?"

He punctuated the remark by stabbing Athanasios in the breast with his long, alabaster forefinger.

"Oh, I've talked about this with Arik, too," Athanasios responded. "It's just that for me, somehow, my life seems inextricably tied to the past. I can't even explain it very well. I have this sense that if I knew who my parents were, I'd suddenly have a much better picture of *why* I am, and that it would make all the difference in the world to me, that it would clarify things, somehow."

"Why should that be?" Melanthrix posed.

He cocked his head as if listening to the spheres, to some unseen music that no one else in the world could possibly hear.

"I don't know, Melánty," the priest admitted. "It matters to *me*, I guess. Perhaps if I find the answers to *my* questions, I'll be able to answer *your* question."

"Well, should you fail to find an answer to either of our questions," the old man stated, "you can be *our* child, for we would be proud to acknowledge you."

Athanasios laughed out loud.

"I bet you would, you old reprobate," he responded. "Come along now, let's go find some food. You can join me for dinner and tell me of your plans for my continued fostering."

"So we shall, my boy, so we shall," said the philosopher, as they walked off together.

From a shadowy alcove in the hall, the brothers Kiríll and Zakháry watched with fitful jealousy, waiting for the devil to find his way back into Hell.

CHAPTER THIRTY-ONE
"WHAT YEAR IS THIS?"

Late that evening, after the king was carefully sedated by Polyxena, the queen took herself to the Chapel of Saint Hyakinthos, where she met with Patriarch Timotheos and Archpriest Athanasios. Joining them were the Princes Kiríll and Zakháry, and Captains Kérés and Fösse, with ten each of their men. All but the priests and queen were heavily armed.

"I again ask all of you," she said, "to understand full well what we attempt to do here tonight. Some would dare call it treason. I dare to call it patriotism. The reasons will not matter if we're caught. Are you with me?"

There were rumbles of agreement from all of them.

"Then please bless our enterprise, holiness," she begged.

Timotheos touched each of them with sacred water, and then gave them his special benediction.

"It's in God's hands, now," the queen iterated.

The patriarch led the way to a private alcove in his apartments in the abbey, where they transited a few at a time to the Chapel of Saint Ambrosios the Base, located within the Keep of Legalsó Vár in northwest Paltyrrha, near the city wall.

The "Hole," as it was popularly called, had been built during the time of King Matvéy two hundred and fifty years before, to house both high- and low-security prisoners of the state. The more transient populace of the prison was located in the top layers, erected above street level, where the detainees could be easily moved in and out by their jailers. Sensitive clients, however, including political prisoners, were housed deep within the bowels of the gaol, in sections mined far beneath ground level, where access could be tightly restricted.

The queen's entourage was dressed quite plainly, the patriarch and Athanasios being clothed merely as black-robed chaplains, and the princes outfitted as additional guards following the captains. The queen, of course, appeared as herself.

Polyxena marched forthrightly out of the chapel, and straight to the first of a series of guard stations, dutifully followed by the two priests and her security troops.

"The Queen of Kórynthia to see Prince Arkády, Princess Arrhiána, and Princess Sachette," she demanded in a stern voice, handing over a pass signed by the king.

The sergeant on the other side of the iron gate looked askance at the little group, and pointed at them with the rolled-up piece of paper.

"Who're these?" he asked.

"Two priests and my personal guard," she replied.

"And who are *you?*" she inquired.

The sergeant squirmed and looked down again at the pass. He couldn't read, although he would never admit that.

"Umm," he said, "sorry, majesty, I just have to ask certain questions. Please go right on through."

He unlocked the gate, and swung it open. As they passed the guard, Prince Kiríll suddenly hit him from behind, knocking him unconscious. They pricked him with a pin smeared with the "*kókk,*" which would keep him out for another few hours, and hid him in an alcove. One of their own guards traded clothes with him, pocketed the master keys, and took up the previous occupant's station. Then they relocked the gate before proceeding, carefully preserving the pass.

Prince Kiríll had been here several times before, in the role of gaoler, and he knew the general layout of the place.

"They'll be in two different wings," he advised. "They keep the men and women separated. We need to go down seven levels on the left side to find Prince Arkády."

At Level Two they came to another guard station, this one staffed by two men.

Again Queen Polyxena demanded entrance, handing over her pass.

"This is dated a week ago," the sergeant noted. "And it only allows passage for two persons."

"Oh, I never pay much attention to these things," the queen replied, "and I don't think anyone else does, either. The clerks write so many of them that they tend to repeat the same language. You know the rule, sergeant: I'm not supposed to go anywhere without my security detail. King's orders. Of course, if you want me to bother him and bring him over here, I'm sure...."

"Very well!" the guard acknowledged. "We'll pass you through. Gensrick," he ordered, "unlock the gate."

As soon as they had entered, their troop pulled out weapons, disarmed the two guards, drugged them, exchanged clothing with them, dragged them off into an alcove, and left two of their own sitting in their place at the entrance. Then they relocked the gate, and continued on down to the next section.

The third and final security check was encountered at Level Six.

The guard stationed there took one look at the queen's pass, and gave it back to her.

"Sorry," he said, "this isn't valid here. You have to have a special pass just for this section."

"Really?" Polyxena responded, batting her eyes. "Nobody told me that, and I haven't had to use one on my previous visits. Of course, that was during the day, and you weren't here then."

"Nevertheless," the guard replied, "I can't pass you through without the proper paperwork. Also, no weapons are allowed beyond this point. No exceptions. Sorry, but it'd be my job."

"But I came all the way here just to see my children," the queen explained. "Can't you let me in, or at least bring them here to see me?"

"Well, as I explained," the man indicated, "this is the high-security level, and we don't allow anyone in here without a duly authorized pass."

"I certainly hate to get the king out of bed," she whined, "but if that's the way it is...."

She turned and nodded slightly.

"Highness," the guard said, "I couldn't even let the king...."

There was a whir in the air and a flash in the dim light, and suddenly the end of a knife was sticking out of the man's eyesocket. He slumped forward.

Then Zakháry used his abilities to tease the keys out of the guard's pocket. The locks here were protected against mental intrusion of any kind, and could not be picked except by mechanical means. He unlocked the door, and they trooped through. The patriarch immediately gave the guard an abbreviated version of the last rites. Again, they exchanged uniforms and dragged the body off, leaving one of their own in place.

Kiríll checked the master map.

"This way," he said, heading down to Level Seven.

The stench in this section was almost overpowering, although one did become used to it after a time.

The prince used his ringflame to compare the numbers over the cells to the master list.

"Sixty-eight," he read. "No, that's Rössvald. Ah, here it is, sixty-nine."

His brother Zakháry used the master key to unlock the door, and swung it back.

"Kásha," Kiríll whispered.

"Kir! Is *that* really you?" his brother gasped.

Then he was out and embracing his mother and brothers.

"God, how good it is to see a loving face again," he said with relief. "But, what about Rhie and Chette?" he asked.

"They're next," Kiríll stated. "What do you know about your neighbors here?"

"Almost all of them are political prisoners," Arkády indicated. "If we want to get out of here alive, I strongly suggest you free as many as possible, and arm them. But be careful: the guards make regular patrols through this level. There should be another one coming by here in a few moments."

Zakháry ordered Kiríll and Kérés to take half the remaining men and go to the righthand wing of the structure to rescue the women. Meanwhile, he and Captain Fösse and their remaining troop set about freeing the other prisoners of Levels Six and Seven, beginning with Rössvald.

The haggard old man staggered out of the cell, looking wildly around him, his gray beard straggling down to his waist.

"What year is this?" he croaked, barely able to talk.

"Year XLI of King Kipriyán," the queen replied.

"My God!" Rössvald gasped, "I've been here nearly four decades."

"Who imprisoned you?" Arkády inquired.

"The regents," the prisoner noted, "I...."

The rest of his remarks were lost as a guard came ambling around the corner of the passageway, saw them, and drew his sword.

"To arms!" he yelled. "To arms!"

Then he attacked them, but the experienced Fösse cut him down immediately.

"Come," he said, "we need to move fast now."

More and more prisoners were now joining them. Fösse tossed the dead guard's weapons to several of the younger ones, who obviously had just been recently incarcerated, and were still in reasonably good physical condition, certainly well enough to fight.

One by one the cells were opened. Some of the detainees were incapable of walking, while others were dead. Several of the units were empty, including one supposedly inhabited by Zéléný, the well-known political satirist, who had left behind the detailed picture of a forest landscape drawn perfectly on one wall, a makeshift, burnt-out torch lying at its base.

Then a half dozen guards suddenly attacked them from both sides, and they were fighting for their lives. When one of their own men, the soldier Pál, was injured, falling heavily to one side, a prisoner grabbed his weapon and stepped in his place.

The six *gendarmes* were quickly overpowered, four of them being killed.

Within an hour they held Levels Six and Seven, and all the prisoners there had been freed, including the Princesses Arrhiána and Sachette, and the Lords Vydór, Báltoff, Emming, and Beÿkö.

It was Zakháry who brought them the bad news.

"The alarum has spread to the upper levels," he said. "I suspect the entire guard will be called out soon, if it hasn't been already. They've got the passageway beyond the control gate at Level Six sealed off. There's no possible way we can get through."

"We can't force it?" the queen inquired.

"Remember," Kiríll noted, "that this place was designed to resist sieges or rebellions, from any sector. The corridors were deliberately made narrow and easily blocked. No, we can't escape back the way we entered."

"Then it's over," Polyxena stated. "Kipriyán will have us all executed, and a reign of terror will begin. God help our poor country!

"Will they have sent to the palace yet?" she asked.

"No," responded Kiríll. "The governor here will certainly have been notified by now, and he'll try to keep any word of the rebellion from spreading outside of this complex until he has us all in his grasp. Otherwise, questions could be raised about how we got in here in the first place, and he could easily lose his head."

"Who is he?" Arkády queried.

"Lord Lásky," his brother indicated. "A real dolt. He was given this post as reward for his service in the barbarian wars. His 'service' consisted of quartermastering two brigades. The real commander is his deputy, Sir Lóngin von Zumpt. He's a nasty bastard, mean as a badger. If he has his way, we'll all be tortured before the king even hears about it."

"Nice," Arrhiána commented. "However, there's another way out."

"What!" they all gasped simultaneously.

"We've got plenty of accomplished Psairothi here," she noted. "Let's just make a transit mirror, and we'll get all of these folks to safety."

"But how?" Arkády blurted out. "We have no gold."

"No," she agreed, "but we have plenty of high-quality steel, and if we can generate enough energy to melt several of the swords together, we might be able to get a surface shiny enough to reflect and refract light."

"Oh, dear sister, I've never heard of anything like this being done before," Arkády stated.

"What choice do we have?" she posed.

"None," he responded.

Then Arkády turned to his brother: "Zakháry, round up the two captains, and send them up to Level Six to mount our defense. I assume it'll take Lásky a while to get organized up above. Then you and Kir and Chette and Mother and Rhie and any of the other adepts that can be found must clear an open area in the lower keep that's both level and self-contained. I'll lay out a dozen of the best quality swords. Let's get to it!"

Soon they had brushed off a relatively even area of the stones in the one large room of this section, and built a dirt and brick embankment around it.

"Normally," Arkády said, "we would set certain defenses about the area, but I don't think we have the proper implements with us, or the time. So we'll make do with what we have. Now, who will direct the working?"

"You should, Kásha," his mother proclaimed.

"No, I'm too shaky from the bad food and conditions down here," he replied. "So is Arrhiána. One of you will need to do this."

"I'm too old, son," Polyxena noted, "and Kiríll and Zakháry, as strong as they are, lack the finesse for this kind of work."

"Let me," Sachette pleaded.

"You've been here as long as we have," her brother stated.

"You think that because I'm blind I'm capable of nothing,"

the girl replied. "Like father, you see me as damaged. I'm not, Kásha. *This is my element.* I live in the dark. Always. I have for many years. I'm a night dweller. I see both wonders and horrors there that you can only guess at. My world is my mind. Let me do this. Let me contribute."

He looked at her in the dim light as if envisaging her for the first time. He took her pale hand in his and kissed it gently.

"Very well, Chette," he agreed. "*You* will control the working."

The group of nine adepts—Arkády, Arrhiána, Sachette, Polyxena, Kiríll, Zakháry, Timotheos, Vydór, and Athanasios—sat in a circle and joined hands. Each centered him- or herself on their *psai*-ring, entered a trance, blanked out any stray thoughts, and allowed Princess Sachette to weave their energies into one fabric.

She carefully took the individual strands of their lives, and focused them on the floor between them. The swords, which had been laid there side-by-side, began to glow a dull red, pulsating with their synchronized heartbeats. They could hear the "boom, boom, boom" of the blood rushing through their veins, as the princess changed the nature of the metal, allowing their energies to penetrate and smooth the iron within, turning it white, and then melting and shaping the flowing steel. Sachette reached out one bare foot, seemingly stretching it far beyond the bounds of human possibility, and using it like a trowel quietly and quickly to smooth the surface of the white lake, charging it with psychic energy as it began to cool. Then it was finished.

Prince Arkády called all of the prisoners together except those guarding the hallway on Level Six.

"Who'll be first?" he asked, raising high his torch, peering down at the odd metal construct to determine if his reflection was actually visible.

"I will," Sachette responded.

And before the prince could say nay, she stepped to the middle of the red-hot working, spit on it to cool the metal to a bright, gray sheen, and then felt with her toes for the leys that she knew were there.

"This is how you must do it!" she exclaimed, flashing an image to them through her *psai*-ring.

Then she vanished, sinking right through the floor to her destination.

One by one the remaining mages sent the prisoners to private destinations, until the area was clear save only for their own small group.

"Zakháry," Arkády instructed, "please fetch Captains Kérés and Fösse. Let's get out of here!"

The prince was back in a moment with their troop.

"I gummed up the lock with mud, highness," Kérés reported. "It will take them a while to get through."

"Good work, captain," Arkády commended. "All right," he added, "we're going straight to Tighrishály Palace. Put poor Pál's body in a cell; we'll retrieve it later. Now, let's go."

They transited out in three groups, leaving the area completely deserted for the prison guards to find.

CHAPTER THIRTY-TWO
"A GREAT MYSTERY TO THE BOTH OF THEM"

But just a few moments later, the artist Zélénÿ walked back through the drawing in his cell, only to find his door wide open and the place unnaturally quiet. Very, *very* carefully, he peered out into the corridor, looking both ways several times. All of the other units on his block had their doors ajar and were clearly vacant. This disturbed him so mightily that he went back into his cell, closed the door, and retreated to one corner, huddling in the shadows until the guards finally found him the next morning, shining an amber light onto his haggard face. His presence there remained a great mystery to the both of them.

CHAPTER THIRTY-THREE
"I'M GOING TO KILL YOU, SON"

Queen Polyxena, Prince Arkády, and their small group of supporters gathered in the former's quarters at Tighrishály Palace in the waning hours of the night. Their plan was quite simple: they would secure the king in his apartment while he still lay sedated in bed, and then quickly assume control of the seat of government. If confronted by the palace guards, they would say they were accompanying the queen as part of her special security detail.

But no one questioned them at that early time of the morning, and everything went perfectly, until they reached the king's quarters. His bed was empty, and they found no trace of Kipriyán anywhere.

"I thought you said you'd drugged him?" Zakháry asked his mother.

"I did!" she emphasized. "He should have slept till *hektê*. I just don't understand it."

"What'll we do?" Kiríll pleaded. "He must *know* something. Maybe Lord Lásky fetched him after all."

"*Stop!*" urged Arkády. "We know nothing of where he went or why, and until we do, there's no use speculating. Kérés, I want you to check Kórynthály and its environs, particularly the royal tombs. Fösse, do you have any means of quietly finding out whether the alarum has been given yet over the prison outbreak?"

"Yes, highness," the captain replied. "I have a few friends

among the local *gendarmerie* who are discreet enough, but at this hour.... Well, I just don't know who might be on duty. Not many, I suspect."

"Do what you can," the prince ordered.

"Kiríll and Zakháry, you two can still be seen in public without raising any suspicions," he added. "I'd like you to search the palace with the remaining guards. Did anyone bother to ask the two men just outside the door whether they saw the king leave?"

"I did," Polyxena replied. "They were awake, or so they claim, and no one left after I."

"Then he either had to transit out," Arkády sighed, "or he blurred their minds. Father Athanasios, I'd like you and the patriarch to check the cathedral, unless you think it's too risky, holiness."

"At this hour, none of the brethren will be awake," Timotheos replied.

"Very well," Arkády said, "let's all meet back here in an hour."

They hurried away to their respective chores, while Arkády, Arrhiána, Sachette, and Polyxena remained behind to plot their strategy.

"Any ideas, ladies?" the prince inquired, collapsing onto a nearby couch.

Polyxena had prepared a pot of tea and a light meal.

"Yes, run away," Arrhiána snorted. "My old dingy palace at Aszkán is beginning to look better and better to me. Seriously, I'm starting to wonder if Kiríll is right, that father somehow got wind of this."

"I honestly don't see how," their mother replied. "I've been extraordinarily careful, and I prepared and administered the drug myself tonight. It should have knocked out a horse. No, I think this is just another sign of his growing mania. I tend to believe that he's wandering around in Paltyrrha somewhere, perhaps not even understanding what he's doing."

"Whatever the reason," Arkády stated, "we need to find him

before daylight. The longer this goes on, the better the chance that Lásky or one of the other hardliners will get to him first. I don't have to tell you what that would mean."

He grinned up at both of them.

"For now," he continued, "I'm about to collapse from exhaustion. Wake me in an hour."

He immediately went to sleep, his soft, gentle snores indicating the depth of his weariness. Sachette soon joined him.

"Perhaps you'd best lie down, too," Polyxena said to her eldest daughter.

"I'd love to, mother," Arrhiána replied, "but I'm just too keyed up to rest."

And so they talked quietly to one side while waiting for the others to return.

But the Princess Sachette dreamt that she was in the Church of Saint Ióv in Kórynthály, where she had often played as a child, before the incident which had rendered her sightless. She floated over to the black marble tomb of Tighris the Founder, and rubbed the onyx mosaic which covered it.

Suddenly she became aware of a great armored figure standing next to her. She felt no fear, only an overwhelming sense of awe that she should be honored by such a presence.

"Why have you come to see me, daughter?" the man inquired.

"To find my father," she said.

"And who might that be?" he continued.

"Why, King Kipriyán the Conqueror!" she exclaimed.

"'The Conqueror,' eh?" The warrior laughed, long and loud. "A mighty title for a very little man. Yes, I remember him now. The last time he saw me, he was just a boy, and very much afraid. I think he's still afraid."

"Why?" Sachette asked.

"Because he guessed the truth," the king sighed, "and the fear that gripped his heart so tightly then has never left him. And it never will, daughter."

He coughed into his hands, and from his breath he created a pinwheel which he set spinning above the tomb.

"So does the wheel of fate turn, and turn again," he intoned, "and grinds mortal men down in its revolutions. Alas, I can do nothing to save him. He has chosen his fate, and it must work through to its ultimate conclusion."

"And what might that be, grandsire?" she inquired.

He laughed, not unkindly, and took her right hand in his.

"You're quite inquisitive for a Tighrisha," the great warrior smiled, "and unusually gifted, even by our standards. Your brother will become the most illustrious example of his race, and your elder sister will shine almost as brightly, setting down the history of our family in a way that separates truth from fiction. But they will pay a fearsome price for their fame, for the wheel has a way of exacting its own toll, and of insisting upon a balance in the end."

"And little Sachette?" she cried, "what of her life?"

He turned her hand over, and gazed sadly upon her palm.

"I will not lie to you," the man said, "your time upon this plane is shorter than theirs. What you make of it, what any man or woman makes of it, lies entirely within these hands of yours."

He took both of her small hands in his large ones, and placed them around either side of the spinning wheel.

"Feel here the pulse of life," he instructed, "and then choose wisely, my daughter."

His voice sounded hollow now, and she felt that he was beginning to fade.

"Wait!" the princess said, "I need your help."

"Look to yourself," he replied faintly, "and to God Almighty."

Then he was gone, but the wheel kept spinning before her, and she saw things in her mind that she had never before envisioned, and witnessed great empires coming and going, and their leaders crumbling to dust with them; and she realized then, for the very first time, that her blindness had become as much of an excuse for herself as it was for her relatives who had put her away. She raised her head to the cross shining in its mystical light at the beginning of the end of the old church, and she knew what she should be, and how far short she had fallen.

She pledged then to dedicate the rest of her life to Jesus Christ, to become His bride in truth as well as fiction, and to return to the Holy Church all of the peace it had freely and unselfishly given unto her.

She touched again the great wheel of life, and felt therein her father, he whom she had been seeking, and the great Tighris, and King-to-Be Arkády her brother, and Princess Arrhiána her sister, and so many, many others, and she knew, in a way that they would never understand, what their lives had been and would now become. She knew then a great pity for her sire, the King Kyprianos, a pawn in the game of kings, he who had thought himself a king, but had never understood what game was being played. She forgave him the awful things that he had done and would do to her and hers, and prayed most earnestly that God the Father would ultimately agree.

And still the wheel turned. She bent over and kissed the tomb of her ancestor, the black marble cold upon her lips, and felt the sharp twist in her side. It was the beginnings of the consumptive complaint, she knew, taken from the damp depths of Legalsó Vár, but the knowledge did not bother her. She would do what she could do with the time that she had, and then her life would be harvested, along with all the rest.

Poor Arkásha, she thought, *the eldest of Papá's children, yet he will outlast us all. What a terrible fate to live so long!*

Then she returned to her parents' apartments in Tighris, Palace, gradually awakening from her deep sleep.

Most of the wayfarers had now returned. They had found nothing.

"I know where to find him," Sachette exclaimed. "I know where he is!"

"Where?" asked Arrhiána.

"The Tower of Glass," her sister replied.

"What!" Kiríll stated. "Why would he go up there in the middle of the night?"

"He's looking for something," Sachette indicated. "He won't find it. We must go to him soon."

Kiríll started to say something, but Arrhiána held up her hand.

"What is he looking for, Chette?" her sister asked.

"Courage," Sachette said, "honor, all of the good things he's lost. They've been taken from him."

"Who took them?" Arrhiána continued.

"The Dark-Haired Man," her younger sibling replied. "That's what Papá thinks. He doesn't understand that there's a dark-haired man waiting inside all of us. He's afraid."

"I must go to him," Arkády suddenly interjected.

"Yes, Kásha," Sachette indicated, "you and no one else, or all will be lost. Take care, my dearest brother."

He hugged her tightly, and then ran off.

He used his ringflame to light his way up the winding stairs of the tower.

When the prince reached the top, he let his fire die and carefully eased himself out onto the open platform, next to the image of the Silver Bird. It glowed faintly in the pale starlight, almost as if it were lit from within. On the railing opposite sat his father, his legs draped over the trailing edge. He was humming something to himself, staring out into space.

"That you, Arkásha?" he stated. "'Course it is. Who else would come traipsing up here after me? True blue Arkády, the fair-haired heir. Tell me, my boy, how did you ever get yourself out of that 'Hole' I stuck you in? Never mind, doesn't matter. Nothing matters. You've come to get me, haven't you, one way or the other? Why don't you just push me off the edge, and be done with it? At least that would be clean, in a manner of speaking. No messy trials. No uncomfortable executions. No weeping women. God, I hate weepy women.

"You know," the king continued, "Melanthrix said you'd do something like this, and I just wouldn't believe him. I said, really I did, that no matter what happened, it wouldn't be you, that I could trust my eldest boy to do the right thing. Guess I was wrong, eh?"

"What are you doing up here, father?" Arkády asked quietly.

"Doing?" Kipriyán replied. "What do you mean, *doing?* I came up here to piss all over my beautiful city of Paltyrrha, to show them all that I could do any damn thing I wanted to. And there's nothing any of you can do about it, either."

The king jumped up on the ledge, carefully turned around, and then pulled a dirk from his belt. He smiled very sweetly.

"And now I'm going to kill you, son," he said, jumping down towards the prince.

He stepped forward, one methodical step at a time.

"Just so we know who's king around here," he murmured. "I gave you your life in the first place, and now I'm taking it back."

He abruptly lunged at the prince, who deftly leapt across the stairwell opening, using the Silver Bird for leverage.

"Damn you!" Kipriyán yelled. "You're so goddam noble all the time. How could I ever have sired such a prissy little prince?"

He struck again, this time hitting the Silver Bird and crying out in pain as the sculpture suddenly flashed a brilliant white. The king shook his hand to remove the sting, and then began stalking his son once more. There was very little room on the platform, and Arkády knew that it was only a matter of time before his father would corner him. He had to think fast!

Then an idea came to the prince, while he was dodging yet another blow, this one grazing him slightly on the arm. As he rolled to one side, the prince centered himself and uttered a spell of transformation. He abruptly rose to his feet arrayed as a huge, shaggy monster covered with straggly black hair.

"Ahh!" moaned the king, waving his hands and dropping his knife as he backpeddled rapidly away from the hideous apparition.

When his knees hit the stone railing, he lost his balance, and his hands began flailing about in a futile effort to keep himself from going over backwards.

Arkády desperately lunged out for him, just managing to grasp one swinging foot as his father toppled over the edge. There was a "klunk" as the king's body slammed into the stone side of the tower, knocking him unconscious, and the prince thought his arm would break from the strain of holding his burly father's heavy body.

He called upon all of his resources, and focused them upon the implements adorning the fingers of his outstretched hand. Each flared its signature color in turn, and then slowly, oh so slowly, he dragged the limp figure of his father back up over the railing. Then he collapsed briefly from sheer exhaustion.

A moment later, he sent out a mental call for assistance, and his brothers, who had been waiting down below, quickly came to his rescue. Together they carried King Kipriyán back to his quarters, where he was dosed with the *"szósz"* and *"kókk"* and other such sedatives and put to bed.

CHAPTER THIRTY-FOUR
"THUS DID GOD DELIVER HIS TRUE SERVANT"

Later that morning, which was Sunday and the Feast of Saint Praxedês, the Patriarch Timotheos appeared for the first time in public since his deposition, celebrating the main mass at Saint Konstantín's Cathedral at the hour of *tritê*.

The people of Paltyrrha demonstrated their support for their primate by filling the church to overflowing, the crowds spilling out into the side altars and even into the square. Prince Arkády and his sister Arrhiána represented the royal family, being prominently visible in the first row. Their appearance there caused much comment, for most of the populace had been unaware of their recent release from prison.

In his sermon, Timotheos used as a starting point a text from *Jeremiah* 52:31-32, which said:

> "In the thirty-seventh year of the exile of Jehoiachin King of Judah, in the year Evil-Merodach became King of Babylon, he released Jehoiachin from prison on the twenty-fifth day of the twelfth month. He spoke kindly to him and gave him a seat of honour higher than those of the other kings who were with him in Babylon."

"Thus," the patriarch eventually concluded, "did God deliver his true servant from those who would have persecuted him."

The moral of his homily was not lost on the good people of Paltyrrha.

CHAPTER THIRTY-FIVE
"THEN DOCTOR MELANTHRIX..."

The Grand Vizier Melanthrix finally woke from his self-medicated sleep around midday, abruptly sitting upright with a clear sense of something having gone terribly awry. His head and back ached abominably, and his linen sheet was stained with blood where several of the scabs from the wound he had incurred on the previous day had broken open during the night.

He rose with a groan, ate a piece of ripe fruit, washed his face with warm water, and dressed himself in the garish new robe he had just obtained. But when he went to his door to exit, he found the locking mechanism jammed, and could not release it. Probing the device with his *ley*-ring, he found it packed solidly with mud and clay that had now hardened into an almost rock-like mass.

He used his private mirror to reach the palace laundry, and from there made several discrete inquiries which convinced him that all was lost. His patron had been taken, and all possibility of stopping the change in government had vanished. Had he been his usual self the previous evening, he might have been able to act then, but now it was too late. None of the guards would follow *his* lead, of that he was certain.

He returned to his quarters, and packed his few belongings in satchels, ready to leave if the circumstances should require a quick exit. As the day progressed, and no one made an effort to contact him, he began ferrying certain rare items back to his distant home.

Then Doctor Melanthrix sat down to wait.

CHAPTER THIRTY-SIX
"THIS IS YOUR FREEDOM, THIS IS YOUR LIFE"

Later that afternoon the royal family gathered for a private meeting at the house of Dowager Queen Brisquayne in Kórynthály. In addition to the hostess, also present were Queen Polyxena, Hereditary Prince Arkády and his wife, Princess Dúra, Princess Arrhiána, Prince Zakháry, Prince Kiríll, Prince Andruin, Princess Sachette, and Queen Ezzölla, as well as King Kipriyán.

The monarch had been drugged several times during the night, with the stronger "*szósz*" being reapplied in the morning; his hands were physically restrained in front of him with leather ties. He looked very tired and weathered, and sat slumped in an old, overstuffed chair, his head hanging down.

"We must determine what to do," Prince Arkády began. "I've already spoken to the patriarch, and the church will support whatever decision we make. We must decide today, and whatever we do, it must be announced and promulgated at a meeting of the Royal Council which I've called for tomorrow morning.

"First, let me summarize what we have already accomplished," he continued. "We have freed three members of our family from the dungeon, together with numerous high lords and others who had been sequestered there over the last six months and beyond. We cannot allow them to be reimprisoned.

"Secondly," he noted, "we have taken the king by force after he tried to kill me. All of us were involved in this action except

Dúra and Zölla and Granny. We have drugged the king and held him captive against his will. So long as he *remains* king, these are crimes of high treason against the state.

"Thirdly," the prince added, "we have *de facto* restored the patriarch to his lawfully elected position. We cannot undo this.

"Finally," he summarized, "we have done these things in contravention of the king's will because we believe he is no longer fit to rule. Due to the import of these events and their logical consequences, I must ask each of you to speak in turn and give your opinion.

"Mother?" he said, turning to Polyxena.

The queen rubbed her eyes, and then looked up at her eldest son.

"My children," she stated, "I believe your father is ill, and that he will not recover his balance. Therefore, I think Arkásha must replace him as king immediately."

"I concur," replied Arrhiána. "I don't like having to take this step, but I see no other choice before us if Kórynthia is to survive."

"I too agree," Zakháry added, "but only if that damn'd Melanthrix goes as well."

"I'm with Zack," Kiríll noted.

Queen Brisquayne now spoke up. "Things have gone too far to turn back. The people are tired of war and privation. The women are clamoring for their lost husbands, sons, and fathers. They will not support another such expedition."

"I cannot allow my little Ari to be taken away from me," Dúra cried. "Any man who would do something like that to his own grandson does not deserve to be king."

"Papá has lost his way," Sachette indicated. "If he cannot govern himself, how can he govern a nation?"

Then it was Andruin's turn. "I wasn't here to see what's been happening, but I know what the clergy is saying. To insult and degrade the holy patriarch is a sin against both God and the church. It also sets a dangerous precedent if allowed to stand. Sorry, Papá," he murmured.

Finally, the new Queen Ezzölla had her say. "I don't know," she said. "I hate to see such actions taken against any lawful monarch. At the same time, there have been terrible abuses reported to me. I just don't know."

"Father, do you wish to speak?" Arkády inquired.

The king lifted his head to look at them, betrayal written in his eyes.

"You've already made your decision," he spat, "so why should I bother? Thirty-two years ago I was girded with the sword at Ióv. The great Tighris himself gave me the power to rule Kórynthia, and rule it I have, saving it from the barbarian hordes, leading it back from devastation, rebuilding the land, and bringing it prosperity. Now you want to kill me as my reward. Well, Arkásha, there's no doubt that you finally have the ultimate power within your grasp. So do it and be damned, all of you!"

There was an uncomfortable moment of silence, before Prince Arkády spoke again.

"Very well," he said, "we've given our separate opinions, and we have all agreed, all but one, that King Kipriyán is unfit to rule. So who do we replace him with?"

"You must become king, brother," Arrhiána replied.

"What about a regency?" Kiríll interjected.

"A regency implies that the occupant of the throne will someday return to it," Arrhiána indicated, "and I don't think that's feasible here."

"Then what do we do with Papá?" Zakháry inquired. "I won't agree to having him tried."

"We could give him some special title," Arkády stated, "and an estate nearby as an honorable retirement."

"That would only work," Arrhiána noted, "if the place was closely guarded and we controlled the guards."

"Agreed," the prince said. "Mother, what do you think?"

Polyxena's face was lined from the strain of the last few days.

"That would be acceptable to me," she agreed. "I would, of course, join your father in retirement."

"*Pah!*" Kipriyán boomed. "You go on talking about me in the third person, as if I'm not even sitting here. Why don't you just kill me and be done with it!"

"Because, father," Arkády responded, "I don't want to do to you what you obviously intended to do to me and mine. That's the basic difference between us. I'll give you a simple choice, and I'll offer it to you only once. Agree to renounce the throne unconditionally and irrevocably, or face attainder for treason against the state. You have until the hour of *apodeipnon* to make your decision."

"*Please*, Kipriyán!" his wife pleaded. "We still have our dignity. We still have each other. Please choose life."

The king looked around the room like a trapped animal, his eyes darting here and there, his arms struggling to free themselves from the leather bonds. Finally, he slumped again in his chair.

"Damn you all," he uttered. "Damn you to Hell, Arkády, for doing this to me. After all I gave you...."

Then the king sighed very heavily, and looked over at the queen. "Very well, I will sign the document. Bring it to me by supper."

Prince Arkády let his breath out, his tension finally easing. He nodded to Arrhiána, who pulled out a sheaf of parchment.

"I have it here, father," she indicated, holding the scroll out to him. "This is your freedom, sire. This is your life."

Brisquayne brought pen and ink. King Kipriyán didn't even bother to read the document, but initialed it with his usual flourish. Brisquayne sanded it quickly, and passed it back to Arrhiána, who also examined it.

Then the entire family signed the parchment one by one, carefully putting their names below the king's as witnesses to the deed.

Finally, it was done.

"I am truly sorry, father," Arkády stated, "that we had to do this to you. This is for the better, even if you don't understand that fact now. You and mother will remain our guests here for several days, until we make the appropriate arrangements."

Then he stood at formal attention, the others following suit.

"All hail, King Kipriyán!" he intoned, thumping his breast with his right hand.

"All hail, King Kipriyán!" came the muted replies.

Then Hereditary Prince Arkády bowed deeply to his mother and father, and left the room, being followed, one by one, by each of the royal princes and princesses of the Kingdom of Kórynthia.

A new era had begun.

CHAPTER THIRTY-SEVEN
"THIS IS SO GRAND"

On the following morning, the Feast of Saint Bandreillos, a meeting of the Royal Council of Kórynthia was held at the hour of *tritê* in the Great Hall of the Tighris.

Earlier that day, the Grand Vizier Melanthrix had been rousted from his quarters, and brought before Hereditary Prince Arkády.

"Lord Fértö," the prince had greeted the old man. "There have been a few changes since our last meeting, and I want to make certain that you understand full well the role that you will play this morning."

The philosopher had peered around the room at the score of guards standing at rigid attention.

"Where's the king?" Melanthrix had inquired.

"Indisposed," had come the response.

"We see," the grand vizier had mused.

"I sincerely hope you do," Arkády had stated. "You will read into the official record a document which I will give you. You will make the appropriate statements in response, and register the parchment in your book. Then you will be dismissed from office into an honorable retirement, with the thanks and gratitude of the state and its king."

"We see," Melanthrix had said again.

"Then you will do as I ask?" Arkády had pressed.

"Do we have a choice?" the philosopher had queried.

"What do you think?" had been the prince's response.

"We will do as you require."

Melanthrix had bowed, his silver chains jingling.

"Please escort the grand vizier to his quarters," Arkády had ordered two of the guards, "and remain there with him until the time of the council meeting."

Then he had turned again to Melanthrix.

"Oh, yes, Lord Fértö, we just discovered that there's something wrong with the door to your apartment," the prince added. "It was removed a few moments ago. They'll have it back in place by this evening. My apologies for the inconvenience."

The grand vizier withdrew with a flourish of low bows.

Now the Great Hall was filling with all of the surviving lords and ladies of state, as well as the patriarch, metropolitans, and archbishops and bishops currently visiting Paltyrrha. Representatives of the people were also allowed in the back of the room, to act as witnesses for the world at large.

"My lords and ladies!" boomed the voice of the Hankyárar of Konyály, "His Royal Highness, Arkadios Hereditary Prince of Kórynthia, the Royal Family, and the Royal Council!"

Then the prince and his family and councilors entered, attired in all of their glittering robes, dresses, and tunics.

They seated themselves around a table that had been erected below the king's throne for that purpose.

Doctor Melanthrix abruptly stood at the end of the table furthest from the throne, and picked up a parchment trailing several multicolored seals.

"My lord prince," he intoned as loudly as his voice would allow. "My lord prince, we have before us a special *communiqué* from Kyprianos III, King of Kórynthia."

"Please read us your *communiqué*," Arkády instructed.

The hall suddenly became as still as the day of final judgment, as everyone waited expectantly for the words to come. Then the grand vizier began:

"Kyprianos ɪɪɪ King of Kórynthia, Overlord of Pommerelia, Mährenia, Morënë, and Nisyria, sends greetings unto the High Council of the Land.

"My lords and ladies:

"Whereas we have been beset by the troubles of old age and ill health during this past sixmonth, and

"Whereas we have become burdened thereby with the affairs of state and the necessities of waging war, and

"Whereas we seek to find some solace from these cares after four decades of service to the land and the people,

"Now, therefore, we do hereby irrevocably renounce, reject, and abdicate our throne of Kórynthia in favor of our eldest son and heir, the Hereditary Prince Arkadios Kyprianidês von Tighris.

"Given under our hand at Tighrishály Palace, on the xxɪst day of July in the xlɪst year of our reign.

"Kyprianos Vasileus Kôrynthias

"Witnesseth:

"Arkadios Prinkêps Prôtos
"Kyrillos Prinkêps
"Zacharias Prinkêps
"Andreas Prinkêps
"Briskeina Khêra Vasileia
"Polyxena Vasileia
"Ezzôlla Vasileia Pômmerêlias
"Doura Prinkêpissa
"Arrhiêna Prinkêpissa kai Khêra Komêssa Arrhênês
"Sakhetta Prinkêpissa"

There was a roar of approval from the multitude that rattled the windows and shook the halls. This was a popular announcement indeed. The grand vizier kept motioning for silence, and finally the crowds quieted enough for him to be heard. He held the document up for everyone to see, and slowly rotated it so the seals and signatures were visible, if not legible.

"Highness," Melanthrix continued, "the signature of the king appears genuine, as do the signatures of the witnesses. The seals are also correct. We call upon the witnesses who are present here, and make formal inquiry unto them: did King Kipriyán sign this document in their presence?"

"He did," averred Prince Arkády.

"He did," repeated Dowager Queen Brisquayne, Princess Arrhiána, Prince Kiríll, Prince Zakháry, Prince Andruin, Princess Sachette, Princess Dúra, and Queen Ezzölla. Queen Polyxena was absent tending her husband in Kórynthály.

"Then we must conclude that this document is a genuine communication from King Kyprianos III," the grand vizier intoned.

"What shall we do with it, councilors?" he inquired.

"Record it!" came the universal reply.

With a flourish, Doctor Melanthrix took pen in hand, and very carefully listed the parchment in the official register for the Year of Our Lord One Thousand Two Hundred and Five. Then he pointedly drew a straight line across the page, and wrote in a new header. He held the book up so the people could see, and again revolved in a slow circle.

"The document having been recorded," he stated, "we do declare that the reign of our illustrious King, His Majesty Kyprianos III, has ended in its forty-first year, yesterday being the final day of his rule; and that today, the Twenty-Second of July, shall mark the beginning of the Accession Year of his eldest son and successor, King Arkadios II.

"*Vive le Roi!*" he shouted.

"*Vive Arcadie IIe !*" boomed the councilmen.

"*Vive la Córynthe!*" yelled the crowds.

"All hail our noble King-to-Be, *Arkadios II!*" Melanthrix shouted again.

The cheering went on for half an hour, and spread into the streets of Paltyrrha. The cathedral bells began to ring in celebration, followed by all the bells of the city and Job's Complaint in Kórynthály. There the former king of Kórynthia awoke from his rest and cursed both the new king and the new patriarch.

Finally the commotion in the Great Hall quieted enough so that business could proceed.

"Lord Fértö," the new king ordered, "please call the council to order."

"Yes, sire," Melanthrix obeyed, rapping on the table with his gavel.

"What is the next order of business?" he inquired.

King Arkády rose in his seat.

"The former King of Kórynthia having retired," he stated, "it is our desire that he have sufficient means to make his way in the world. Therefore, we do create him Duke of Tighris, and give unto him an estate of five thousand acres situate near our residence of Kórynthály. Grand Vizier, please prepare the letters patent and deeds.

"Further," Arkády continued, "the title of Arkádiya having become vacant by the unfortunate passing of our beloved brother, the Prince Nikolaí, we do hereby grant unto the Prince Kiríll, our second surviving brother, the County of Arkádiya, with all of the rights, incomes, and appurtenances attached thereto. Grand Vizier, please prepare the letters patent.

"Further," he added, "we do hereby create and declare our beloved eldest son and heir, the Prince Arión, Hereditary Prince-to-Be, and we cancel the orders of our predecessor removing him to Saint Svyatosláv's Monastery."

Then he sat down, as general applause and thumpings of the chest greeted his announcements.

"Do we have any other business?" the grand vizier inquired. "Yes, *Locum Tenens* Athanasios?"

The secretary of the Royal Council arose in his place next to the new king.

"Your majesty," he said, "the sad circumstances whereby I was appointed to the office of *Locum Tenens* of the Holy Church of Kórynthia having been eclipsed by events, I therefore petition the crown to relieve me of this burden, and to restore the Patriarch Timotheos to his proper position."

Arkády smiled.

"We do gladly grant thy request, Archpriest Athanasios," he said, "thanking thee for thy good and faithful service, and we restore the recognition of the crown to the legitimate Patriarch of Paltyrrha and All Kórynthia. Let the patriarch come forward," he boomed.

Timotheos slowly made his way out of the cheering throng, and approached his new king, bowing low to him.

"I welcome you back to the Royal Council," Arkády intoned, "and I hope you will give me your personal blessing in this, our time of trials."

The patriarch came forward and embraced the king, kissing him on both cheeks. Then, grabbing the monarch's right hand, he held it on high, saying to the multitudes: "Witness here the true king now come home to his people!"

Again the crowds roared their approval, shaking the very rafters of the heavens.

Then Doctor Melanthrix spoke softly.

"Sire," he said, "we believe that the Duke of Tighris has need of our services in his new home, and we therefore ask to be relieved of our several offices."

King Arkády nodded his head in agreement.

"You have served us well," he intoned, "and therefore we grant thee thy request, and confirm thee in thy peerage of Fértö. Thou art excused, milord."

Melanthrix removed his chain of office, and stepped around to the other side of the table to tender it to his monarch. Then he bowed, and walked quietly away.

"The office of grand vizier having become vacant," the king stated, "we do hereby appoint Attila Lord Vydór as successor to Lord Fértö."

Vydór made his way to the head of the table, dipped his head, and received the great chain. Then he returned to the end of the table, and took up pen and register, making his first act the recording of his own appointment.

"Sire," the new grand vizier stated, "several seats on the council have now become empty. If it please your majesty, I wish to commend the Dowager Queen Brisquayne to fill one of them."

"So ordered," the king commanded. "Queen Brisquayne, please approach the council table and be sworn."

Arkády administered the oath himself, beaming all the while, and then kissed his step-grandmother on the forehead.

Also nominated were Sir Reszö Rössvald, Prince Andruin, Dowager Queen Polyxena, and several others, all of them approved by the new king.

Finally, the public session was adjourned by King Arkády, being recessed until the private meeting to be held that afternoon. Again, cheers followed the king and the royal family as they made their way out of the hall.

King Arkády and Queen Dúra immediately went up to the balcony overlooking the square, there to receive the accolades of the fifty thousand Paltyrrhi who filled the streets of the city for blocks in every direction.

"All hail King Arkády!" came the refrain, again and again, as the royal couple and their two elder children, Hereditary Prince Arión and Princess Grigorÿna, smiled and waved to the multitudes below.

"Wave, Rÿna, wave," her father urged.

"Oh, Papá, this is so grand," she yelled, barely making herself heard.

They stayed there until the children tired, and then returned to their apartments to rest.

CHAPTER THIRTY-EIGHT
"THE SILENT SOULS OF SAINT SVYATOSLÁV"

The Archpriest Athanasios took advantage of the break to do some further research into his own past in the official Church Archives at Saint Alexios's House in Paltyrrha. Specifically, he was still searching for the date that Arik Rufímovich, now the Patriarch Timotheos, had officially joined the Silent Souls of Saint Svyatosláv.

Arik had not been recorded as a member in the year 1165, but had been listed on the membership roster of 1175. Somewhere in the interim he had left the service of the king and entered into the service of God.

On previous visits Athanasios had already read through the annual registers of the order for the years 1175 and 1174. Now he began working his way through the book for 1173, or IX Kyprianos III. It was a tedious business, for the volume recorded a myriad of mostly financial data, intermingled with appointments, resignations, illnesses, and copies of official letters to and from the abbot. Athanasios had had no idea of how utterly mundane and boring such details could become. He yawned, and read further.

Wait! On May 14th, buried under a list of tax receipts, was the mention of two individuals petitioning Abbot Jován Csigály for entry into the Silent Souls:

Arix Roufim., *ætat.* XXXIII
Abagor Aleks., *ætat.* XXII

There was no question that this was the record he was seeking. It confirmed that Arik had remained in the service of the state for many years after delivering the child Afanásy to Saint Svyatosláv's.

By inference, therefore, Arik had been officially employed by Kórynthia on that mission. It further followed that the subsequent obscuring of the records regarding that transferral had come from somewhere high in the bureaucracy of the government, perhaps from the regents themselves!

Athanasios knew from his previous visits to the archives that no matter how carefully the records had been censored, peripheral details would have remained untouched in some obscure volume. These registers that he had just been examining, for example, contained all kinds of materials that no one who wasn't directly familiar with them would ever possibly imagine to find there. Financial data, for example. Expense claims, to cite another example.

The priest thought to himself for several long moments. There was something here of great importance, could he just grasp the idea.

If the soldier had been dispatched on a long trip to fetch the child Afanásy, and if, as the subsequent ledger entry in the annual of the monastery had indicated, Arik Rufímovich had been delayed *en route*, then perhaps he had filed a claim with the state treasury for his additional out-of-pocket expenses. And maybe, just maybe, whoever had systematically leafed through the records at a later date to expunge all those documents considered relevant to the expedition had not been aware of this particular reimbursement request.

The idea was certainly worth pursuing at some later date. Alas, Athanasios now had to return to the council chamber, so he packed up his things into a neat folder, and hurried out.

CHAPTER THIRTY-NINE
"JUST LET ME TRY"

The second part of the accession council of King Arkády was held that same afternoon in the council chambers in Tighrishály Palace. Lord Vydór, the new grand vizier, called the meeting to order.

Then the king made an announcement.

"We have decided," he said, "to cancel preparations for a second expedition into Pommerelia. General Lord Rónai, I charge you with the task of bringing our boys safely home. You're to withdraw into the two southern citadels we now hold as quickly as possible, and establish secure and stable defenses around them. We should be able to maintain them indefinitely with minimal support. Lockenlöd Castle is another matter, however. Unless it can be relieved quickly, it must be evacuated. What's your recommendation?"

"I think it's irretrievable without a major new incursion on our part, sire," the officer replied. "It's too far away from the pass to be supplied easily, and the natural defenses of the place all fall back on the mountains behind it, while the actual access roads are spread across an open plain that's extremely vulnerable to attack. I recommend that we abandon the place as quickly as possible, but occupy and block the Pommerelian side of the pass with new fortifications, just where it exits the highlands."

Arkády considered the situation for a moment before replying.

"Very well," he finally said. "Proceed with the removal."

"What about the brigades already assembled at Myláßgorod?"

the general asked.

"Hold them there for the time being," the king ordered, "in case they're needed as backup for the other troops. As soon as our soldiers secure the southern forts, send at least some of them home."

"Yes, sire," the officer stated. "And the prisoners we've captured?"

"I want you to arrange an exchange with the Pommerelians, their men for ours," the king ordered. "The numbers should be about equal. Do it just before we evacuate the river plain in the south."

Then Arkády turned to Prince Zakháry: "What news do we have of the political situation in Pommerelia and Mährenia?"

"Our scouts have heard nothing new from Pommerelia," the prince noted, "except that things are just about as chaotic in Balíxira as they are here. In Mährenia, Duke Ferdinand's body was never recovered from the battlefield, but he was declared dead nonetheless, and his eldest daughter, Rosanna, briefly succeeded him. She has now been deposed, but the circumstances remain unclear. Her sister, Rosalla, has been proclaimed the new duchess, under the ægis of her mother, the Duchess-Regent Johanna. Both girls are slightly underaged, but Rosalla's succession will give Johanna another year of control. Otherwise, things seem to be settling down there again.

"Our ambassador in Loíza has just forwarded a letter from the duchess-regent to the king"—he held it up so everyone could see—"which I'll read to you now."

"Johanna, Duchess-Regent and Guardian of the Throne of Mährenia and Ptolemaïs and the Prüffenmark, sends greetings unto her brother, Kyprianos III King of Kórynthia.

"We regret to inform you that our dear husband, Duke Ferdinand of blessèd memory, has entered into his eternal reward, and has been succeeded on the throne by our daughter, the Duchess Rosalla, under the regency of her mother, the Duchess Johanna, until she shall reach her xviiith year.

"Circumstances beyond our control have forced us temporarily to cease hostilities against the Kingdom of Pommerelia. However, we very much fear an invasion from that country in the future, and we therefore call upon the Kingdom of Kórynthia to honor its treaty of mutual aid and defense with the Duchy of Mährenia, and to send reinforcements at once to assist us.

"We further propose that the Duchess Rosalla be betrothed to one of your younger sons, and that the marriage be consummated as quickly as possible to strengthen our cousinly ties.

"Johanna DR.

"Given at our Palace of Loíza on the xvith day of July in this, the ist year of our Regency."

Zakháry added: "There's also a note attached from Ambassador Tamburín stating that Duchess Rosanna, who is not mentioned in the letter, seems to have disappeared from Loíza. No one knows where she's gone, or if they do, they're not saying anything. He suspects foul play."

"Any comments?" asked Vydór.

"I'm willing to go to Mährenia, if my brother isn't," Prince Zakháry commented. "I'm not proposing that we send anyone other than trainers there, but it would be an inexpensive way to outflank the Walküri."

"There's been enough killing," Patriarch Timotheos interjected. "I'm opposed to any further involvement in the area."

"So am I," said Dowager Queen Brisquayne. "We've just been through a bloody war that wiped out the heart of our nobility, not to mention thousands of freeholders and tradesmen nationwide. This should be a time of rebuilding, not foreign adventurism."

"Lord Rónai," the king inquired, "what do you say?"

"All the reports that I've had," the officer noted, "have indicated immense difficulties in getting the Mährenian commanders and their soldiers to work together. They're very independent, and not used to fighting together in large numbers. They tend to revert to form under the least bit of pressure. We could put an awful lot of time and money into this training with very little result."

"That's pretty much what I thought, too," Arkády agreed.

"May I speak?" Zakháry asked.

When the king nodded his aquiescence, the prince continued: "I understand all of the potential problems with the Mährenians, but I still think that the alliance is worth the risk, and I'm personally willing to undertake that risk. I ask for no support from you, my brother, although I will gladly receive whatever you might offer me in the way of monetary or military assistance.

"We have struggled mightily this year on the battlefield. Our men and officers have sacrificed their lives willingly for church and state. Let not their sacrifice be in vain, sire. Grant me this boon. Give me my chance. If I fail, you've lost one wayward prince, who's of little use to you otherwise. But if I win, you've gained an important ally. Just let me try, please."

King Arkády frowned and looked around the table. There was no consensus that he could see.

"Very well," he finally stated, "this is our judgment. The amended treaty of mutual assistance specified as one of its terms that the Duchess Rosanna was to be married to a Tighrishi royal prince, and since that agreement has not been upheld, the pact has already been abrogated by Mährenia, and we are not bound by it. However, we do see an advantage to Kórynthia if we can forge an alliance of blood with their royal family. Therefore, Prince Zakháry, we will grant your request, and allow you to proceed forthwith to Mährenia, there to marry Duchess Rosalla. Father Athanasios," he ordered, turning to the priest, "please prepare a letter of response to the duchess-regent giving our assent.

"Let's move on to the next item on our agenda," the king added. "I've decided to call for a conference of reconciliation and reconstruction, starting in the first week of September here in Paltyrrha, to begin the process of mending the divisions left by the recent war. I ask all of you to think seriously about what needs to be done in Kórynthia in future years, and to forward those suggestions to Lord Vydór, whom I charge with organizing the meeting.

"Some of the problems," he continued, "are obvious to anyone: a need to reform the laws of property rights and inheritance, the absence of sufficient manpower to bring in the crops and to perform other necessary functions, the necessity of changing the succession laws governing transmission of titles of nobility to avoid the problem of too many noble houses becoming extinct due to the depredations of the recent war, and much more.

"I am also determined to erect a memorial to the brave men of Killingford—and yes, that is the name we will use, to remind us of what happened there—somewhere in Paltyrrha or Kórynthály, as well as one to honor my brother, the Prince Nikolaí, late Count of Arkádiya."

Then the king sat down. Prince Kiríll raised his hand.

"I again charge Doctor Melanthrix with high treason," the prince intoned.

The king sighed.

"I understand your feelings, Kiríll," he said, "but I gave the man my word of honor that he would be safe from any reprisals from the state, and would also be allowed to retain his title, if he cooperated with this morning's accession council. It was essential to maintain the legal forms, so that there would be no possible challenge to the succession in the future. Having given my pledge, I must deny your petition. The matter is closed."

"Is there any other business?" Lord Vydór inquired, looking around the room. "Hearing none, I declare this council adjourned."

CHAPTER FORTY
"THE MAN'S LIKE A CAT"

"It's obvious to me," Prince Kiríll said, "that the king's not going to make any move against that quack Melanthrix so long as he's treating Prince Ari for his pains."

"I hear he's moved out of the palace into an apartment in Kórynthály," Zakháry noted. "Lord Fértö, indeed! The man isn't even highborn. Old Fartö, mayhap!"

"I just don't like him hanging around father," Kiríll continued. "I just wonder how much of Papá's illness is due to his meddling. Unfortunately, my little surprise didn't pan out."

"I wondered if that was you," Zakháry commented. "It almost worked."

"The man's like a cat," his brother stated. "Nine damn'd lives, and every one of them evil. I'm determined to try again. I wonder if he'll be attending this proposed conference in September."

"Probably not," Prince Zakháry said. "He would have no reason to come. No, I don't think we'll be seeing much of Melanthrix again, except in our brother's apartments. And I'm not willing to frighten the children by trying something there. I just don't think that's right."

"You won't get any disagreement from me," Kiríll mused. "Then we'll just have to beard the cat in his own lair, won't we? I suggest that we use the same source that I employed last time."

"*La Guilde des Assassins?*" Zack asked.

"Indeed," his brother agreed. "They're professional, strictly confidential, and they accept anyone who pays. I'll make the arrangements myself."

"Then let's hope Doctor Melanthrix has just one more life left to give," Zakháry stated.

CHAPTER FORTY-ONE
"WHEN WILL IT BE OVER?"

But the object of their discussion was at that moment in the Hanging Garden of Queen Landizábel, talking to Princess Grigorÿna and her thirty-two dolls.

"I don't understand why Grandpapá had to go away," Rÿna said.

"It's difficult to explain, my dear," the old man replied.

"But I thought the king had to die before there could be another one," she commented.

"Well, usually that's true," Melanthrix agreed, "but in this case King Kipriyán voluntarily abdicated his rights."

"What does it mean to ab-, ab-uh-di-cate?" the girl asked.

"It means that the king no longer wants to be king, and so he gives his crown to someone else," the philosopher indicated.

"Why did Grandpapá no longer want to be king?" Rÿna pressed.

"Because the king felt bad about the things he had done," he said. "And because he was no longer really a king anymore, and hadn't been for a long, long time."

"How do you become a king, Melánty?" she queried. "Can *I* be one?"

The old astrologer laughed.

"No, my dear," he said, "women are called queens, not kings, and they're usually the wives of the monarchs, not rulers in themselves, more's the pity. The world would be a better place if they allowed queens to sit on the throne of Kórynthia. If that were true, then the Princess Grigorÿna, yes, you yourself, might well become the queen, since you're the eldest child of the reigning king. And a good queen you would make, we think.

"But as to your other question, little one," he continued, "there are many, many stories about how men become kings. Some say that God makes a king. Some say that the order of birth within the royal family determines who will be king, although that has not always been the case with the Tighrishi, who have sometimes displaced the true king with a false one. And some say that a king makes a king. You can make up your own stories, and they will certainly be as good as ours."

"I like your stories, Melánty," Rÿna exclaimed, throwing up her two hands and clapping, "and so does my chorus."

"You do seem to have more of them these days," the philosopher noted, looking over at the four lines of eight dolls each, all gazing up at the great tower.

"Well," she said, "Ouisa keeps inviting more of her friends to join the game. She says it's not over yet."

"And when will it be over?" he gently asked.

"When the king is dead," the little girl replied.

Then all of the dolls slowly turned their heads and looked at him.

"When the king is dead," they echoed.

And Doctor Melanthrix was suddenly very, very afraid.

CHAPTER FORTY-TWO
"HE IS WORTHY!"

A month and a half later, on the Fourth Day of September, which was also the Feast of Saint Moses the Prophet, King Arkády presided over the opening of an unprecedented confluence of the greatest minds of Kórynthia, to discuss the future development of that kingdom. Invited were the best-known statesmen, noblemen, philosophers, writers and scribes, artists and artisans, churchmen, theologians, craftsmen, military men, and musicians, four hundred in all, who gathered together in the Great Hall of Tighrishály Palace.

The king gave the opening address.

"Lords, ladies, and gentlefolk," he intoned. "I have called you here today to begin the process whereby we redefine ourselves as a nation. Kórynthia has suffered a great tragedy. Although some few of our soldiers found their way home this past month after the prisoner exchange and ransoming of officers, it is clear that our losses at Killingford were catastrophic, approaching twenty-five thousand men. Many of the survivors have suffered wounds from which they will never fully recover. Half or two-thirds of the great houses of the land lost a title-holder or heir, and some few had all of their menfolk disappear into the killing fields. The crops currently being harvested cannot fully be captured, because we lack the hands to bring them in. Everywhere the land and the people cry out. We will endure a harsh winter this year.

"All of you here have experienced these losses firsthand," he continued. "You know the depth and the breadth of the problems we face. We are not equipped to cope with a crisis of such dimensions. We must rethink ourselves, and redefine our laws, our customs, our very fabric to provide some hope for the future.

"I ask all of you to contribute your ideas, your good will, and your innovative thinking. These are just a few of the challenges we face:

"*First*, we must reform the laws governing the transmission of land, so that the widows of Killingford will have some means of securing their futures, and will have dowries to provide them with new husbands.

"*Second*, we must reform the laws governing the transmission of titles of nobility, so that the wholesale extinction of the great houses can be prevented.

"*Third*, we must reorganize the army, and create a standing force of professional soldiers that will be able to respond quickly to threats in the future.

"*Fourth*, we need to encourage immigration from neighboring lands to provide the manpower that we need to perform basic tasks.

"*Fifth*, we must strongly encourage the bachelors of the realm to marry the widows and female heirs of Killingford, by offering benefits to those who choose to comply, and by penalizing those who do not.

"*Sixth*, we must encourage new marriages and remarriages through large-scale ceremonies sponsored by the state, with dowries and free land being distributed to these couples to provide them with a basic start in their life together, and the Church must be encouraged to give dispensations for these joint services.

"*Seventh*, we must redistribute the lands of the extinct estates and titles as widely as possible, possibly using them as a basis for dowries for those widows and female children who need them to remarry.

"*Eighth*, we propose constructing a memorial for the dead of

Killingford at Paltyrrha, and another at Kórynthály dedicated to the memory of Prince Nikolaí, our much belovèd brother.

"*Ninth*, we propose the construction of a permanent bridge across the Paltyrrh River to link the old and new parts of the city, and to mitigate against the annual spring floods. Never again can we allow a waterway to divide our country in two during a time of great crisis.

"*Tenth*, we propose the construction of additional permanent roads connecting Paltyrrha with the outlying provinces.

"*Finally*, let all of our people join hands in making the future bright with possibility, for the great and small and all of those in between. Let us spend the next generation building a new Kórynthia, one that will benefit all of the people yet to come."

Then the king sat down. Slowly there came the shouts from the crowd, gathering ever-increasing strength as more and more of the attendees rose in their seats to thump their breasts.

"*Axios! He is worthy!*" they yelled, beating upon the tables and upon themselves. "*Axios!*"

The roar was so loud that it could be heard throughout the palace and even into the streets outside, where the vendors and their donkeys turned and cocked their heads at the unusual sound.

"*Axios!*" they shouted again, and would not be silent. He was worthy indeed.

CHAPTER FORTY-THREE
"NOW WE WILL SEE WHO IS KING AROUND HERE"

But not everyone agreed with that assessment, for at that very moment in Kórynthály, former King Kipriyán was plotting to regain his throne.

Attending him were Doctor Melanthrix, Lord Télen, Lord Munkás, Count Éskak, and Sergeant Poliodór.

"Report!" the king ordered.

Poliodór was first.

"I have secured the loyalty of at least half of the Palace Guard," he stated, "and have arranged that most of the others will be off-duty tomorrow at the hour of *tritê*. My men will be the only soldiers present at the conference, where all the chief men, including your sons, will be gathered together for the opening of the second day. If we control the exits, we control all those attending."

"Excellent," Kipriyán commended. "Lord Télen, what about you?"

"Captain Kérés will be attending the conference," the baron reported, "and I have arranged that his men will be drawn to a disturbance in the church. When they rush in, my troop will bolt the doors until such time as we receive your signal."

"Munkás and Éskak?" the king inquired.

"We'll have our mounted lancers ready at Katonaí Field," the count stated. "As soon as I get the word, we'll enter the city and secure the strongpoints."

At that moment, the door opened to admit another conspirator, Lord Lásky, he who had been humiliated at the "Hole."

"Please accept my apologies, majesty," he offered. "My men are also ready to strike. As soon as the sign is given, we'll lock up the prison tight, and rush to the *gendarmerie* to secure the police force."

"Very well," Kipriyán boomed. "Doctor Melanthrix and I will transit on the morrow to Tighrishály Palace, and then proceed to the Great Hall, where I will finally be restored to my proper place. The traitors will be seized and tried on the spot. You six shall constitute the nucleus of the new Royal Council, with Lord Fértö once again become grand vizier. You all have your instructions. Now leave me."

One by one they exited, returning to their posts, all except Melanthrix.

"Now," Kipriyán said, "Now we will see who is king around here."

Then he smiled his terrible smile, full of crooked teeth and absent of any humor. Doctor Melanthrix just smiled along with him.

CHAPTER FORTY-FOUR
"I SING AN INCANTATION"

Queen Polyxena looked up from her crystal, passing her hand over the globe to clear the image. She knew now what her husband intended to do, and just who was involved. She took a piece of red wax, rolled it into a small ball, and pushed a miniature metal rod into it. This she impressed with a mental message to Queen Brisquayne, outlining the conspiracy as she had viewed it. Then she exited her bedchamber and went out into the garden, closely followed by one of her husband's guards.

She reached into a pocket of her apron, and began scattering grain to the pigeons which gathered by the dozens on the veranda tile, peck, peck, pecking at the bits of food. The soldier Vladlén, clearly bored by the proceedings, sat down on a nearby bench, and shielded his eyes from the hot sun while he dozed.

In her mind the Queen called out to the black-feather'd raven, Lady Milyutÿnis, asking her

> To brave the wild winds and pierce the rough skies,
> Come to her mistress by whichever way she flies,
> Do for her this service which she doth command,
> Lest ill shall prevail and good shall not stand.

"*Mageuô melê*," she breathed through her lips, too softly for anyone save the bird to hear, "I sing an incantation."

A wind began to blow, gently at first, and then harder, ever harder, until the pigeons all scattered to the four quarters of the world, and the guileless guard Vladlén slept on, oblivious to the magic falling 'round his head, and the Lady Milyutÿnis, that great black bitch of a bird, swooped down upon the place and took the message in her beak, leaving only a single ebon feather drifting lazily in her wake as a sign that women's work had been well accomplished that day. The Queen Polyxena daintily stooped down, picked up the leaving, and twined it in her hair. Then there was peace again upon the earth.

CHAPTER FORTY-FIVE
"YOUR LIFE IS IN DANGER"

Elsewhere in Kórynthály, Dowager Queen Brisquayne returned to her home at *hektê* to eat a light luncheon. Although the afternoon was hot, a copse of oak trees behind her house provided a shady spot in which to rest and enjoy the freshening breeze blowing in from Arrhénë. She sat on an old stone railing, feet draped over the edge, and bit deeply into a late peach, the sweet juice running down her double chin.

The most recent word from Neustria was encouraging: her great-grandson was flourishing, and there had been no further sign of Mösza (or Mirza, as she had called herself there) since the incident of the birthing. She knew that Mösza could never return to Kórynthia, that the compulsion planted in her would kill her if she tried, and so Brisquayne felt safer here in her own place than she did anywhere else.

There was a squawk just above her, and the queen turned to see the coal black image of a raven rocking back and forth on one of the lower branches of the tree, its mouth held open by a small object clutched in its beak. Then it hopped down next to her and sauntered over, showing no fear. Brisquayne held out her hand, palm up, and the bird dropped a nugget of wax into it. It squawked again, and flew off.

The queen crushed the wax pellet gently between her thumb and forefinger, and felt something hard inside. She carefully worked the metal casing out into the open air, and then concentrated her mind, probing the little message pod by pressing her *psai*-ring against it.

Quayne, she heard Dowager Queen Polyxena's voice in her head, *Kipriyán intends to retake the throne tomorrow, with the help of Doctor Melanthrix, Count Éskak, Lord Lásky, Lord Télen, Lord Munkás, and Sergeant Poliodór. They will occupy key points both in the city and here in Kórynthály, and then strike during the first session of the second day of the conference. Please warn the king. Also, my dear, I sense a movement in the æther directed at you personally. Your life is in danger, so please take care. I send this message via my faithful friend, Lady Milyutÿnis, and I remain your loving daughter-in-law, Polyxena.*

So the old bastard hasn't learned his lesson yet, Brisquayne mused. *Well, we'll see about that!*

She tossed the peach pit into the trees. Rubbing her hands together to get rid of the juice, she headed back towards the house, where she used her private *viridaurum* to transit to Tighrishály Palace.

She caught Princess Arrhiána just outside her apartments, as she was leaving for the second session of the conference.

"I wonder if I could see you privately for a moment," Brisquayne inquired.

"Of course," Arrhiána responded, sensing her urgency.

They returned to the princess's carefully-protected study.

"Just before leaving Kórynthály," the dowager queen said, "I received this pod from Xena. I think you'd better touch it."

Brisquayne handed over the pellet.

After reviewing Polyxena's mental message, Arrhiána sent a runner for the king, with a note asking him to come at once without making an obvious exit from the meeting.

A quarter of an hour later, King Arkády joined them. After "reading" Polyxena's warning, he ordered an impromptu meeting of the Royal Council for later in the afternoon, after the second session of the conference had ended, ostensibly to review the first day's events. He also ordered Lord Lásky to appear before the council to give a report on security measures needed at the keep of Legalsó Vár. Then he sent for Captains Fösse and Kérés.

Fösse reported first, and was informed of the situation.

"Can you handle Sergeant Poliodór?" Arkády asked.

"Now that I know about their plans and have a good idea of who's been turned, yes, sire," the officer replied.

"Take whatever measures that are required," the king ordered.

Arkády handed the soldier a handwritten paper.

"This gives you my personal authority to command any troops within the city," he said. "Be discrete and be ruthless, captain: I do not want the traitors to know that *we* know, until we spring the trap. And make certain that only the guards loyal to me are in attendance at the council meeting this afternoon."

"Yes, majesty," the captain responded, and hurried out of the room.

Captain Kérés reported next.

After bringing the officer up-to-date, the king inquired: "Can you handle the situation at Kórynthály?"

"Absolutely, sire," the soldier promised. "When Lord Télen strikes, we'll surround him and his men, and arrest them on the spot. There'll be no advance warning to the conspirators."

"Good," the king stated. "Proceed, captain."

After Kérés had departed, Arkády turned to the two women.

"That's as much as we can do now," he indicated. "Please join me at the council meeting late this afternoon."

CHAPTER FORTY-SIX
"WHAT DIFFERENCE DID THIS MAKE?"

At the beginning of the afternoon session of the conference of reconciliation, much discussion was devoted to a proposed reformation of the laws governing the transmission of titles and estates, and the king asked the Archpriest Athanasios to research the topic, and then report back to the group several days hence with his findings. The cleric immediately departed, glad to have a break from the seemingly interminable speeches and pontifications of all the learnèd gentlemen.

He went again to Saint Ptolemy's House in Paltyrrha. This squat gray building served as the State Archives of Kórynthia, housing a variety of official civil and military records, indeed, all such materials except those falling under the provenance of the church.

Instead of working on the king's project at once, however, the priest decided to devote an hour or two to his own quest to discover his origins. He started with a volume of the military *Annales* from the year II Kyprianos III, or A.D. 1166, beginning with the month of April. He read through three months' worth of receipts, travel claims, orders, reports of scouts and spies, and other miscellanea before finding something of interest.

In the middle of the volume he noted a cryptic expense voucher:

"*2.VII.* CP Areek R., DD. 12 s. 25 o., add. exp., jrn., Apr. II K III to Tôrtous, per *OB* AY K III 228."

Athanasios interpreted this record as stating:

"*Second of July.* Captain Arik Rufímovich, Detached Duty, is reimbursed 12 staters and 25 obols for additional expenses incurred on a journey in April of 1166 to the Emirate of Tôrtous, per *Order Book* ACCESSION YEAR Kyprianos III, p. 228."

Why, the priest wondered, would Arik have gone on such a distant journey, save to retrieve the child Afanásy?

He then pulled the volume of the *Order Book* series covering the last half of the year 1164, the ACCESSION YEAR of King Kipriyán III, and turned to page 228.

Buried in the middle of the page was a simple one-paragraph statement:

"*15.IX.* Ordered by the Regents, that Mösza P. be sent abroad for her health and continuing education."

This had to be the reference. But where was the proof? He checked the shorthand index at the front of the book, and noticed several other volumes and pages cross-referenced to the main entry.

In the tome for I Kyprianos III (1165), the Master of the Exchequer was ordered to pay 75 *s.* to Nasr ad-Din ibn Abdalláh, Emir of Tôrtous, for the reimbursement of physician expenses for "*PM.*" Halfway through the same year, the book recorded the repayment of living expenses for two unnamed persons to the same ruler. A similar notation appeared in the following year, but in 1167, recompense was made for one person only. The vouchers continued through the year 1169, and then stopped, without explanation.

Princess Mösza was his mother? There was no other possible

interpretation. She had either died in the year 1169, or had departed for parts unknown. He wondered if there would be a stone for her in the royal graveyard at Kórynthály.

But who was the father? And why such secrecy? There had been plenty of illegitimate Tighrishi born over the past two centuries, although most had either been ennobled and given a small fief, or publicly sent to the cloister. Of course, such things were frowned upon when women were involved, particularly when they were unmarried.

Suddenly something occurred to him, and he was thunderstruck.

My God, he thought to himself, *I'm first cousin to King Kipriyán. But what difference did this make to them? Why couldn't I have been told?*

He had a feeling that there was more to the mystery than he had already uncovered, but at least he now knew the name of one parent. He would keep searching assiduously until he found the other.

CHAPTER FORTY-SEVEN
"HAVE YOU TESTED IT?"

Late in the afternoon, after the conference had adjourned for the day, the members of the Royal Council quietly filed into chambers for a review of the day's events. They were not prepared for what they heard from King Arkády.

"What!?" shouted Prince Kiríll. "He's doing *what!?*"

Expressions of outrage filled the room.

The king explained what steps he had taken to counter Kipriyán's proposed *coup d'état*, adding:

"We still have the lancers of Munkás and Éskak to consider, but if they can't enter the city, they'll be temporarily neutralized."

"I can handle *that* little business," Kiríll interjected.

"Good," the king commented. "I want the ringleaders arrested and sent to Legalsó Vár. Speaking of which, I've ordered Lord Lásky to appear before this council meeting to report on the security improvements he's made at the keep. I expect he's waiting outside right now. Captain Fösse, be prepared to follow my lead. Call for Lord Lásky," he added.

"Call for Lord Lásky," echoed out into the hall, as the guards, who had been carefully selected by the captain, escorted the Governor of the Royal Prison into the room.

"Thank you for coming on short notice," the king smiled, motioning the diminutive baron to sit. "We're all interested in hearing about the new security measures you've instituted."

"Yes, your majesty," he stated, shuffling some notes he

had brought with him. "Well, sire, in the wake of the unfortunate break-out of several months ago, we have inaugurated new checkpoints and examinations of passes. I can now say with some assurance that no one who has been incarcerated at Legalsó Vár will ever escape from it again."

He paused, suddenly embarrassed, for it was the very king sitting before him who had managed to break out of Lásky's prison so recently.

"Are you quite certain, Lord Lásky?" Arkády inquired.

"Absolutely, sire," the little man replied. "Why, I'd stake my life on it."

"But have you tested it?" the king pressed.

"I don't understand," the governor replied. "How can we possibly do that?"

"Well, you might try imprisoning someone who really knows how the system works, and see if that individual could successfully get away," the monarch posed.

"I, uh, don't think that would be practical," Lásky indicated.

"Oh, I think it would be most efficacious," Arkády ventured, "and I have just the candidate for the initial experiment."

"You do?" the prison supervisor stated.

"Yes, Lord Lásky, *you*," the king said. "You would do very nicely indeed."

"I don't understand," the baron responded.

"I'm quite sure that you do," King Arkády noted. "Lord Lásky, I charge you with high treason, in that you did conspire with the Duke of Tighris to restore him to the throne and murder your legitimate monarch. How plead you?"

At that question, two guards seized the governor and pulled him from his seat, knocking it backwards in the process. There was a loud rattle as the chair toppled over.

Lásky's face went completely ashen. His hands began to tremble, and his mouth moved up and down as he tried to speak.

"You have but one chance to save your miserable little life, Lásky," the king stated, "not to mention preserving your titles and estates for your family. Confess everything, name all of your co-conspirators to this council, detail your plans, and you may spend the rest of your days in your own prison, with your wife retaining your property. Otherwise...well, you do know the penalty for treason, I believe."

It didn't take the little man very long to reveal everything that they needed to know.

CHAPTER FORTY-EIGHT
"A SMALL SCARAB LURKING SOMEWHERE IN THE BACKGROUND"

Later that evening the King Arkády hosted an unveiling of the restored tapestries of Jaél. Since being brought from the citadel of Myláßgorod, courtesy of the new Count Zygmunt, the *objets d'art* had been carefully cleaned, repaired, and hung by trained artisans, and now they glowed in all their revealed beauty before an audience of carefully-selected connoisseurs. The king paraded about, displaying features of this piece and that, like a proud father.

The works had been placed in a room of the east wing of the palace that had been specially cleared of its previous trappings and furniture, and redecorated to accommodate Jaél's set of masterpieces. And now that they could be clearly viewed, it was obvious even to the most obtuse of onlookers that masterpieces they were indeed.

Beginning with the first panel to the right of the entranceway, the tapestries depicted the rise of the Psairothi tribe in Atlantis, the persecution of the "Anointed Ones" in that ancient land, the prophecy of doom uttered by the great seer Ishmaél, the flight of the persecuted minority to the east and the west, the wrath of the old gods visited upon Atlantis, and the sinking of that continent beneath the waves.

The king also had restored the one tapestry of Jaél which had previously hung in Tighrishály Palace, and placed it at the end of the sequence. It depicted a scene from what must have been another, related set of weavings, showing the war of the gods over the fate of Atlantis, and how the losers were cast down into the pit and imprisoned there, until that day when someone should release them and let loose their fury upon an unsuspecting world.

This was the first time that Arkády had seen the old panel since it had been cleaned and repaired. He now looked upon the grotesque images of the old gods ranged in rows on either side of their dungeon, and suddenly he recognized the place as the one where Mösza had taken him so many months before. He shivered in the warm air.

"Striking, isn't it?" Arrhiána commented.

"Obscene," the king retorted. "I can almost feel their eyes moving upon me. One has the feeling that it was either done from life or from the memory of one who was present."

"What do we know about the artist?" she inquired, linking her arm with his while she examined each work.

"Very little," Arkády stated. "In his *Historia Nisyrias*, the ancient historian Mikhaêl, writing about the ninety-nine 'biographs,' states that 'Iaêl son of Ismaêl'—and we don't even know if this is the *same* 'Ishmaél' as the ancient seer—'mastered the nine ancient magics of the Psairothi, and then created a tenth, the magic of weaving, which had never been considered before him. He fashioned during his life many great tapestries and other works of fabric, even, it is said, a dress of shivery electrum thread for Stephaélla the Sorceress.'"

"Then these panels are supposed to contain magic of a sort?" Arrhiána asked.

"Such is the legend," her brother replied. "I've tried probing them, but I get no feeling from any of them, except a kind of tingle sometimes."

"Each of them has a small scarab lurking somewhere in the background, I notice," she said.

"That's his sign," Arkády noted. "All of the ancient artists used such symbols to identify their work, instead of the monograms or signatures common now."

"They're so alive!" she exclaimed. "Each of the faces shows a personality that I wouldn't have believed possible in a fabric composition. I wonder how many threads per inch he used, and what kind of loom was employed."

"I tried to determine that as well," the king admitted, "but got nowhere. All I can tell you is that the density is much greater than that in an average weave, and the cloth is like nothing I've ever seen before. It has an ability to retain and display color that is simply extraordinary. Once, late at night when I couldn't sleep, I came down here and let myself in. Only half of the panels had been cleaned by then, but I started looking at the second one over there, and suddenly it was an hour later. I don't remember anything of the intervening period."

"I wonder if any more of these exist," Arrhiána mused.

"We could find out," the king stated. "Let's send out a call to the furthest reaches of the kingdom, asking that all tapestries be inventoried by their owners within the next six-month, and that these lists be returned here to you. If we spot any likely candidates, we can examine them ourselves, and make the owner an offer he can't refuse."

The princess smiled most prettily.

"That sounds almost threatening, Kásha," she noted.

"Yes, I'm a very mean king," he agreed.

"Still," she said, "it bothers me a little that we have no idea what kind of magic was employed, or, more to the point, what it was intended to do other than to make these scenes come vividly alive. Isn't there any clue in Mikhaêl?"

"Of a sort, but no one knows what it means," he indicated. "'*Hyphainó, skarabaie, kai mageuó,*' or 'I weave, scarab, and I make magic.' According to Mikhaêl, it was writ on Jaél's tomb, summing up his essential philosophy. I confess, it doesn't make much sense to me."

"I wonder," she mused. "Could it have something to do with the scarab symbol itself?"

"Perhaps," Arkády indicated, "but how?"

"I don't know," the princess admitted, "but I'll think of something. However, we'd better get back to our guests. I see Antónia Lady Vydór standing over there, chatting with Sir Werner von Brüst, and making very certain that he won't miss any of her finer features. Hovering on his other side is Lady Millitsénta Prüdníka. Why don't you go over and smile that sweet smile of yours and give them the grand tour?"

"And *I* see Lord Hölleröller," he pointed out, "standing there with his large mustachios and double (no, triple!) chin hanging down almost to his oversized belly, who is said to own three large manor houses and estates in Grüninsel, and who's recently lost his wife to the fickle flux."

"Pooh!" Arrhiána retorted. "Fickle flux indeed!"

CHAPTER FORTY-NINE
"YOU ALWAYS DID
ENJOY THE KILL"

"Gad, I hate these things," Kiríll groaned, as they left the exhibition of tapestries. "These grungy old hangings, and we're supposed to say 'ooh' and 'ahh' at each and every one, and then be nice to all the fat old lords and ladies tottering around, if they even *can* totter. I mean, did you see Lord Vydór, that old sot, making his ga-ga eyes at Lady Dûffus?"

"Just be glad you're not the king," Zakháry agreed. "You'd have to go to every one of these bloody things, and then smile and bow and smile again."

"Which is just what you'll be doing in Mährenia soon," his brother noted.

"Yes, but at least *I'll* be the one setting the agenda," Zakháry replied.

"When exactly are you leaving?" Kiríll wanted to know

"As soon as the conference is over, and I can arrange for a regent to oversee my fief here," Zakháry said. "Not long, I think. I need to get settled there before the snows arrive."

Then he changed the subject. "What do we do tomorrow, Kir?"

"Well, dear brother, our dirk-toting friend from Tôrtous has just arrived," Kiríll stated, "and I shall arrange a pass for him to attend the conference on the morrow. And if he should fail, then I think we must try again ourselves. Melanthrix has proven to be the traitor we always suspected he was. He deserves to die. They *all* deserve to die. I've already made special plans for Munkás and Éskak."

"I can just imagine," Zakháry laughed. "You always did enjoy the kill, brother. What about father?"

"He's irretrievable," Kiríll noted. "If he survives, then it's back to Kórynthály with him."

"And if he doesn't?" his brother inquired.

"Then it's back to Kórynthály with him!" Kir responded, laughing.

CHAPTER FIFTY
"HE'LL KILL ME"

On the next morning, the Feast of Saint Bêrtinos the Abbot, the third session of the reconciliation conference began promptly at *tritê* with a blessing and an address by the patriarch. In his homily, Timotheos urged the participants to strive for unity, and to keep always the loving-kindness of God foremost in their minds as they wrestled with the great problems of the land.

At that very moment in Kórynthály, a soldier named Didím came running up to Captain Kérés, saying a fire had been reported in the ancient Church of Saint Ióv, and would he please come quickly.

Kérés had not gone to the conference that morning, as originally scheduled, pleading an indisposition incurred the previous evening, when he and several of his fellow officers had visited a local tavern, and pretended to drink themselves nearly senseless.

Instead, the captain had arranged for a special troop of lancers to be split from the forces of Munkás and Éskak at Katonaí Field, ostensibly for training maneuvers, and had then arrested the commander and officers of the troop and replaced them with his own men. The ordinary soldiers he had quietly deployed around the outskirts of Kórynthály Estate during the middle of the night.

Corporal Didím again pleaded with the captain to bring his men quickly, lest the church burn down. And indeed, Kérés could see smoke billowing up in the distance. Instead, however, he abruptly pulled his sword, swept the tip right up under the man's chin, and ordered him to confess the conspirators' plans or lose his head, then and there.

Curiously, Didím suddenly learned how to obey his orders most promptly. Based on the information thus gathered, Captain Kérés sent one troop here and another there, and flagged a runner to go to Sergeant Émilman in the nearby forest.

Time to close the trap, he thought to himself, *and God help them all if they actually* have *burned down the church!*

Soon Lord Télen was in custody, together with his chief officers, and Kérés had deployed the common soldiers from the renegade's force to help put down the blaze started in an outbuilding of Saint Ióv's. Fortunately, it was soon brought under control.

Then the captain ordered Télen brought to him, and again drew his sword.

"You can't intimidate *me!*" Télen blustered.

Kérés idly flicked his wrist, and the baron's left ear popped off, spinning into the dust by their feet. Télen screamed, and grabbed the streaming stump of his ear with his right hand. The captain smiled.

"I haven't a great deal of time," the officer said, still grinning, "but I try very much to enjoy my work, and I'm willing to work very hard indeed right now to make you talk. I need to know exactly how you intend to signal Duke of Tighris that you control Kórynthály, and I need you to send the appropriate sign or message at once. I will check your response against those of your officers. So tell me, dear Télen, how many appendages do you wish to lose today?"

As it happened, the baron had no real desire to add much to the toll, only contributing the other ear and the small finger from his left hand, and very quickly provided all of the details requested. Captain Kérés thoroughly and speedily verified the details by interrogating one of the baron's senior officers, who only lost a nose, and then ordered Télen to write down the code word.

"He'll kill me!" the baron stated.

"He won't be in a position to kill you," Kérés responded. "*I,* on the other hand, am quite willing to torture you before I kill you, if you fail to obey my every command. *Now!*"

The message was quickly dispatched by runner to be slipped under the front door of the ex-king's manor house.

As soon as Kipriyán received the missive giving the "all safe" sign, he and Doctor Melanthrix transited to the laundry in Tighrishály Palace.

The former monarch breathed in deeply, savoring the sweet odors of the lower depths of the great castle.

"Ah, it's great to be home, Melánty," he said.

Elsewhere in Tighrishály Palace, Captain Fösse was conferring with one of his men, Constable Warka.

"Have you found Sergeant Poliodór yet?" he inquired.

"Not a trace, sir," the guard responded. "Some of his men are missing, too. We think they're holed up somewhere in the building, waiting for the king...that is, the Duke, to appear."

"Very well, keep looking," he ordered.

Then Fösse went into the Great Hall to report to King Arkády.

"I'm a little worried, sire," he indicated, after the king took him off to one side for privacy. "Poliodór and at least one squad of his guards are still unaccounted for, and we're expecting the Duke of Tighris and Melanthrix at any moment."

"Just stay on the alert, captain," the king stated. "I assume that all of your men are in place, including the archers?"

"They *are,* majesty," the officer replied, coming to attention and saluting.

"Then we can do nothing else but wait for events to unfold," Arkády noted. "Carry on."

"Yes, sir," Fösse said, hurrying off to confer with his sergeants.

In the king's apartments, Queen Dúra paced back and forth, back and forth, waiting for news, brushing away an occasional tear. She had pleaded to attend the conference at the king's side, but had been refused.

"The most important thing to me right now is *your* safety and that of our children," Arkády had emphasized.

"Please take me with you," she had begged. "I should be there, Arkásha."

"It's too dangerous," he had repeated, as if she hadn't spoken. "I have a runner hidden away in the hall where he can watch the proceedings. If I'm killed or captured, he will rush here to warn you. Under such circumstances, I want you to take Márissa and the children, and transit immediately to your brother's palace in Austrasia. You'll be safe there. Later, Arión can try regaining the throne, but that will be his decision, not mine.

"To accomplish my task," he had told her, "I must know that both you and they are secure. Help me, dear love, please help me."

"Just don't die, Kásha!" she had pleaded. "Just don't leave me alone!"

He had grabbed her then by her shoulders and held her tight against him, smothering her objections against his mantle. He could feel the dark, feathery fingers of her hair idly caressing his chin.

"Never, my Drúsha, never," he had whispered into her ear. "We will always be together, here and in the aftertime. Always. Old Death has no claim on us. Whoever goes ahead will wait there for the other, patiently and with love. My vows bind me to your spirit forever."

"And mine," she had softly replied.

Then she had stood on her toes and kissed him on the mouth, resolving to do what he said, but hating every moment of the interminable wait, wondering what had happened, what *would* happen at the conference, and whether she and her family would have to flee suddenly to escape the assassin's knife.

"What's the matter, Mamá?" asked Princess Grigorÿna, her eldest daughter. She had Ouisa tucked under one slender arm.

"What?" her mother replied, still lost in thought. "Oh, I'm sorry, dearest. I don't know where I'm at today. I was just wondering how the conference is going, that's all."

"Ouisa says everything's going to be all right," the little girl assured her.

She ran up and gave her mother a hug.

"I know it is, Rÿna," the older woman stated, "but sometimes mothers just have to worry a little bit."

Wives, too, she added to herself, *oh God, wives must worry, too.*

CHAPTER FIFTY-ONE
"I CAN'T HOLD IT"

Meanwhile, down in the laundry former King Kipriyán was conferring with Sergeant Poliodór.

"I'm a little concerned, majesty," the soldier was saying, "about Captain Fösse and his men. I was unable to secure them before reporting, simply because they were not where they were supposed to be, and because the captain technically outranks me. I do have three squads of guards ready to spring the trap here in the palace, about thirty-five men in all, so I'm still confident that we can do this. But you must make the final decision."

Kipriyán sighed.

"We've gone too far to turn back," he said. "No matter what happens, the die has been cast, and we all know the consequences of failure. We must either take or kill Prince Arkády immediately, or we're lost. Let's get on with it."

They then began transiting a few at a time to a little-known and -used alcove mirror at the rear of the Great Hall, where the other two squads already were waiting for them.

"Is everyone ready?" Poliodór asked.

When his men responded in the affirmative, he nodded to the ex-king.

Then Kipriyán said: "For God and Kórynthia!" and started into the hall.

Over his shoulder, he murmured softly to Melanthrix, "Stay close to me, Melánty. Use your powers when necessary to support mine."

Amidst the press of hundreds of attendees, the conspirators attracted little attention until they neared the table at the center of the room where the Royal Council sat. Then Lord Vydór spotted the former king leading the soldiers towards them and immediately sounded the alarum.

Before he could even raise his defenses Vydór was blasted from his seat by a bolt of green energy from Kipriyán's outstretched swordhand. Dowager Queen Brisquayne, who was sitting next to the grand vizier, responded with a blast of her own, knocking the weapon away from the ex-king.

Doctor Melanthrix kept Kipriyán from falling backwards to the floor, and with his left hand sent a charge of ruby lightning right at the queen's breast, blowing her out of her seat and over the council table, straight into the arms of the Princes Kiríll and Zakháry. King Arkády sent back a surge of yellow fire at the sorcerer, who warded it off with a wave of his hand.

Then Sergeant Poliodór rushed his men forward in a direct physical attack on the councilmen. Several arrows from the hidden emplacements at the edge of the hall struck down the advancing rebel guardsmen, but quarters were simply too close thereafter to employ such distant weaponry. When they realized what was happening, Captain Fösse's men tried desperately to push their way through the throngs of citizens trying to leave the hall, but with only partial success.

The royal princes soon found themselves fighting for their lives against three or four attackers apiece, using the table and their own backs as aids in the increasingly savage fight. Father Athanasios was confronted by a sword-wielding rebel, who raised his arm and was on the verge of cutting down the cleric when a red beam, apparently aimed at the king standing behind him, zapped the guard.

Patriarch Timotheos was already tending to the wounded, trying to comfort them until help could arrive, while the battle surged around and over him. At one point, he looked up from Queen Brisquayne to see Sergeant Poliodór preparing to stab Prince Kiríll in the back with his sword, muttered "God forgive me" under his breath, raised his hand as if to give a benediction, and fried the sergeant where he stood with a beam of violet energy. Princess Arrhiána cut down another guard with a wave of amber light.

As the chaos spread over the floor of the hall, up in the king's apartments the Princess Rÿna was listening to something that her doll Ouisa was telling her. Then she got up, went into the room where her brother Ari was resting, and suddenly pinched him on the arm to the point where he screamed out in pain. In the main room, Queen Dúra jumped up and came running.

"Call Doctor Melanthrix," she ordered her daughter.

"Yes, Mamá," the girl replied, and grabbing hold of the little silver bell in both hands, clutched it between her palms as if to pray, crushing it so hard that the blood flowed from her flesh onto the hard silver casing.

"Oh, come to me, Doctor Melanthrix," she whispered, and flung her two hands up into the air to either side, the bell tumbling away from them end over end straight up towards the ceiling, ringing and ringing and ringing, as if the world itself were coming to an end.

"Ahhhh," screamed the philosopher, clapping his two hands to each ear, while the battle surged around him. It felt as if someone had stuck a needle right through the middle of his head, causing it to reverberate in waves of sound and terror. He knew what this was, he knew what it meant.

Off to one side, one of the so-called conference attendees smiled to himself, deftly drew a silver-coated throwing knife from its hidden sheath, and in one bold stroke sailed it thirty feet across the room right into the sorcerer's back.

A look of great surprise passed over the face of Doctor Melanthrix, before he fell straight forward onto his face, hitting the floor with an audible "thump."

Still the battle ebbed and flowed, as Kipriyán continued to hit his opponents with strokes from his recovered sword and with bolts of energy, but his rebel supporters had now diminished to no more than a dozen, the rest being scattered about the floor like so many discarded pieces from a game, dead or insensate.

Then Arkády was facing his father head-to-head, but the old king's strength was fast dissipating, and he found it harder and harder to raise his sword for yet another blow.

"Die, damn you!" Kipriyán exclaimed, trying for one more killing swing. As his sword descended, Arkády blocked it, swung the weapon to one side, and neatly disarmed his father.

"Yield!" he ordered the older man.

"Never!" Kipriyán responded.

Then Arkády drew back his arm, wielding his own sword around in a mighty circle, and brought the flat part of the weapon down on his father's helmet, knocking him senseless.

"Surrender!" he yelled to the handful of remaining rebels. "Surrender or die!"

Seeing the inert form of the rebel king stretched out before them, they suddenly stopped what they were doing, and one by one dropped their weapons. Captain Fösse and his men rounded up the six remaining guards of Poliodór's troop, and hauled them off to a waiting room.

"God's death!" the king uttered, looking around him at the bodies strewn all over the council table and floor. He shook his tousled head in frustration.

"Kir! Zack! Do you live?" he yelled.

"Here, brother," shouted Prince Zakháry over the din. He was cradling his brother's head in his arm. "Kir's been hurt, but I think he'll be all right. Where's the physician?"

At that moment Fra Tibor appeared, together with several assistants, and they immediately went to work on the ex-king.

"When you've finished treating him, sedate the duke," Arkády ordered, "and then have him bound."

Patriarch Timotheos and Father Athanasios continued to provide spiritual aid and comfort to anyone who needed them.

"Arkády!" Arrhiána called out urgently. "Over here."

The king hurried to his sister, who was bending over the prone body of Dowager Queen Brisquayne. There was a dark singe mark spread across the front of her dress, radiating out from a central point between her breasts. She was breathing heavily.

"Kásha," Brisquayne managed to utter, "you must stop the evil. You must find a way to preserve the land. Promise me."

"I will, Granny," the king said, taking one of her hands in his. It was cold.

"Then I die content," she gasped.

"You're not going to die, Granny," Arrhiána cried.

"You're a good woman, Rhie," the old queen whispered. "You always were. Tell my girls that I love them, that I thought of them at the end."

Then she paused a moment.

"I can see the light, Kásha," she said. "I must go now. Another is calling me."

Then they felt her pass into the beyond, the gates of Paradise swinging wide to admit her.

Not far away, another, grimmer death was approaching. Arkády and his sister heard a groan, and looked up to see Doctor Melanthrix roll onto his side, grimacing with the effort. They left Brisquayne to join a circle that was slowly forming around the old philosopher, including most of the surviving members of the Royal Council. Arkády felt Father Athanasios come up behind him.

Fra Tibor looked up from the astrologer's prone body and shook his head.

"If I pull the knife, he'll die immediately," the doctor noted. "Too many organs have been damaged. And there's something strange about his anatomy. I can do nothing."

Then he moved on to another patient who had greater need of him.

The patriarch came forward to offer his services, but Melanthrix weakly waved him away.

"I gave up that nonsense a long time ago," he wheezed, "and it's too late to start again now."

"It's never too late," Timotheos responded. "God has infinite mercy for repentant sinners."

"Not for me, father," Melanthrix replied. "Never for me."

He groaned again, and a ripple seemed to wash over his face.

"I can't hold it," the philosopher murmured.

Then he began to change, slowly at first, and then ever more quickly. Different faces and different bodies appeared seemingly at random on his form—men and women of all ages and sizes, as well as a wolf, an eagle, a large snake, a scorpion, and several other beasts—one coming after another in rapid succession, until the changes were happening so fast they could not even be comprehended by the onlookers. Finally, ultimately, he became the body of an old, tired woman with the hilt of a knife sticking out of her back.

Mösza! King Arkády screamed inwardly, his rings flaring bright red, *Aunt Mösza!*

She looked up in his direction, and smiled grimly.

"Well, my boy," she gasped between breaths, *"'Ego deum genus esse semper dixi et dicam coelitum.'"*

And then, after a pause: *"'Ego pretium ob stultitiam fero.'"*

She coughed, blood bubbling daintily from between her lips.

"Not long now," she said, chest heaving. Her voice rose to a high pitch: *"'Exoriare aliquis nostris ex ossibus ultor!'"*

Then she shuddered and expired.

"What was that all about?" Arrhiána asked. She put her hand over her brother's. "What did she say? Who is she?" she added.

The Archpriest Athanasios appeared just behind them to offer his assistance.

"She spoke in the Romanish tongue," the priest noted. "I know some of that language, and can make a rough translation: 'I have always said and will say again that there is a race of gods.' And secondly: 'I am well rewarded for my folly.' And thirdly: 'Rise from my ashes, avenger, rise!' I don't know who she is, though; I've never seen her before."

No one else could identify her, and the king could say nothing, being bound by the oath that he had given to the Covenant of Christian Mages. So her name remained Melanthrix, and Arkády ordered her body carefully wrapped in a blanket and taken to her old quarters, where it was laid out on her bed and the room sealed. He insisted, however, that no one actually touch her bare flesh.

The monarch next turned his attention to the prone body of Lord Vydór, who was being tended by several physicians, with Lady Antónia hovering nearby, almost hysterical with worry.

"Will he live?" Arkády and Vydór's wife both inquired simultaneously.

"I think so," a very harried and frustrated Fra Tibor responded.

"We're doing the best we can, sire," he sniped, returning to his work.

"Oh my goodness gracious," Lady Antónia declaimed. "Oh, oh, oh, save him, majesty, oh please save him. Please, sire."

She draped herself over the monarch to the point where he had to have one of the guards pry her loose.

Then Arkády sought out Prince Kiríll, who was stretched out on the council table, and was being bandaged by a young woman the king had never seen before.

"How is he?" he asked.

"He'll be just fine with a little care and some rest," the lady replied, without even looking at him.

The woman continued to work steadily, wrapping a bandage around the stricken man's chest, and then knotting it tight.

"There," she muttered, before looking up straight into the king's eyes.

"Majesty!" she exclaimed, quickly bowing her head. "I didn't know it was you."

"You were rather busy," the king noted, smiling a thin smile. "And I'd rather have you devote your attentions to Kir than to me. What's your name?"

"Mála Lady Teuschpach," she quietly responded.

"The daughter of Yevséby?" Arkády asked, and when she demurely nodded, continued: "I grieve for your loss. Who inherited the title?"

"No one, sire," she said, sadness filling her voice. "The honor reverts to the crown. I am the last of my line, for my mother collapsed when she heard the news, and was struck senseless. She will never leave her bed again.

"But we had no one else to represent our small district at this conference, so few of our men survived," she continued, "and so I was chosen by the Council of Teuschpach to come to Paltyrrha. With the little money that I had, I hired a nurse to care for my mother while I was gone. And that is all my story."

"Mála Lady Teuschpach," the king responded, loudly enough for Kiríll and Zakháry to hear, "in gratitude for the service you have performed this day for my brother, I hereby create you Baroness Teuschpach, and grant to you all of the estates previously owned by your father, with remainder to the heirs of your body whatsoever. I will have the grand vizier prepare the letters patent when he is well enough to do so, but the creation is effective from this instant."

Mála knelt and kissed his hands.

"Thank you, majesty," she intoned, before turning back to her patient.

Then the king asked for reports on a thousand different subjects, remembered at the last to send a note of reassurance to his Drúsha, and gradually, very gradually began putting his house back in order.

CHAPTER FIFTY-TWO
"SOMETHING NOT QUITE RIGHT ABOUT THE CORPSE"

A few hours later, the king and his sister, the Princess Arrhiána, met privately in her apartments in the palace. After they had discussed several matters, King Arkády ordered their father brought to him.

The deposed king had to be dragged in by the guards. Although obviously ravaged by the effects of the drugs he had been administered, he was still able to spit at the both of them when he was deposited in the chair opposite.

"So, father," Arkády indicated, "still fighting me, eh? I'm sorry for that, and I'm sorrier still that I must now order you confined completely to your house. You will have no visitors other than those authorized in advance by me. Your transit mirror will be removed, your rings taken from your fingers. No written communications will be allowed from your establishment, coming or going. You will be kept drugged so that you can't use your powers. The guards at your estate will serve only under *my* orders, and those orders will be specific, and not capable of being countermanded by yours, ever. They will be instructed to use force, if necessary, to ensure that my orders are carried out. This is my final word on the subject. Take him away!" he said.

Then King Arkády turned to his sister: "What about Brisquayne's daughters?"

"I've sent a messenger informing them of their mother's

death," she noted, "and they'll be arriving on the morrow, with all their family, including the King of Neustria. They'll remain through the funeral, and then return home. Gad, how I'm going to miss that dear old lady!"

"She was a very special person," Arkády agreed, "whose spirit will continue to dwell in all our memories. I've decided to name the room where the tapestries were hung after her."

"She'd like that, I think," Arrhiána stated. "What are you going to do about Melanthrix?"

"I don't know," the king replied. "There's something not quite right about the corpse, which is why I ordered it to remain inviolate. I think I'm going to have to handle that little problem all by myself."

"Who *is* she, Kásha?" the princess inquired. "I had the sense in the hall that she was speaking just to you, and the even stranger notion that you knew exactly who she was and what she was talking about."

"I'm afraid I can't say anything further on this particular topic," Arkády replied. "I've given my word."

"But who...? No. No, never mind," she finally acquiesced. "I know that face that you're giving me. What will you do about the other conspirators?"

"They'll be given a fair trial," he stated, "and then they'll be executed, all except Lásky. He'll be allowed to abdicate his title in favor of his younger brother, and then be condemned to a lifetime of servitude in the very prison that he used to govern. I find a certain ironic justice in that sentence. By the way, what's the latest word on the grand vizier?"

"Antónia told me that he'll survive," Arrhiána indicated, "but it will be a long and painful recovery. He was very seriously burned.

"Kásha," she continued, "I want you to think very carefully about what I'm going to say. I don't trust father, not anymore. If he can find a way out of his cage, he'll do so, and he'll be back with an even larger and more dangerous insurrection in the future. He's gone mad in a way that can never be reversed.

I urge you to find some means of controlling him better than by leaving him on his estate."

"I've thought about the problem a great deal, Rhie," her brother replied, "and it comes down to this: if I err on the side of generosity, then so be it. I will not kill my own father, and I won't imprison him, either. As long as there's some small hope of reforming him or turning him back to the true path, I must take that chance."

"And Kórynthia?" she asked. "Are you willing to sacrifice the kingdom on the slight chance that father will redeem himself?"

"I'll give him one more opportunity," the king said, "a very tightly controlled opportunity." He grinned, ever so slightly. "I'm no fool, Rhie, really I'm not. But I have to try. I won't go down the same path that he did."

"I've never thought you a fool, brother," Arrhiána sighed, "no, never that. Of all of us, you are the noblest, the one person by whose mark the rest of the family now measures itself and will continue to measure itself in the future. No, brother, don't ever lose those ideals."

The king just laughed.

"I'm no saint, Rhie. I just try to do the right thing. Occasionally I succeed, with the help of you and so many other good souls; all too often I fail, sometimes very spectacularly."

Then he rose from his seat.

"Now come, little sister," he urged, "we have so much to do and so very little time in which to do it. We need to arrange for far too many memorial services, and the conference needs starting again. A country demands rebuilding. Time's a-wasting."

CHAPTER FIFTY-THREE
"THE BROTHERHOOD OF TIGHRIS LIVES AGAIN"

That evening, the one known as Tau called the first meeting of the Brotherhood of Tighris held in six months. Only five members of the original nine reported that night to the island of Loryùppa.

In the chamber of the Enneaphon, Tau began by relating the formula of passing.

"My brothers and sisters," he intoned, "I bring you good news and bad. Four of our members have passed into that great adventure beyond life itself. Their names can now be mentioned in this assembly. The Patriarch Avraäm IV, who led us as 'Alpha,' perished shortly after Killingford. Let his *nomen* be inscribed among the immortals, let his name be etched upon these hallowed walls."

Then he cut the name of his patron onto the surface of the chamber.

"Axios!" came the muted response.

Similarly, he celebrated the lives of "Kappa," or Fra Jánisar Cantárian, and "Gamma," or Gorázd Lord Aboéty, both of them foully murdered.

Finally, he reached the fourth name.

"My brethren," Tau continued, "the next name on our list is that of 'Mu,' whom we now know was once the Princess Mösza, but who also postured as the philosopher called Doctor Melanthrix."

The one who was called "Thêta," or Father Athanasios, slumped in his cold stone seat, stunned as the import of what Tau was saying began sinking into his consciousness.

Tau waved his hand to quiet the outbursts of his companions.

"I now believe," he indicated, "that this sorcerer was the individual who tried to destroy our organization from within. Therefore, I move that Mösza's name be purged from the roles of the Brotherhood, and that she be cursed by generations to come for the witch that she really was."

"Agreed," came three responses.

"Thêta, what is your vote?" Tau inquired.

Suddenly Athanasios realized that Timotheos was talking to him.

"I—I must abstain," he finally choked out.

"And I vote yea," Tau noted. "The motion is carried. Now, brethren, we must elect a new leader, and then proceed to search out new membership to fill our ranks. Are there nominations for the post of Alpha?"

Athanasios was finally alert.

"I nominate Tau," he replied.

Timotheos waited a few moments, and then asked: "Are there any other nominations? Very well, hearing none, I declare Tau duly elected."

He sighed.

He moved to the largest of the nine stone chairs, and intoned the ancient formula: "I am the Alpha and the Omega. The one who was known as Tau is dead."

Then, looking around at the others, Timotheos added: "This meeting is adjourned until we can recruit and inaugurate four new members. Please let me know privily of any promising acolytes that you may find, and I shall question them closely. The Brotherhood of Tighris lives again."

"Amen," they replied in unison, and began filing one by one into the transit alcove.

Only Alpha, he who had once been Tau, remained behind.

"Why, Mösza?" he spoke to no one in particular, "why?"

CHAPTER FIFTY-FOUR
"DON'T LEAVE ME HERE!"

At midnight, the King Arkadios made his way to the chambers of the late Princess Mösza, she who had also been known to the world as Doctor Melanthrix. There he put to sleep the men standing guard outside the door with an idle wave of his hand, unsealed the old philosopher's room, and quietly entered.

He stepped to the bed, where Mösza's body was neatly laid out, and picked it up, being careful not to touch any of the exposed flesh.

What are you doing? came the little voice.

Ah, he replied, *I thought you might still be in there, Auntie.*

Where are you taking me, Arkásha? came the plaintive query.

Just for a little ride, the king noted.

He carried the body down several levels, stopping once to regain his breath, using back ways that were little frequented even during the day. They met no one.

Then he moved to the other wing of the palace via a narrow passageway accessed through a sliding door located behind a floor-length wall hanging. He finally came to Queen Brisquayne's Gallery, as it would now be called, where Jaél's extraordinary tapestries were on permanent display.

He closed the door behind him with his foot, and placed the body of Mösza in the middle of the floor. Then he lit his ringflame, and went over to the panel depicting the Pit of the Demons. During his last visit here, Arrhiána had given him an idea that he wanted to try.

The king deliberately centered himself, and then focused his mind on the scarab device located in one corner of the artwork. He imagined it as alive, and touched it with his *psai*-ring, sending his energy surging through it. He was gratified to see the small image begin waving its six tiny legs. As the beetle suddenly scurried up within the hanging, it seemed to give life to the tapestry, and Arkády could feel a cold breeze and dank smell oozing from the picture. Then he retrieved the body of his great-aunt, and stepped into and through the image.

Where are *we?* she screamed.

Don't you remember, Auntie? he asked. *You brought me here once.*

Noooo! came the cry of terror. *Arkásha, don't leave me here!*

I'm sorry, Mösza, I truly am, Arkády thought, *but what else can I do with you? If I put you where you can be found, you'll move on to someone else, won't you? And then this will start all over again. I just can't take that chance.*

Please, Mamá, please! she pleaded. *I promise to be a good girl, really I do. I know I was bad once, but you've punished me for that already. Don't send me away, Málya, please don't. It wasn't my fault. Nésty said that she didn't care, that she had hurt him, that only I could help. I didn't know, brother, I didn't. I believed him. And then he started to laugh, and he called me thin and ugly and strange, and he laughed some more. All I wanted was to be loved by someone. Please don't send me away, Mamá, please!*

Arkády put the body carefully down on the altar, laying it out on the crosspiece, but again avoiding direct contact with the flesh. He tried not to look at any of the grotesque images lining the dank chamber.

Mösza Karlománovna von Tighrisha, he intoned, *Princess of Kórynthia, Countess of Rábassy, and Shaikha of Salaleh, rest thou in eternal peace.*

Waaiitt! she screamed again. *You don't know what they'll do to me. Stoppp! You can't do this. You can't leave me here, Zee. Víktor, save me, please, save me. Kyp, you must help me. Kásha, please, I'll do anything, I'll give you the secrets of life and death, I'll tell you how to transmute into shapes. Maaaamáááá!*

Then the king sensed movement of a sort all around him, of evil presences reaching out to one of their own.

Saaave meee! Mösza shouted to Arkády. *Pleeaase!*

But nothing could save her now, for she was damned, not only by her own nature, but by her own choices as well. The spirits dwelling in this place sucked her soul out of her corpse like a dog working marrow out of a bone, and they made her one of their own.

The being called Huzzíyas then spake unto King Arkády: *Why dost thou linger here, mortal man?*

I bow my head in sorrow and in shame, the king replied.

Sorrow shall be thy lot in life, it whispered, *but still thy fate transcends this one's emptiness by a degree unmeasurable to man. Leave us to our pain, mortal, for that is all we have.*

Then King Arkády centered himself, and bowing his head, walked straight through the ouroborean transit mirror home to Paltyrrha, leaving his regrets behind. It was the Feast of Saint Eleutherios, and a new sun was rising in Kórynthia.

CHAPTER FIFTY-FIVE
"COME TO ME IN
THE PIT OF DEMONS"

On the final day of the year, which was also the Feast of
Saint Sylvestros, the depowerment of the ex-King Kipriyán
took place at the Church of Saint Ióv in Kórynthály. The former
monarch had to be dragged from his house, and then bound and
gagged, for he would not go willingly to what he perceived to be
the slaughter of his especial perceptions and powers.

Only a handful of witnesses were present to see the
unusual ceremony. These included the King-to-Be Arkády,
the Hereditary Prince-to-Be Arión, the Princess Arrhiána, the
Prince Kiríll, the Prince Andruin, the Princess Sachette, the
Dowager Queen Polyxena, Queen Ezzölla, the Queen-to-Be
Dúra, the Royal Council, and the Holy Synod. Among the latter
was the recently-installed Metropolitan of Örtenburg, the hieromonk Athanasios Hokhanêmsos.

The former king was lashed to the top of King Tighris's tomb
in the nave of the Church, and the members of the royal family
took their places on either side of the ancient memorial.

The great Sword of Tighris was carried in by six burly Albány
guards, who set it on a table in front of Tighris-Mögila, removed
the jewel-encrusted scabbard without touching the metal, and
then left.

The outstretched body of the living ex-king was carefully
covered with a single piece of raw white silk, except for the
face, which was left bare. This was overlaid with cloth-of-gold

emblazoned with the crouching ochre tiger of the Royal House of Tighris. A belt of diamonds signifying his rank completed his uniform.

"Let us pray," intoned Patriarch Timotheos, being seconded by the Holy Synod, which now consisted of the Metropolitans Mêtrophanês, Konôn, Kyriakos, Eudoxios, Zôïlos, Aphrikanos, Athanasios, Nôe, Serapheim, Symeôn, Dositheos, and Hypatios.

The solemn mass began. Clouds of incense swirled into the bright morning air. Then the Eucharist, the bread and wine representing the Body and Blood of Christ, was distributed to the communicants, as each of them solemnly presented him- or herself before the altar to receive the greatest gift of all from the hands of the primate.

As the service began winding towards its conclusion, the Thrice Holy Patriarch of Paltyrrha and All Kórynthia moved to the head of Tighris's tomb, with the Holy Synod standing in two lines flanking the prone but squirming body of the former monarch.

Timotheos lifted his hands in supplication, saying: "Whereas it hath pleased Almighty God to remove our Sovereign King and Lord, the High and Mighty King Kyprianos, Third of that name, from his throne and from his station, let there be remembrance of his name for thrice times thirty generations, let the metropolitans and the lords and all the children of the church cherish his memory as king from generation to generation, for ever and ever."

"Amen," echoed those present.

"We beseech the Archangels Gabriêl, Mikhaêl, Raphaêl, and Ouriêl to sanctify our former king at the feet of the Almighty. May God receive him and welcome him into His family."

"Amen," came the universal response.

But amid such signs of peace, the former King Kipriyán began screaming to himself in horror, as the great figures of the angels suddenly surrounded him, forcing him to face the cancers eating away at the inside of his immortal soul.

It seemed to the old king that the face of the Archangel

Gabriêl began transforming before him, changing to the image of his daughter Sachette as a woman-girl of thirteen years.

He tried to turn his eyes away, tried to shout a universal "No!," but the angels gave him no mercy, forcing him back to the searing icons of his memory. He saw himself kissing the girl and stroking her, and he remembered, oh yes, reveling in the excitement of tasting forbidden fruit, and then, oh God, then, as she suddenly realized that something was terribly, horribly wrong with her dear Papá, he recalled the girl dashing from him in terror, and running headlong into the stone pillar, knocking herself unconscious. And when she woke, oh Kipriyán the Conqueror, aye, when she awoke, her world had become a world of eternal blackness, a blackness that he alone had smeared all over her delicate soul. His loathing for himself reached new heights.

"He has put aside the cares of this world," the patriarch continued, "he has need of them no more. Therefore, Kyprianos von Tighris, we take from thee thy riches, for they mean nothing in the Kingdom of Heaven."

A monk removed the belt of diamonds from atop the ex-king's living body.

And Kipriyán remembered the field of grotesquely charred corpses that was Killingford, recalled the destruction that he had caused, the widows he had created, the houses he had rendered extinct, the tens of thousands of accusing souls now pointing their fingers at him (he could see them, every one, hovering just behind the spirits of the angels of God!), and all to satisfy his own hunger, nay, his *lust* for power. Oh, he remembered every little detail, all right!

"We take from thee thy titles and thy honors, for thou art mere clay before the Majesty of God."

The emblazoned cloth-of-gold was removed.

Then the ex-king recalled what his grandmother and his great-uncle had done in his name, and what they had told him, and what he now knew to be true, that he had never, ever been the consecrated King of Kórynthia, but had only sat in the place of another who had been unjustly deprived, and he blasphemed, oh, he squirmed, and "sister" Mösza called to his soul from the depths of Hell itself, saying, "Come to me, my brother, yes, come to me in the Pit of Demons."

"We take from thee thy sight, thy breath, and thy speech, for thou dost not need them in Heaven."

The Thrice Holy Timotheos traced the sign of the cross in chrism on the former king's forehead, nose, and lips, burning him with the holy oil.

Ayyyy!, he cried to himself. And Kipriyán the ex-king, he who was surnamed the Conqueror, knew the bitterness of what he had become and whom he had wronged, and how he had used them all, every one, to further his own ambition, and he raged, yes, he raged at the restraints, because, he knew, if freed, by perdition's gates, he knew he would do it all over again!

I defy you, God, Kipriyán yelled into his gag. *I defy you all!*

"And we take from thee thy power, for it is not thine to keep, but belongs to another."

The patriarch closed his eyes and placed his left hand on Kipriyán's breast and the right on the sword, and then a glow began to engulf them both, running quickly through the spectrum of colors. Timotheos's face changed and briefly assumed the form of ancient Tighris's, and then the light swept down the ex-king's body, draining from it through Tighris-Timotheos into the Great Sword just beyond.

There was a collective sigh from everyone in the Church. It was over. Job's Complaint sounded one plaintive lament as the family sadly filed out through the great bronze doors.

But it wasn't over yet. As they brought the bound body of the old king out into the sunlight, and released his gag, he began cursing the patriarch and his own family in such a foul and filthy way that everyone there turned their backs on him, and said to themselves, and publicly averred, that nevermore would this be, that he was now as dead to their hearts as he had become to himself.

CHAPTER FIFTY-SIX
"HE WAS NO LONGER A CHILD"

That afternoon, for the first time in many months, the Metropolitan Athanasios found his way back to Land's End in the maze at the heart of the Hanging Garden of Queen Landizábel. The air was warm and still, the skies clear. The weather mages had been busily at work during the preceding week to make certain that the girding of King Arkády with the sword would proceed without difficulty on the morrow. Tucked under the priest's arm was the folder containing the results of his family research.

This *annus horribilis* was finally, mercifully winding to a close. The year that had seen so many deaths, as well as the deposition of a king and the passing of a revered patriarch, was about to become history.

He looked back upon the past twelve months with almost a sense of amazement. So many friends gone, so many new ones made, his carefree existence vanished, and new responsibilities added. And, finally, a possible ending to his quest for himself and his origins.

Athanasios sat down on the stone bench under the queen's statue and opened the folder, spreading his work around him.

What did he really know? he thought to himself. *What could be inferred?*

His mother, the Princess Mösza, had been with child during the year 1164, as a generation of handsome young Kórynthi soldiers was marching off to another, earlier war in Pommerelia.

Then had come the disaster at Dürkheim—how familiar this sounded!—and the news of the deaths of King Makáry and his two eldest sons, both without surviving heirs.

The third son, the young Prince Kyprianos, had been made king under the joint regency of his grandmother, Dowager Hereditary Princess Zubayda, and his great-uncle, the Prince-Bishop Víktor, until he had come of age some five years later.

Princess Mösza's condition had then been uncovered by the regents—it could scarcely be hidden—and she had been packed off to the Emir of Tôrtous, where she had borne a male child, Maksím. The boy had been taken from her several years later by Arik Rufímovich (now the Patriarch Timotheos), while in the service of the state, and then deposited at Saint Svyatosláv's Monastery, where he had been given the name Afanásy.

This much was certain.

But *why*? Why keep everything so secret? Plenty of illegitimate Tighrishi had been sent to the abbey or the convent, without so much as a comment being expressed by anyone in the royal family. What made the difference in his case?

It had to have something to do with his father. He reviewed his original list of soldiers from the *Gardes Élites*, and decided that the only two who might have mattered were Prince Néstor or King Karlomán, the elder two sons of King Makáry. If Mösza had had an incestuous relationship with one of these boys, her nephews, who were only a few years removed from her in age, then any male offspring of this couple, illegitimate or not, would have had a claim to the throne of Kórynthia in advance of King Kipriyán's.

He re-examined the evidence of the torcs. The only names from this short list that matched the symbols he had seen on *his* torc was that of Néstor, then Hereditary Prince of Kórynthia, and his wife, who would have been the logical recipient of Néstor's memorial. Athanasios tried to recall what he remembered of the fate of Princess Diávola. She had suffered an accident of some kind, of that he was certain, a fall perhaps, or something else very unusual.

He sighed. The only way that Mösza could have gotten the memorial meant for Diávola was to dispose of her rival for Néstor's affections. Perhaps that was the real reason for her exile.

And had Athanasios been acknowledged at that time by the palace, then the priest would have been declared the true king of Kórynthia, not King Kipriyán, his uncle. He shook his head in sorrow. All of this—the great war, the deaths of so many men, the deposition of the king—had occurred because of one woman's pride and fear and desire for revenge. Her anger had eaten out her insides, and left nothing but a shell of hate behind. She had never even been willing to acknowledge her son directly, although she had carefully positioned herself, in the guise of Doctor Melanthrix, to nurture his career and take her vengeance upon the man who sat in the place her son should have occupied.

The priest felt suddenly nauseated. He had never desired such a role in life, in fact would now find it utterly abhorrent to his existence. He had neither the temperament nor the patience to rule a kingdom, and he was wise enough to know that much about himself. Even now, he feared being inadequate in his new role of administrator of a major archdiocese. He would do the best that he could, but he was no Timotheos.

He gazed into the serene eyes of Queen Landizábel, and he realized that his *real* father, by any measurement that could be made in life, was Arik Rufímovich, he who had taken the boy Afanásy by the hand, and who had kept him from straying down the path that Mösza had wandered. Arik had watched over him, nourished him, cherished him, given him advice, showed him the way, had spent time with him whenever the boy needed it, even when the soldier-monk had had very little latitude of his own. Arik had been his father and the Church his mother, and Athanasios felt no regret at the thought. He had been blessed by God as few in the world ever have been.

The hieromonk picked up his papers, and put them back in the folder. He had no need for such things now. He was no longer a child, and so he should put away the conceits of a child. It was time to be about his father's business.

CHAPTER FIFTY-SEVEN
"I WILL NOT REVEAL THY MYSTERIES TO THINE ENEMIES"

I have raised a monument more enduring than one of brass, and loftier than the pyramids of kings; a monument which shall not be destroyed by the consuming rain, nor by the mad rage of the north wind, nor by the countless years and flight of ages.

—Horace

Anno Domini 1206
Anno Juliani 846

On the first day of January, which was also the Feast of the Blessèd Virgin Mary the Mother of God, the city of Paltyrrha and the citizens of Kórynthia celebrated the installation of a new king. New Year's Day had long been the traditional date for the girding of the monarch at the Church of Saint Ióv in Kórynthály, and it also marked the official beginning of the anointed one's reign.

The day dawned clear and warm in Paltyrrha. For weeks the mages had labored to produce the mild temperatures and cloudless skies that greeted the multitudes that morning. This was the first such girding in some four decades, and the crowds looked forward to it with great anticipation.

The King-to-Be was roused an hour before dawn, and escorted to the traditional milk bath to purify his body and soul for the events to come. No food or drink had passed his lips since the previous day.

Four of his family and friends had been chosen to shield him in all his innocence, unprotected as he was from outside influences. These included the Princes Kiríll and Andruin, Metropolitan Athanasios, and Mailhoc Hereditary Lord Vydór, eldest son of the grand vizier. It was their privilege to become the King-to-Be's moving guard.

Athanasios donned the red tunic studded with *rubraura* that signified his role as Hagios Kônstantinos, who takes precedence over his three brethren in the *killijálay* as patron saint of the House of Tighris. They took their stations surrounding King Arkadios—Kiríll in *flavaurum*-touched gold as Holy Petros in the front, Andruin in *viridaurum*-flavored green as Holy Andreas in the rear, Mailhoc in *albaurum*-sprinkled white as Holy Ignatios to the left, and the metropolitan to the right—and began synchronizing their *psai*-rings.

This technique required a great deal of training to master, and was generally practiced only by those adepts of a certain age of life, from the years of fifteen to forty-five. Before that time one's control was insufficient to maintain a link for long, but the process used up so much energy if sustained for any length of time that only the relatively young had the stamina to continue the protection beyond a short period.

"*Prôtos*," Athanasios said, setting his controls in place.

"*Deuteros*," replied Kiríll, linking his psychic energy with the first.

"*Tritos*," added Andruin.

"*Tetartos*," said Mailhoc.

Now came the difficult part. The King-to-Be, as the one being protected, had to center the magical hood over himself: "*Hê-nô-me-nos*," he breathed, a syllable at a time, as he gathered together the four strands of their souls one by one and wove them into a single unit. A faint, milky-white shadow suddenly popped into the air above them.

The King-to-Be's servants now covered his frame in a simple, lightly-woven white linen tunic and *shalvar*, overlaid by a white woolen *zuban* coat, its only decoration an embroidered Tighrishi tiger etched in ochre. A black silk sash was wrapped tightly about his waist, the fringed ends hanging free to the left. Finally, they brought in the pure white leather *stivalia* and harness and fitted them to the monarch with silver clasps. A comb was run quickly through his unruly hair. He looked at each of them somberly and nodded. They were ready.

They proceeded very deliberately through the corridors of Tighrishály Palace, moving at a steady, even pace so they would not lose contact with each other. Although they could in theory have maintained the link for a distance of about ten paces apart, the closer they were to each other and the more regular the spacing maintained, the easier it was for each to keep focused on his task. They had all practised this very delicate balancing act for many weeks.

At the entrance awaited the great carriage of state, all gilded in gold and *lapis lazuli* and drawn by four matched pairs of white Ras ash-Shamra stallions, with postilions astride the near four. The steeds snorted and stamped their feet, tossing foam with each swing of their heads in anticipation of their activity.

As was his privilege, Athanasios preceded the King-to-Be into the carriage and out the other door, there to perch precariously on the step. Mailhoc took a like position on the left, Kiríll mounted the driver's box, and Andruin the rear of the carriage.

And then they were *off!*, moving down the *Avenue du Saint-Constantine* to Paltyrrha-by-the-River, where the barge was waiting.

The superbly fitted white *caïque* was decorated in ochre and black encrusted with gold, topped by a raised canopy of scarlet velvet embroidered with Tighrishi tigers, and fringed with golden tassels positioned to act as their swinging tails. Great Arkadios took his seat upon the golden throne, sitting straight and stolid and silent; below and beside him his shadows flanked the King-to-Be on all four quarters.

As they moved upriver one could hear the "swish-swish" of the twenty-eight massive oars as they pulled through the brown waters of the River Paltyrrh, the beat of the master's drum providing an almost hypnotic accompaniment to the barge's sensuous glide. Following them in procession were other craft containing the Hereditary Prince-to-Be, Queen Dúra, Princess Arrhiána, Princess Sachette, Queen Ezzölla of Pommerelia, the lesser adjuncts of the House of Tighris, and all of the high lords of state and their retinues.

The air was scented with perfumes from the flowers especially grown for the occasion. As they passed near the *Quai de Saint-Basile*, the Royal Guard stood rigidly at attention, bared *kiliçs* held smartly in their right hands in salute to their liege and master. The huzzahs of the sailors lining the decks of the multitude of small boats and barges moored on both sides of the Paltyrrh River resounded again and again over the water, echoing off the walls and buildings on either side.

Some five miles upriver the procession of boats docked at the *Quai de l'Amirauté*, where the *Padishah* Arkády alighted with his escort and was welcomed by a band of trumpeters, their bronze instruments flashing in the light of the morning sun as they blew a glorious fanfare of exaltation.

There awaited the king's favorite steed, a black stallion called *Daïs*, or Firebrand, which had to be restrained by its handlers from rearing and plunging until the calming sphere of the Moving Guard enveloped it. The bridle seemed woven of liquid silver, and heavy silver medallions adorned nearly every surface of the high-cantled saddle, gleaming in the sunlight against the perfection of a beautifully woven, red woolen blanket of intricate design. The destrier quieted immediately as its master mounted.

Then the King-to-Be proceeded up the cobbled *Avenue des Rois*, still flanked on all sides by the Moving Guard, and closely accompanied by a squad of armed Circássi soldiers. Tens of thousands of well-wishers lined the way, many of them waving ochre-and-black pennants that had been distributed to them earlier in the day.

At the Church of Hagios Ióv, the Chief of the Hankyár Derviches, Frigyes Lord Zsitvay, kissed the monarch on his left shoulder, and the Thrice Holy Patriarch Timotheos welcomed the procession into the holy see of the Tighrishi. The celebrants left their shoes at the entrance and slipped on cloth sandals, walking the prescribed twelve paces forward in company with the Hankyárar of Konyály, whose privilege it was from time immemorial to gird the sword of Tighris on each new king. Grand Vizier Attila Lord Vydór greeted the king with a salute, and in the name of the lords and people of Kórynthia bowed low to kiss the hem of the king's *zuban*.

In the center of the church, directly beneath the great dome, lay a black marble tomb covered with mosaics of onyx and a thin layer of fretted silver as delicate as the lace of a woman's gown, which contained the relick'd bones of Great Tighris, founder of the royal house which yet bore his name.

For the purposes of *killijálay*, the investment ceremony, the patriarch and the twelve metropolitans of the Holy Synod had placed a ceremonial table of finely-polished walnut draped with a cloth of purple velvet at the head of the tomb. The sounding of a single clear note from Job's Complaint signaled that the hour of *hektê*, or *sext* in the Roman tongue, had arrived and the girding should now commence.

Six great Albány guards slowly entered the Church bearing the sword of Tighris on its solid silver salver. Fashioned of a bronze-gold alloy, the scimitar was as long as a man is tall, curved at the end and weighing some fifteen stone, sheathed in black metal encrusted with rubies, emeralds, sapphires, opals, and *lapis lazuli*. The hilt was cunningly wrought into an intricate twirl of metal; when passed in front of a light, it created a shadowy *tughra* spelling out the name Tighris.

The Albánys carefully lowered the sword onto the table in front of the tomb, pointing towards the altar, then gently removed the sheath without touching the blade, and exited the church. The Patriarch assumed a position between the table and the tomb, at the point of the sword, while the King-to-Be, the Hankyárar, and the grand vizier stood at the hilt. The four Pillars of the Realm, which is to say, the Moving Guard, glided to each of the four quarters—Athanasios to the right of Great Tighris's tomb, Mailhoc directly opposite in the North, Andruin behind the *Padishah*, and Kiríll at the far end of the tomb.

The Thrice Holy Timotheos chanted: "Glory be to Thee, God the Father, glory be to Thee, Eternal Son, glory be to Thee, Holy Spirit, by whom all is sanctified. World without end."

The congregation responded: "Amen."

Incense began swirling above the congregation in patches of strongly scented fog, making patterns knowable only to God.

Then the patriarch spoke again, lifting his hands toward the air above their heads: "I call upon thee, Holy Konstantín, to stand rightly with us in joy and gladness at this *killijálay*, to sanctify thy servant, Arkadios."

A wind began to whine through the church, lifting the hair of the men and the coverings of the women and stirring the solemn robes of the monks. A glow began forming in front of their eyes. Athanasios's arms lifted involuntarily behind him and stretched into something else, light and feathery and almost weightless. His legs grew, his body lengthened, his face changed in ways that cannot be described. He saw and did not see, he felt and did not feel, he heard sounds that were not sounds, he breathed the air of another plane that had no air, he *knew* suddenly whom he had become. Through eyes that were not his own he watched his brethren, the Saints Pëtr, Andréy, and Ignáty, take form, standing there ten feet tall, as silent and strong as the Pillars of the Church they represented.

And then Timotheos spoke again:

"Lord and Master, Our God, who has established in Heaven the orders and armies of angels and archangels to minister to Thy Glory, grant that with us there may enter those holy intercessors who serve and glorify Thy goodness. Shelter us under the shadow of their wings, drive away every foe and adversary."

Then he carefully pressed the tip of the sword with his right index finger, drawing a drop of blood.

"'And the star came and stood above where the child was'," he continued. "Make beautiful, O Lord, this instrument of Thy will. Thy glory has covered the heavens, and the earth is full of Thy praises. Strengthen now Thy servant Arkadios, clothe him with beauty, remember him with Thy blessings. For when Thy servant Tighris did walk upon this earth, he promised to nurture his sons forever. Send down Thy Holy Spirit to watch over us. Give us a sacrifice of Thy praise and bless Thine inheritance."

Then the patriarch reached behind him with his right hand and touched the monument with his blood.

"Holy Deathless One, come thou forth from thy tomb!" he shouted.

The crowd gasped, for at that moment the tomb of Tighris rattled, and the lid slid back from the coffin. A shadowy, translucent figure garbed in strange robes and ancient armor slowly rose upright.

And it seemed to King Arkády that the form of his ancestor then turned to him, and asked: "Why have you come here? Your father still resides amongst the living."

"Because he broke covenant with the land," the king replied.

"So he did," Tighris stated. "But yet he abides."

"He would have destroyed Kórynthia," Arkády noted. "I could not allow that to happen."

"And what would you do that is so different, oh King-to-Be?" his ancestor inquired.

"I will build in this land a place of prosperity for all who wish to come here," the king declared. "I will preserve the peace, and oppress neither the few nor the many."

"These are worthy aims," Tighris continued, "but what will this accomplish that has not been done before? The king who follows you and the king who follows him may not be cut from the same piece of string. There is a dark stain in our line that cannot be eradicated, for it is the other side of the transit mirror in which you see yourself reflected. The great talents which I have given unto you and yours also carry with them equal potential for use or abuse. Certain of my children have been warped into something abominable and hideous in the sight of God and man. Those who cannot master themselves will ever use their powers for evil. So tell me, oh son of Tighris, what you will do to preserve the land forever."

Arkády was taken aback, for this was not the ceremony he had been expecting. But he thought very hard about the problem, before finally admitting, "I do not know. But I will try to find a way."

"That is, at least, an honest reply," Tighris said.

There was a hint of gentle laughter in his voice.

"Very well, my son," he continued, reaching out with his arm to touch the new king upon his head, "you'll do."

Now, all of this happened in the merest instant of thought, while time itself ceased to exist, so that no one watching the proceedings saw anything untoward, or was even able to blink a single eyelid.

And then the spirit merged itself with the form of the patriarch, who intoned:

"The grace of God, that always strengthens the weak and fills the empty, does here appoint Arkadios ho Tigridês to be your lawfully girded king. Let no man challenge the will of God. Let no man doubt the choice of Tighris. Prepare thou the girdle."

The Hankyárar brought forth an empty scabbard and belted it around the King-to-Be's waist, whispering in his ear, as was the custom: "Remember, lord, that thou art mortal."

Then the form of Tighris touched the great scimitar and a ripple of silver light flowed from his finger into the weapon. "If thou hast the power," he said, "Then pick up thy sword!"

In one smooth motion Arkády grasped the scimitar in both hands and pointed it straight up at the dome above. A beam of purplish light sprang from the tip of the weapon, penetrating through the roof into the sky where the crowds outside could see the proof of his empowerment, the beam slowly changing colors through the entire spectrum. Within the church it seemed as if the stain spread from where it touched the inside of the onion-shaped dome slowly down around its skin, eventually coating the interior walls with a fine shimmering glow; and outside it was the sky itself that seemed to take on a range of pastel colors, very like the shimmering of the Great Northern Lights.

"Axios!" shouted the grand vizier, "he is worthy!"

Three times the words echoed through the church and the crowds outside.

"Axios!" the princes and lords roared in a grand huzzah of acclamation.

"Axios!" the metropolitans all concurred.

The light slowly died, and the huge stone lid on the tomb of Great Tighris gradually closed itself. Then Holy Timotheos said:

"We do beseech thee, Lord, with humble mien to spare our Great King Arkadios, Second of that name, for three times thirty years, that with a clean and understanding heart he may rightly speak the word of faith as Guardian of the Realm. Preserve him in health, O Lord, in honor and in length of days, faithfully dispensing Thy word of truth. Fill him with the Holy Spirit and the grace and wisdom that he needs to govern the realm."

The King Arkády responded: "I will offer to Thee incense and rams. All my garments smell of myrrh, aloes, and cassia. Let my prayer be as incense in Thy sight."

Then he carefully laid the Great Sword of Tighris back on its table.

The Hereditary Prince Arión approached with the smaller Sword of State, sinking to his knees and handing it to his father with these words: "My lord king, accept this gift beyond price, given to us until the end of time."

The king sheathed the sword, replying: "Peace be unto thee, my son, peace be to all the lords of the land and to all the children of the church. I do anoint thee my lawful successor. Lord, make him this day a sharer in Thy mystic supper. For I will not reveal Thy mysteries to Thine enemies, nor like Judas give

Thee a kiss, but like the thief I say to Thee: Remember me, O Lord, in Thy kingdom. Remember me."

Finally, the grand vizier brought the Crown of State on its cushion of velvet, handing it to the Thrice Holy Patriarch Timotheos. The king bowed his head before the living symbol of God on earth, and received his temporal crown, the ancient diadem of plain hammered gold that has adorned the brows of Tighrishi kings since time immemorial.

Then a choir of monks sang their song of rejoicing, and the newly-consecrated King and his entourage exited the rear of the Church, continuing up the *Boulevard des Tombeaux Tighrises* to pay homage to the monuments of their ancestors.

The Great King Arkadios II had finally come home.

CHAPTER FIFTY-EIGHT
"WE'RE ALL PAWNS, MY DEAR"

That evening, a sumptuous banquet of celebration was held in the Great Hall in Tighrishály Palace in Paltyrrha.

On the east wall of the hall was ranged a longtable filled with some of the surviving members of the royal family. At the center sat the new king, Arkády, flanked on the right by his eldest son and heir, Hereditary Prince Arión, and by his wife, Queen Dúra, on the left. Other spots at the table were occupied by Princess Rÿna, Prince Siegfried, Princess Numméla, their governess, Lady Márissa, Princess Arrhiána, Zakháry Duke of Mährenia, Prince Kiríll, Prince Andruin, and Princess Sachette. The Dowager Queen Polyxena had chosen to remain in Kórynthály to care for her husband. The younger two children were returned to their nursery following the opening remarks.

Across the hall was set another longtable, which wrapt itself around to the Pommerelian side, and was filled with the chief nobility of Kórynthia, including Valentín Count of Arrhéné and his uncle, Sándor Count of Yevpatóriya, Rufín Count of Susafön, Zhéleva Countess of Görgoszák, Maurin Count Kosnick, Attila Lord Vydór and his son, Lord Mailhoc Vydór, Ladislav Count of Zándrich, Paul-Bernhardt Graf von Luristán, Bonica Countess of Myrrhás, Zygmunt Count of Myláß, Issakhar Count of Westmark, Mála Baroness Teuschpach, General Rónai Lord of Borgösha, General Reményi Lord of Karkára, and their consorts, among many others.

A third, much shorter table was placed along the left

side of the hall, and included the pretender of Pommerelia, Queen Ezzölla, together with her escort, Swithven Count of Langendoss. Also at her table were seated her *cousine* and heir presumptive, the Princess Ariélle, together with her consort, Albián Graf von Spírrë, and their two surviving sons, the fifteen-year-old Hereditary Graf Balthazár and Lord Deménty. Riél, as she was called in the family, also descended from the late Prince Dominík, third son of Gérman IV von Forellë, late King of Vorpommern, in the days of yore when that country had still been independent of Pommeralia. King Gérman's wife had been Króya Princess of Kórynthia. Another member of the family, Mordán Count of Leigrés, was also seated at the Forellë table.

Completing the square on the south was a fourth long-table, where the lords spiritual sat, including the Thrice Holy Timotheos, Patriarch of Paltyrrha and All Kórynthia, together with all twelve of the Metropolitans and Archbishops comprising the Holy Synod.

A throng of servers, retainers, and guards hovered behind the tables, awaiting a word from their patrons and masters. Banners flaunting the arms of state and church covered the walls. Scattered around the tiled floor on the alternating black-and-white squares were performers, pantomimists, troubadours, and theatricians. Every so often they would exchange places to vary the entertainment from table to table. In one corner was ensconced a group of players, their instruments producing a series of light airs designed to soothe the savage beasts.

"My lords and ladies," shouted King Arkády, "a toast!"

He raised high his chalice.

"Vive la Córynthe!" he proclaimed.

"Vive la Córynthe!" was the response.

Then Duke Zakháry rose in his seat.

"Vive le roi Arcádie!" he boomed.

"Vive le roi Arcádie!" they all agreed.

"Vive le duc du Moravie!" Prince Kiríll yelled.

"Vive le duc du Moravie!" came the reply.

And the congratulations and toasts continued for at least another hour, until everyone was properly cheery.

Then King Arkády motioned again for silence.

"I have the great pleasure to announce," he intoned, "the betrothal of the Hereditary Count Balthazár Albiánovich, second in line to the Throne of Pommerelia, to my eldest daughter, the Princess Royal Grigorÿna Arkádiyevna."

There were cheers of approval on all sides, particularly from the much diminished table of the Forellës, for the marriage of state signalled to them the continuing support of Kórynthia for their ongoing cause.

"Furthermore," the king smiled, "It is my great honor to announce a second betrothal tonight, this time of my younger brother Prince Kiríll, Count of Arkádiya, to Mála Baroness Teuschpach."

This was clearly a love match, and the ladies of the court were not lax in showing their pleasure at the proclamation.

"Axioi!" they shouted, "they are worthy!"

"Let the couples come forward and be blessed by the patriarch," the king continued.

Prince Kiríll and his love and Lord Balthazar and his intended came to center floor, the players withdrawing to the corners, and Patriarch Timotheos joining them a moment later.

The cleric intoned, "A man shall leave his father and mother and shall cleave unto his wife, and they shall be one flesh. He who finds a virtuous wife finds a good thing, sayeth the Lord. Her price is far above rubies. The heart of her husband does safely trust in her. Her husband is known in the gates, when he sits among the elders of the land. Strength and honor are her clothing. In her tongue is the law of kindness. She looks well to the ways of her household, and eats not the bread of idleness. Her children rise up and call her blessed. Favor is deceitful and beauty is vain, but a woman who fears the Lord, she shall be praised. Give her the fruits of her hands, and let her own works praise her in the gates.

"Therefore," he continued, "do I sanctify the promises that

are fearfully and wonderfully made here tonight. O Lord, seal these oaths upon the true hearts of Thy children. Make their love as strong as death itself. Let every day that they live give praise to Him that created us. Let the two lands rejoice in festivity. Amen."

The couples returned to their places, and Timotheos rejoined his old friend Afanásy, sitting just to his left.

Then the king spoke again.

"These are but the first of many such ceremonies that you will see this year," he indicated. "I have asked the patriarch to preside over the joining of five hundred couples in the Cathedral of Saint Konstantín on the first day of June hence. The Conference of Reconciliation was but the initial step towards the reunification of the land. We must all strive to help each other, to build new bridges to those around us. One of these structures will be known as Saint Vasíly's Bridge, and it will mark the first time that Old Paltyrrha and New Paltyrrha will be permanently joined together. It is these connections, between man and wife, between old city and new, between the land and its people, that will help remake our kingdom into an earthly paradise once again.

"Vive la Córynthe!" he added, and huzzahs rang unto the very rafters of the building.

The king sat down and turned to his eldest son, Hereditary Prince Arión.

"How are you feeling, my son?" he asked, putting a comforting hand on the lad's thin shoulder.

"I'm all right, Papá," Ari assured him, "just a little sleepy."

He stifled a yawn. The day had been a long one for the six-year-old.

Arkády felt a slight tug at his sleeve, and looked down into the upturned face of his eldest daughter, the Princess Royal Grigorÿna. She was clad in a sheer silk shift of palest green, which emphasized her reddish-gold hair and fair coloring.

"Oh, Papá!" she whispered, her bright blue eyes shining like twin sapphire crystals in the reflected lights. "It's just like a fairy tale!" she said.

The king looked over the top of his daughter's titian curls, and caught Dúra's eye. His wife smiled back at him. Their little girl was now betrothed.

Rÿna squeezed her father's hand again, and gazed out at all the beautifully dressed and coiffed lords and ladies. She decided right then and there that in the future, she would seat her most noble doll family at longtables placed in a square, rather than in one or two rows facing each other, as she had done in the past.

Yes! she reflected, *that would be much more useful.*

Down the longtable to King Arkády's right, the Princess Arrhiána was talking to her younger sister, the Princess Sachette.

"Have you made any decisions yet?" she asked.

"Yes, Rhie," the younger woman said, "I've decided to go back to the convent later this month, but not to linger idly in my cell all day. I want to work with the crippled soldiers of Killingford, particularly the blind. Many of the survivors of the war were severely burned, and those who returned badly need our assistance. I've had to fight some of the same dæmons which now plague these men, so maybe I can do them a little good."

"I know you can," Arrhiána agreed, "and if there's anything that I or the palace can do to help, please tell me. To start, we can send you wagonloads of medicines and bandages, as well as additional physicians."

"Most of these men just need someone to listen to them," Sachette noted. "If I can do that much, then I'll have contributed something of value to the world."

Arrhiána glanced to her right as a burst of raucous laughter came from the Forelli table on the north side of the hall.

The newly-minted Queen of Pommerelia, Ezzölla I (long may she reign!), was having a gay time with her current beau, Swithven Count of Langendoss, an effete gentleman of some forty years of age.

The ancient House of Langendoss had fallen on somewhat reduced circumstances of late, due to the proclivity of its title-holders to wager their fortunes annually on the running of the horses at the Nördmark Summer Fair. Alas, their judgment of horseflesh was as limited as their sense of business, and so the current count found himself suddenly without the means to present himself most appropriately to the world at large. Fortunately, what Swithven lacked in acumen was more than offset by his charm and good looks, and his casual *savoir-faire* and saturnine appearance captivated all of the ladies whose presence he chose to grace. Now he was sniffing after bigger game, and responded with a barking laugh at some would-be witticism from his unsuspecting bride-to-be.

He slyly glanced to his left, smiling and raising one perfectly trimmed eyebrow at one of the ladies at the next table, where some prime horseflesh of a very different nature was presently on display. He had noticed the king's sister, Princess Arrhiána, earlier in the evening, beautifully dressed in a scooped-out gown of pale blue satin that displayed to great advantage several of her prime assets.

Ah, he thought to himself, *if only....*

Further down the king's table, Lady Mála nudged her *fiancé*, Prince Kiríll, and nodded towards the Forellës. The prince spotted Langendoss's leer, smiled to himself, and then pulled out a long, curved dirk, with which he pointedly began cleaning his fingernails. He caught the light from a nearby chandelier on his knife, and flashed it across Swithven's perfect eyes. The count looked over quickly, then started when he caught the prince's hard glance, and lowered his eyes back to his plate. *King's private preserve*, he thought to himself, and laughed again at one of Ezzölla's jokes.

Across the room, Lord Maurin was poked awake by his wife, Lady Nolána.

"Did you see that?" she asked, "why, that old reprobate, Langendoss."

"What?" Maurin said.

He had obviously missed whatever little drama she was referring to. He yawned again. Normally, he had no problem downing tankard after tankard of cheap soldiers' ale, but all these toasts and all this fancy wine had just been too much for him.

"Well, have we had enough of playing courtier yet?" she added.

"All this folderol," he exclaimed, shaking his head. "Gad, I get tired of these games. I sometimes feel like we're just so many pieces on a checkered board, being moved 'round and 'round by all of these 'great men.'"

She laughed. "We're all pawns, my dear," she noted. "But *you're* not supposed to become aware of the fact."

"Well, it's too much for me!" Maurin stated. "I want to go home again, where I know who I am and how things stand, and where I can play the game on my own terms, without all of this 'high drama.' I need to understand the rules if I'm to have an advantage."

"Oh," Nolána replied, "I thought you already did have an advantage."

She smiled up at him sweetly, and bumped his muscled thigh with her warm, soft one.

He grinned back at her. "Seems that I do!" he acknowledged. "But what good's an advantage if you never get a chance to exercise it?"

"I see, good sir," she said, "so it's exercise you want now, is it? Well, I think we may be able to accommodate that request, too, a little later in the evening."

"I hope it isn't too much later," he retorted. "I'm apt to fall asleep on you."

"I don't think so," she mused, smiling again. "I think we can take care of that little problem just fine."

"Before we go, Lána, I'd like to say goodbye to Father Athy," Maurin stated. He pointed to the table housing the lords spiritual. "I can see him just over there, to the right of the patriarch."

She sat bolt upright, and laughed out loud.

"Oh, you mean 'The Hieromonk and the Donkey,'" she said. "That tale just gets funnier every time you tell it."

"Please don't repeat that to Father Athy, oh please," Maurin pleaded, his face abruptly turning red. "If he ever found out that it was me, I'd die of the humiliation. The troubadours have even made it into a ballad, I hear."

"Really?" Nolána squealed. "Oh, you must have them play it for us sometime."

But Patriarch Timotheos, who had been watching the repartee at a distance, spoke softly to the metropolitan sitting on his right.

"Athy," he said, "who's that pretty woman over there next to Count Kosnick? I can't quite make her out."

Metropolitan Athanasios squinted at the distant longtable. Ironically, as he sprang into middle age, he was finding his longer sight becoming much clearer, even as he experienced more difficulty in reading simple scrolls up close.

"That's Lady Nolána," he noted, "the new countess. I've only met her once. She seems like a very fine lady, full of life and laughter."

"You must introduce me later," the primate indicated.

He rubbed his eyes, trying once again to peer across the room, and Athanasios suddenly realized for the first time that his friend and mentor had grown old, just in this last year.

Is this what the burden of office will do? he asked himself. *Is this what I will become?*

He had a vision then of a long line of mitred men standing in rank, perhaps a hundred or two hundred in all, fading away into the distance on both sides of their table, and he realized that he was seeing the past and future patriarchs of Paltyrrha, from the very beginnings of the Holy Church in Kórynthia into some unforseeably dim future.

"What is it, Athy?" his mentor asked.

"Nothing, Arik," he replied, smiling at his father. "Nothing at all."

The hieromonk marveled at the resonances between this scene and the one held here exactly a year ago to the day. But where that banquet had marked the beginning of a twisted venture into warmongering and the useless deaths of tens of thousands, this new one promised a renewal of life and faith itself.

Perhaps, after all, there was much to look forward to in this new year. Perhaps all of the death and destruction and despair that he had witnessed this past twelvemonth was for some good purpose, even if that purpose was known or knowable only to God. He would trust in that future and in that God, because to do anything else would be to give in to the despair that had claimed his mother and old King Kipriyán.

There were many different roads to choose in life, and many different possibilities. Here, in this room, he could see around him the joy and tragedy, the comedy and triumph, that filled man's very existence. Here were stories of passion and betrayal, of faith and hope, of every good and ill thing that humanity could possibly devise. This was his play, and these were the players. Not pawns to be moved on a board, but real men and real women, to cherish and love and break bread with. Life was very good.

His attention was diverted by a singer who stepped to center floor, and began a quiet, unaccompanied piece that soon had captivated everyone. No one knew who she was or where she hailed from, except that her name was Lady Milyutÿnis, and that her hair was black and long and swayed in time with the music.

And this is what she sang in a voice that surpassed all sweetness:

> One generation passes away,
> And another takes its place,
> One great king gives up his sway,
> And another joins the race.
>
> Oh where has my Ambrózy gone?
>
> A primate goes to his reward,
> And another takes his place,

A dark-souled mage defies the Lord,
And vanishes without a trace.

Oh where has my Ambrózy gone?

The kings, they say to war we go,
And tell each man to grab a sword,
My love runs off to beat the foe,
And perishes at Killingford.

Oh where has my Ambrózy gone?

Oh why must we repeat our chord,
And bless each man who dies?
But I remember Killingford,
Where dear Ambrózy lies.

Oh where has my Ambrózy gone?

One generation passes away,
And another takes its place,
One bright sun has set this day,
And never shall I see his face.

Oh where has my Ambrózy gone?

One great soul has passed beyond
The shining shore of never,
Oh where has my Ambrózy gone?
The earth abides forever.

CHAPTER FIFTY-NINE
"I HAVE COME FOR YOU AT LAST"

To everything there is a season,
And a time to every purpose under Heaven.
—*Ecclesiastes*

Anno Domini 1219
Anno Juliani 859

On the Feast of Saint Sylbestros in the xivth year of Arkadios II King of Kórynthia, a mounted monk swathed in muddy green robes and a brown greatcloak paused before the massive gate of Saint Svyatosláv's Monastery in Zándrich. With the sigh of a man who has reached his ultimate destination, he leaned over his saddle and banged his iron-tipped staff on the bronze doors. His breath steamed out from under his hood, billowing up in white clouds under the pale golden moonlight.

A small hatch in the adjoining wall popped open and a rough voice yelled down: "Who seeks entrance to Holy Svyatosláv?"

"Brother Kyprianos von Thánátü," he replied. "Hieromonk of Most Holy Epiphanios, who seeks present audience with the worthy Archimandrite Ludwík t'Örvös."

"Holy Svyatosláv embraces you," the voice replied, "and the monk Zôsima welcomes you to our simple home. Enter this place of God in well-deserved peace."

Then the visitor was led through the gate, and taken to an

anteroom off the abbot's quarters, where Abbot Ludwík joined him a half hour later.

"Welcome, Brother Kyprianos," the cleric stated. "How may I help you?"

The visitor pulled a paper from the arm of his robe, and handed it to the abbot.

"This pass gives me the authority to see the hieromonk Pantaleôn, who is under your care," the man said. "You will note that it bears the seal and signature of the Thrice Holy Patriarch."

"This is highly unusual," Ludwík commented. "The hieromonk has had no visitors since arriving here, and I was ordered to allow none but our own brethren access to him."

"Who gave you that order?" Kyprianos asked.

"The patriarch," the abbot admitted. He examined the document thoroughly once again. "This does appear to be in order," he stated. "I will make the appropriate arrangements for you to meet with Brother Pantaleôn on the morrow."

"With all respect, archimandrite," the visitor stated, "I wish to see him *now*."

"But it's evening!" Ludwík exclaimed, aghast at the notion. "Our brethren are saying their prayers, even as we speak. Ours is a working community, Brother Kyprianos. We retire early and rise early. It's out of the question."

"Again, with due respect, Abbot Ludwík," the monk insisted, "this document gives me that right. Or did you fail to note the words, 'Brother Kyprianos speaks and acts with our authority,' just above the patriarch's signature. I *will* meet with Brother Pantaleôn within the hour, and privily, if you please, right here in your antechamber. Also, neither you nor your fellow monks will disturb us. Is that clear?"

"Perfectly!" the prelate spat, disgusted at this raw display of power. He sent Brother Hovhannês to fetch old Pantaleôn, and then withdrew.

A few moments later the elderly hieromonk was deposited at the entrance to the antechamber, and Hovhannês slammed the door shut just behind him with a pointed "bang."

"Wh-who are you?" came the tremulous voice of the blind man. He felt with his hands in front of him, trying to penetrate the emptiness of the air.

"Let me help you," Kyprianos responded, taking the outstretched arms, and leading Pantaleôn to the abbot's very own padded chair near the fire.

"Ohhhh, it's so warm in here," the hieromonk breathed. "This is heavenly." He leaned toward the fire, allowing the glow to warm his thin limbs.

"I'm told, brother, that you enjoy an occasional game of *les échecs*," the visitor indicated.

"Yes, yes, I have played a game or two in my time," Pantaleôn noted, "but no one here ever wants to sit down with me. They all have something else more important to do, all but me. And on the rare occasion when someone *will* play with an old man, well, they lose, and then they don't want ever to do it again."

"I'll play with you," Thánátü offered. "Perhaps I can challenge your sensibilities more fully."

"Would you?" the hieromonk replied. "Oh, that would be glorious. Why, I'll even offer you white."

"That is most generous of you," the visitor said. "I accept."

There was a board and pieces already set up on a nearby table, and the traveler simply moved the entire configuration so that it was setting between the two men.

"Are you ready?" Thánátü asked.

Pantaleôn felt with his hands to establish the positions of the two lines of eight pieces marking the black players, and then extended his senses across the board.

"Yesss," he hissed, "this will be no problem at all!" The old monk smiled to himself.

Kyprianos moved his white pawn to king's pawn four, and Pantaleôn reached out to play the opposing move. But when the monk touched his black counter, his hand was riveted to the board, and his eyes rolled upward into their sockets as a surge of energy swept up his arm into his body, momentarily driving out his consciousness. When he could see again, he had been transited somewhere else.

He was standing on a flat plain hatched with strange cross-marks. Surrounding him on either side were his comrades-in-arms, all dressed alike and ranged in two lines. His body was covered in black armor and his left hand gripped an upright sword. On the opposite side of the field he could see another group of warriors clothed from head to toe in white armor, also in two lines. Two of the soldiers, one of each color, had already faced off in the center of the plain.

Pantaleôn instinctively tensed, looking right and left for any danger to his king, then almost fled the field when he saw the long black hair writhing and moving as it hung behind his monarch's helmet. The king's head turned down and looked right at him, and Pantaleôn noticed that there were two red glowing spots where the eyes should have been.

"What's the matter, little king?" the monarch hissed, a forked tongue flickering out from the opening in his armor, "S-snake got your tongue?"

And then the hieromonk would have run, run as fast as his legs could carry him, run anywhere but this awful place of death, except that he couldn't. He was nailed to his square, unable to leave it, because it wasn't his move. He was still looking at his terrible monarch when he noticed a movement out of the corner of his eye. A white metropolitan had moved in front of the white pawns onto the field opposite him.

"Your turn, little king," the black monarch said.

Pantaleôn found himself moving diagonally to the dexter side of the board, attacking the piece. He could only move when it was his turn, and then only in ways prescribed by the rules; other-wise, he was stuck within the confines of his square. Men began to fall as the game progressed, but here, instead of cleanly being removed from the board, they were struck down by the awful weapons of war, with limbs and heads being hacked off and blood spurting everywhere, and men and horses groaning their death rattles and crying piteously for help which never came.

But still the game remorselessly moved toward its completion, as the number of players steadily diminished through deliberate murder and assassination.

A white pawn moved within his range, and suddenly Pantaleôn lunged at it, wielding his sword with deadly accuracy, striking him down mercilessly. He stood there gloating while the soldier bled all over the square, crying out: "My brother, my brother, why hast thou forsaken me?"

He would have continued his attack, but there was nothing he could do: he could not cross the boundaries surrounding him on all sides. He was doomed to repeat what he now knew was an old, old game.

Despite the monk's best efforts, the black king was soon besieged within a protecting ring of his few remaining warriors. Pantaleôn could hear the dark monarch raging as the noose drew ever tighter around them: "I defy you, I defy you all!"

But as the white king passed nearby, suddenly Pantaleôn swiveled with all of his strength, trying somehow to strike through the right wall of his square, but he could not move from his ever-fixed place. The face of the black monarch turned toward him, hissing, "S-strike the traitor down." The remaining black warriors began closing in on all sides, and the monk knew he was doomed.

"Why?" Pantaleôn cried out with all of his remaining strength. "Who *are* you?"

Then the black king swept back his hood, finally revealing his hideous aspect.

"I am the Dark-Haired Man, o Kipriyán the Conqueror," he said. "I have come for you at last."

CHAPTER SIXTY
"SHAH MAT!"

The hour of departure has arrived
And we go our ways,
I to die and you to live.
Which is better, God only knows.
                    —*Apology*, Plato, quoting Socrates

Anno Domini 1220
Anno Juliani 860

On the next morning, the Feast of the Blessèd Virgin Mary, the Abbot Ludwík finally found the strength to enter the antechamber, and there he beheld a most terrible sight. The monk Pantaleôn sat straight upright in his chair, a look of terror etched on his face, his right hand rigidly grasping the black king on the game board. The monarch was tilted to one side, as if about to fall over.

"Shah mat'!" Ludwík exclaimed, and then called for Brother Hovhannês and Brother Thaddaios to help. The body was icy cold. This man had been dead for a long, long time.

The abbot had the body secured and washed and taken to the Chapel of Saint Miráks, where a requiem mass would be said for the repose of the monk Pantaleôn on the very next day, with burial, as per the written instructions that Ludwík had previously received about this inmate, in an unmarked grave among the deceased brethren of the Silent Souls.

He also ordered a search to be made of the monastery compound and grounds, and the brothers dutifully spent the rest of New Year's Day combing every room, nook, and hiding place in the abbey. The stranger's clothes were found folded neatly in the cell assigned to him, and his horse was still tethered in the stable. But of the mysterious hieromonk surnamed Kyprianos von Thánátü, there was no sign.

It was a great wonder in Zándrich, which is still talked about to this day.

EPILOGUE
"THANK GOD *THAT'S* OVER"

Anno Domini 1242
Anno Juliani 882

"Thank God *that's* over," Queen Grigorÿna muttered under her breath, taking care not to wake the other occupant of her bed. She could hear the rough snoring of Hastur Duke (*ad personam*) of Paltyrrha and Royal Consort. It reminded her of a pachyderm's lament that she'd first heard at the Zoölogeion in Alexandria—and probably had as much meaning to it!

She carefully eased her way out from under the plush coverings, and walked naked to the open window. The slight breeze of a late summer evening helped scour the pores on her skin, and carry away some of the sooty detritus of—she shuddered at the thought—their love-making. She whispered a spell of renewal, and slowly began to regain her *équilibre*. She breathed in and out very heavily for a half dozen—a dozen—cycles, and gradually her energy and composure returned. In just a few moments she appeared to shed ten years of age.

The marriage itself had been the highlight of the social season—well, truth be told, of a *decade* of social seasons in the Kingdom of Kórynthia—with the actual revelries being spread over three weeks of nonstop feasts and fêtes and folderol, culminating in the afternoon's slow-motion ceremonial at Saint Konstantín's Cathedral, presided over by the Patriarch himself. Everyone, including her new husband, seemed to be very happy with the setting, with the bonding, and with the outcome.

But that was nothing, nothing at all, compared to the humiliation of her semi-public deflowering this evening by her new Duke Consort—the hasty Hastur. Fortunately, she'd found an herb in Mösza's old *pharmakeia* that gave a new meaning to the order, "be upstanding," and the old man had come through with his usual stern uprighteousness. Gad, never again! Of course, there was no possibility of a child, but no one else needed to know that fact. Indeed, she was counting on her courtiers, noblemen, and councilors all to anticipate constantly the imminent prospect of an heir being born to the second reigning female monarch of the Obsidian Throne. Ha!

Well, she'd already made other plans. Little Lord Ferdy, grandson of Grand Duke Zacharias, had already been designated her primary heir in her will; and, if the Great God allowed, would eventually be adopted by the Queen with a more suitable dynastic name.

She returned to her bed, and planted a suggestion in her new husband's brain that he sleep soundly till the middle of the morning, when, revived, rested, and refreshed, he would return to his quarters in the East Wing, full of self-satisfaction over his unexpected performance of the night before—and never questioning her absence.

Then she donned a white undershift and a robe of power, removed herself to her private transit alcove, and slipt betwixt the leys, pulling on one strand in particular. She vanished with a slight pop of air.

But Hastur Duke of Paltyrrha sighed, rolled over on his back, snorted a few times, and then opened his eyes and sat up in bed, smiling to himself.

The witch is gone! And while the cat was away, the mice would play.

He stretched his limbs, watching them crack as they straightened and smoothed out. He flexed his right leg backward at a right angle, something which in an ordinary person would have snapped that individual's kneecap—but then, he *was* no ordinary person. Indeed, he wasn't even Duke Hastur, that silly old goat!

He flung back the quilt that had covered his flesh, and ambled over to the Queen's *albaurum* mirror—her transit device—admiring his own nude reflection therein. He was tall and thin and albino in coloring. He grunted, and his now-full head of hair suddenly turned a deep jet black, so dark that one could almost lose one's soul in that bottomless pit of soulless tar.

"'Ware the Dark-Haired Man!" he said, making a gesture with the fingers of his right hand.

And the visage staring back at him morphed into the face of a harmless and gentle old matron, smiling benignly at the thought of the little thing that she'd accomplished.

"Were you successful, my old friend?" she asked.

"Oh, yes, dear Mösza," he said. "You're going to be a grandmother!"

AFTERWORD
"I LEAVE A FEW DOORS OPEN"

Anno Domini 2012
Anno Juliani 1652

One of the things that old authors tell young authors is never to fall in love with your own works, but to maintain enough of a distance from your own creations that you can actually edit, rewrite, and improve them. Of course, I do edit my novels and stories, and so does my dear wife and soulmate Mary, whose wise counsel has improved many of my tales.

However, I've never been overly successful myself at following that particular adage, although I do realize that certain of my fictions are better than others. So, I sometimes wind up preferring Brand X over Brand Y, for no obvious reason except that one represents what I would like to read in some *other* writer's work—or that another appeals to what I consider important in both life and letters. Or, occasionally, just because it seems to me that one has more energy than another.

My literary sins of omission and commission are many, I'm certain, but this trilogy of historical fantasies, which was called *The Dark-Haired Man* in its first, integral incarnation, remains among the favorites of my own work.

The experience of penning this narrative is one of the highlights of my life. It just seemed to write itself, with a gush of creative fervor that's never been repeated. Yes, I'm a better writer now than I was back then, and yes, I understand the art of wordmongering more than when I started; but, gentle reader, this one made such a bleat of joyous arrival that it remains an affectionate favorite of mine—and always will.

I love the setting, I love the characters, I love the magic that I created; and all of it seemed to mesh together as if another hand had fashioned it out of the æther for me. I have no idea whence it came: it just appeared, every night, over the course of two months and two days of nonstop writing—and, *mirabile dictu*, it worked.

I used pieces of my own memories and background and reading and...and, well, just everything. *And it worked!*

As with all of my creations, some readers approve of my fiction—a few very highly—and some don't—a few very stridently. Sorry, but I can't please everyone all the time, or even a few of you at any time. I write, in the end, for myself and for Mary, and if even one of you out there likes what I do, well, that's a bonus to me.

I divided the original novel of *TDHM* into this trilogy to try to make it more salable in the present market, which is heavily oriented towards ebooks and audiobooks. In the process, I've expanded the running story of Princess (later Queen) Grigorÿna as a frame for the three books, and I've had a great deal of fun doing this. I tried to sync her later character with that of the young girl who's warped at an early age by her association with powers beyond her ken, and I think I was successful at doing that.

As usual, I leave a few doors open here. Whether or not I will ever have the time or energy to walk through those several entry- and exit-ways is very uncertain. I had sequels planned to the original work that have never materialized, although I have written elsewhere of Nova Europa and the magical universe in which it's lodged.

When I finish the division of the original novels into thirds, this next year, there'll be a dozen finished glimpses into this most interesting of fictional vistas. Maybe, just maybe, there'll be more someday. I do hope so.

If you like my little creations, please do let me know. I would love to hear from you. I can be found at my website,

www.robertreginald.com

—Robert Reginald
San Bernardino, California
28 December 2012

ABOUT THE AUTHOR

ROBERT REGINALD was born in Japan, and lived in Turkey as a youth, plus a half dozen different U.S. states. He starting writing as a child, and penned his first book during his senior year at Gonzaga University. He settled in Southern California in 1969, where he served as an academic librarian for forty years. He currently edits the Borgo Press imprint for Wildside Press, having turned in more than 1,200 volumes in seven years, and has also penned more than 137 books and 13,000 short pieces.

His fiction titles include: twelve Nova Europa historical fantasies in four trilogies (2004-13): *Melanthrix the Mage, Killingford, 'Ware the Dark-Haired Man, The Righteous Regicide, The Virgin Queens, The Prince of Exiles, Brother Theo's God, Questions and Questings, Whither Goest Thou?, The Cracks in the Æther, The Pachyderms' Lament*, and *The Fourth Elephant's Egg*; The War of Two Worlds science fiction trilogy: *Invasion!, Operation: Crimson Storm*, and *The Martians Strike Back!* (2007/2011); a science fiction novel in The Human-Knacker War series: *Knack' Attack* (2010); a future dystopia, *Academentia* (2011); two Phantom Detective period mysteries: *The Phantom's Phantom* (2007) and *The Nasty Gnomes* (2008); a comic mystery, *The Paperback Show Murders* (2011); and three short story collections: *Katydid & Other Critters: Tales of Fantasy and Mystery* (2001), *The Elder of Days: Tales of the Elders* (2010), *The Judgment of the Gods and Other Verdicts of History* (2011).

He's also edited several anthologies: *Choice Words: The*

Borgo Press Book of Writers Writing on Writing (2010), *Yondering: The First Borgo Press Book of Science Fcition Stories* (2011), *To the Stars—and Beyond: The Second Borgo Press Book of Science Fcition Stories* (2011), *Once Upon a Future: The Third Borgo Press Book of Science Fcition Stories* (2011), *Whodunit?: The First Borgo Press Book of Crime and Mystery Stories* (2011); *More Whodunits: The Second Borgo Press Book of Crime and Mystery Stories* (2011), *The Christmas Megapack: Yuletide Stories* (2012), and *The Second Christmas Megapack: Yuletide Stories* (2012).

You can find him at:

www.robertreginald.com